Animal:
The Beginning

Animal:
The Beginning

K'wan

www.urbanbooks.net

Urban Books, LLC
97 N18th Street
Wyandanch, NY 11798

ISBN 13: 978-1-62286-997-8
ISBN 10: 1-62286-997-4

First Mass Market Printing July 2016
Printed in the United States of America

10 9 8 7

Distributed by Kensington Publishing Corp.
Submit orders to:
Customer Service
400 Hahn Road
Westminster, MD 21157-4627
Phone: 1-800-733-3000
Fax: 1-800-659-2436

Prologue

For Marie Torres' twenty-three years on Earth, nothing had ever been easy for her. Growing up as a poor young girl in Harlem, she had always had a rough time, fighting for everything she had or ever would have. Her upbringing had been harsh, and she was no stranger to pain, but if you compiled every physical and emotional pain she had gone through, none of them compared to the pain she was in at this moment.

She was lying on her back in a hospital bed, fitted with a lumpy mattress, with her feet planted in two steel stirrups. The overhead light above her bed beat down on her like a tiny sun, causing her to sweat, but every time she flung the thin blanket away, she got cold. Nurses stood around her bed, checking her vitals and occasionally dabbing her forehead, while a doctor sat on a stool between her legs, prodding her vagina and assuring her that everything would be all right.

She didn't believe him. He wasn't the one lying spread eagle with a small person tearing through his pelvis.

"Jesus, why does this hurt so badly?" Marie shrieked. Her tanned face was covered with sweat, and her long, curly hair was plastered to her forehead.

"You're doing great, Marie. Just keep pushing." One of the nurses patted her hand.

Marie batted her hand away. "If I'm doing so good, then why the hell is he still in there?"

"Ms. Torres, I need you to be calm. The baby is at an awkward angle, and I'm trying to turn him back around, so we can get him out," the doctor informed her.

His fingers probed deeper into her vagina, trying to get hold of the baby. It had been the most peculiar thing; the baby had started to crown and then went back in, as if he wasn't ready to come out yet. In all his years in medicine, he had seen some incredible things, but never a baby changing its mind mid-birth.

"If his ass won't come out willingly, then cut me. Damn it! I just need him out!" Marie wailed. She grabbed the hand of one of the nurses and looked up at her with pleading eyes. "Why is this hurting so bad?"

"I honestly don't know, Marie," the nurse admitted. "It's not usually this bad with women who've given birth before, but everybody is different. They say it's the youngest that always give you the most grief," the nurse joked.

Marie didn't laugh. When she'd had her first child, he'd slid out within a matter of hours, and there wasn't much pain. A few stitches and a few days of rest, and it was back to business as usual with Marie, but not this birth. Even early in her pregnancy, the life growing in her stomach had gone out of its way to make her miserable. It was bad enough that she couldn't get high while she was carrying, but she'd also gained seventy pounds and was tortured with morning sickness until her seventh month of pregnancy. Now, she had finally come to the end of her misery, and the baby sought to extend it by refusing to come out.

"Look. Cut me or whatever you gotta do. Just get this li'l muthafucka outta me." Marie gripped the bedrails. It felt like the baby was tearing into her walls with its fingernails, trying to keep from being dragged out.

"We can't give you a caesarean. You have to do it vaginally," the doctor told her. "Now, I've almost got the baby into position. On my word, you're going to push with everything you have, all right?"

"All right! Just get it out!" she shouted.

"One . . . two . . . three . . . push!" the doctor urged.

Marie pushed, and when the baby didn't come out, she pushed some more. She pushed so hard that she shit all over the hospital table and on the baby, but she had finally managed to pop it out. She collapsed back on the pillow as the doctor snipped the umbilical cord and handed the baby off to the nurses to be cleaned up.

Once they had wiped the baby down and suctioned the feces from its nose and mouth, they wrapped it in a fresh blanket and brought it over for Marie to see. It was a beautiful brown boy with a head crowned by thick black curls. Even at less than a few minutes old, the baby's eyes seemed to be full of life and awareness.

"Look, Marie. It's your son." One of the nurses brought the baby boy over to Marie's bedside.

Marie turned her tired eyes to the bundle in the nurse's arms. "So you're the li'l thing that was clawing out my damn insides." She reached up and tickled the baby's chin with her finger. To everyone's surprise, the child giggled and wrapped his chubby fingers around her digit.

"Have you picked out a name?" the nurse asked.

"Yeah. I'm gonna call him Tayshawn," Marie said, thinking of the man who had impregnated her. "That's about the only thing of his daddy's he'll have. My baby boy ain't gonna be no killer. He's gonna grow up to be a doctor or lawyer."

"Would you like to hold him?" the nurse offered.

"After the way he split my ass open? Hell no!" Marie used her fingers to comb her hair back into a ponytail. She was sore but felt one hundred times better after having pushed the baby out. It was like having the best bowel movement in the world. "You can hold Junior for another minute. Right now, I need a cigarette."

"But, Ms. Torres, this is your son," the doctor said, shocked that the woman had declined to hold her child in favor of a cigarette.

Marie rolled her eyes. "I know, and that means I'm stuck with him for twenty-one years or until he gets outta my house, so he'll still be my son after I have my cigarette. Now are one of y'all gonna find me a Newport somewhere, or do I gotta get my bloody ass up outta this bed and find it myself?" She looked at the doctor and nurses.

The nurse cuddled the baby to her and hurriedly left Marie's bedside. She joined the huddle with the doctor and two other nurses and shook her head.

"I don't know why these little girls keep coming in here, popping out babies that they don't want anything to do with."

The doctor shook his head. "Well, let's go in the waiting room and break the good news to the father. Maybe he'll be a little more excited."

"There is no father that we know of," another nurse informed him.

The doctor's heart sank. He had been working in the hospital for a few years and had seen plenty of girls like Marie, and it never got easier to let the babies go home with them knowing how slim their chances of making it were.

"What should we do, doctor?" the nurse holding the baby asked.

The doctor looked back at Marie, who was glaring at them, obviously still waiting for her cigarette. He looked back to the nurses and the baby they were huddled over so protectively and spoke frankly with them. "There isn't much we can do except put him in the nursery with the others and pray he's got more than a snowball's chance in hell at a better life than what his mother's looking to offer."

"Poor kid, born into the world with the deck already stacked against him. Such a shame." The nurse nuzzled against Baby Tayshawn's cheek.

"Not a shame, an epidemic," the doctor said as he shook his head sadly.

PART I

—He Without Sin—

Chapter 1

It was September and damn near ninety degrees that day. The sun beat down so mercilessly on the Harlem streets that the asphalt began to melt and made the sidewalks feel like you were walking on stale pastries. The big kids headed to the local swimming pool to try to get their last dips in. It was the last weekend the pool would be open before they closed it for the fall. The younger kids who couldn't travel by themselves had to find more practical ways to keep cool. One of the kids borrowed a wrench from the maintenance closet in one of the buildings, opened the fire hydrant, and released a stream of water into the street. The kids danced in the streets happily as they were provided with some much-needed relief from the heat. All the neighborhood kids played in the free-flowing water—all except one.

Young Tayshawn sat on a bench under the shade of a tree with his nose buried in a book. His curly hair jutted up from his head at all sorts of uneven angles because it hadn't been cut since the school year ended. His T-shirt was two sizes too big and slightly yellow around the neck, but for the most part, it was clean. He wore a pair of tattered shorts that had once been jeans, until his mother cut them off just above the knee. They had been handed down from his older brother, as all his clothes were. The only thing he wore that hadn't been pre-owned was a pair of white Pro-Keds that his mother had bought him the day before from the discount store. He was supposed to be saving them for the first day of school that Monday, but he couldn't help himself, so even after being told numerous times not to wear them, he'd snuck outside in them anyway.

In the neighborhood, Tayshawn was somewhat of an outcast. His mother and stepfather were notorious baseheads who spent more time chasing their demons than they did tending to the children. The parental neglect was apparent in Tayshawn's appearance and behavior. His clothes were always knockoffs or hand-me-downs, and he was lucky if his mother stayed sober long enough to do the laundry. Often he would have to go to school wearing the same clothes for a week straight. This made him an easy target for the cruel kids. They always teased him about his appearance and poor hygiene, saying that he smelled like an animal.

The teasing was so bad that Tayshawn had started cutting school just so he wouldn't have to deal with it. The school had sent countless letters to his house about his attendance, but his parents were too high to bother opening them. To Tayshawn's parents, he wasn't much more than a government check. The only person who seemed to care about him was his big brother, Justice.

Justice was a problem child. He was constantly getting in trouble for petty crimes around the neighborhood, and most of the older people couldn't stand him. They often whispered about how he was a bad seed and would end up dead or in prison, but that was only because they didn't understand.

Justice was no angel, but crime had not been his first career choice. Justice was a good student, but when the drugs took hold of his mother and stepfather, he had to start making power moves. He dropped out of school and took it to the streets to become the man of his house and the protector of his little brother. Justice did what he could to hold it together, but at the end of the day, he was still a child himself, so there was only so much he could do. The brothers often lay awake, ignoring the growling of their stomachs, dreaming of the day when they would escape the hell they had been condemned to.

"What you reading?" A soft voice drew Tayshawn from the story he'd been so engrossed in.

He looked up and was surprised to see that it was a young girl named Noki. Anokia, known as Noki to her friends, was the youngest daughter of the Japanese couple who owned the fish market on the avenue. Noki was the only one of her five siblings who had been born in the United States, and it showed in her walk, talk, and the way she dressed. She was rocking fatigue cutoffs and a white tank top, with white shell-toe Adidas and no socks. Her long black hair was in its usual style—neatly done box braids. Tayshawn had had a crush on Noki since she moved into the neighborhood, but he had never had the courage to say anything.

Tayshawn held up the tattered book cover so Noki could see it. "*Huckleberry Finn*."

Noki frowned. "Why you reading that white people bullshit? You need to be reading Malcolm X."

"You mean that guy who got killed a long time ago?" Tayshawn asked. He was familiar with the name but didn't know much about him other than the little bit he'd picked up in social studies during Black History Month.

"Malcolm was more than just some dude who got killed. He was an icon and a great leader of black people," Noki said passionately. "When white people had their feet on the necks of the downtrodden blacks, Malcolm stood up for them. He didn't buy into that submissive ex-slave shit; his philosophy was that if Black wanted more as a people, then they had to demand it. They killed him for his beliefs."

"Wow," was all Tayshawn could say after Noki's history lesson.

Noki shook her head sadly. "How is it that I'm Japanese and I know more about the black experience than you?"

Tayshawn just shrugged. "Did they teach you that in school?"

"Nah, I learned it from my older brother. He's got tapes of all these black leaders hidden in a box under his bed. Sometimes I sneak them out and listen to them, and that's how I got turned onto people like Malcolm X, Stokely Carmichael, and Sonny Carson."

"Why does he hide them if they're just tapes?" Tayshawn wanted to know.

"Because my dad would kick his ass," Noki said seriously. "You have to understand. We come from a different culture, and my parents are old school in their thinking. When they were growing up, the ideals of people like the Black Panthers could've gotten them branded traitors and executed. What my brothers and I call motivational, they call propaganda. That's why I love America so much, because I'm free to be whoever I want to be." She twirled one of her braids around her finger for emphasis.

"What you doing over here talking to my girl?" A kid named Apple interrupted their conversation. He had been playing in the fire hydrant with the other kids, until he saw Tayshawn and Noki talking.

Apple was the local bully, and most of the kids were terrified of him. He was older than they were and bigger, so he used fear to control the other kids in the neighborhood. You were either down with Apple's gang or a victim of their antics.

"I'm not your girlfriend, Apple, and we weren't doing anything but talking," Noki told him.

"You are too my girlfriend. You just don't know it yet, and I don't want you talking to this dirty little nigga," Apple barked. "What the fuck is that in your hand?" He turned his attention to Tayshawn.

"Nothing." Tayshawn tucked the book behind his back.

"Don't look like nothing." Apple snatched the book from him. Water dripped from his thick jaw onto the pages of Tayshawn's book as he read the title. "*Huckleberry Finn*? What kinda gay shit is this?"

"It ain't gay. It's a story." Tayshawn reached for his book, but Apple held it out of his reach.

"Why don't you leave him alone, Apple?" Noki yelled at him.

"Because I don't like niggas in my neighborhood reading gay shit." Apple laughed, running his hands through the pages, purposely wetting them.

"Give it back," Tayshawn demanded.

"I ain't done looking at it," Apple told him as he turned and walked back toward the hydrant.

"Just forget about the book and let him have it," Noki suggested. She knew Apple was purposely trying to start trouble.

"I can't. It belongs to the library, and if I lose it, I won't be able to pay the fine, and they won't give me any more books," Tayshawn told her as he got up and followed Apple. "Stop playing and give me my book back, Apple. I don't want it to get wet."

He could feel his heart quickening in anticipation of the confrontation he knew Apple was dragging him into. By now the kids who had been playing in the water had stopped to watch the confrontation, so Apple wanted to make a good show of it.

"I forgot. You're afraid of water. That's why you smell like a monkey cage every day." The kids erupted into laughter. With each giggle, Tayshawn felt smaller and smaller. "I think this book could use a bath." He inched toward the water.

"Don't!" Tayshawn lunged for the book, but he was stopped when Apple grabbed him by the front of his T-shirt.

"Shut up, punk. Matter of fact, I'm gonna wash you and this dirty-ass book."

Apple grabbed Tayshawn in a bear hug and lifted him off his feet. The frail boy struggled, but Apple had a grip like a grown man. Apple forced Tayshawn to his knees in the water, letting it hit him in the face full blast. Tayshawn screamed and choked, but Apple continued to hold him there while the other kids looked on and laughed.

When Apple finally let him go, Tayshawn scrambled away from the water like a frightened rabbit. His hair was matted to his face, and his clothes were completely soaked. What truly broke his heart was when he looked down and saw that the water had loosened the glue on his knockoff sneakers, and the sole was coming apart. Tayshawn was hurt, and he was angry. The laughter of the children around him filled his ears.

Noki stood off to the side, looking at him pitifully. The look of disappointment on her face hurt him more than anything else. He looked up at Apple's smiling face, and a veil of red slid down over his eyes. The next thing everyone knew, Tayshawn had sprung to his feet and was on Apple's ass.

Apple was caught off guard when Tayshawn came at him like a feral cat, scratching, clawing, and biting. He tried to grab Tayshawn's throat, but the smaller boy sank his teeth into Apple's hand. Two of the other kids grabbed Tayshawn from behind, allowing Apple a chance to compose himself. He delivered a vicious right to Tayshawn's jaw and followed it with a left to his gut, dropping him. For good measure, Apple gave him two kicks to the ribs. Tayshawn lay on the ground in the fetal position, glaring up at Apple like a wounded dog.

"You crazy little muthafucka. You don't only smell like an animal, but you act like one too. From now on, your name ain't Tayshawn; it's Animal!"

"Animal! Animal! Animal!" the kids all chanted as they laughed.

Tayshawn got to his feet and ran away as fast as he could. Even as he entered the building where he lived, he could still hear the children's voices screaming, *Animal! Animal! Animal!* . . .

Chapter 2

Tayshawn stepped off the elevator on the third floor and walked toward his apartment, leaving a trail of wet footprints in his wake. Tears ran down his cheeks, mixed with excess water from the hydrant. His whole body hurt from the beating he had taken from Apple, but it was his wounded pride that made him cry. He hated Apple for what he had done and vowed to get back at him.

As he stood in front of the door to his apartment and prepared to knock, the door came open and out stepped a man whom he knew from the neighborhood. He was wearing a black Raiders fitted cap and black T-shirt with a thick rope chain with a large medallion that rested on his chest. His dark blue Levi's jeans were creased down the middle and lay almost perfectly over the front of his white-and-red Nike Cortez. Poking out from his back pocket was a red silk handkerchief. He looked down at the soaked young boy

and smiled, revealing a mouth full of gold teeth.
The shiny grills had always fascinated Tayshawn,
and he loved to see the older head smile. His
name was Tango, and he was *the man* in their
hood.

Tango was a sporting young dude who had
migrated to New York from Los Angeles a few
years prior and started a rapid climb up the
underworld ladder. He was a different kind of
cat from a different part of the world, so the
young kids flocked to him, more out of curiosity
than anything. They would sit around for hours
listening to Tango tell war stories about his life
in L.A. and *Piru Love*. He made it all sound so
poetic that, in a short period of time, he had
gathered a good-sized crew who spread his
drugs and his beliefs throughout their projects
and the neighboring hoods. By the time some of
the established New York hustlers realized what
was going on, Tango and his gospel had already
infected their neighborhood. His crimson flag
was firmly planted.

"What up, young blood?" Tango rubbed
Tayshawn's head, as he always did when he
greeted him. He looked at his wet hand and
frowned. "Damn! Where are you coming from?
The pool?"

"No," Tayshawn said.

He kept his eyes on the ground so that Tango wouldn't see that he had been crying. Tango was one of the cats in the hood they all looked up to, and Tayshawn didn't want him to think that he was weak. Tango lifted Tayshawn's head and looked into his eyes. "What's the matter, shorty? Somebody fucking with you?"

"Yeah, that punk-ass nigga Apple was messing with me, so we had a fight, but he beat me up," Tayshawn said shamefully. Just thinking about it upset him, and his eyes watered up again.

"Hey. Ain't no need for them tears, young blood," Tango said sternly. "You got your ass kicked, but the important thing is that you fought back. It's a cold and ugly world out there, kid, and only the strong survive. If you get knocked down, you get back up and keep swinging. No matter how big your enemy is, you've got to fight. This way, people will know you ain't no sucker, and the next one won't be so quick to try you. Stand strong at all times." He placed his fist on Tayshawn's chest. "And never anyone's victim. You hear me, young blood?"

"Yeah," Tayshawn said.

"Cool."

Tango pulled out a knot of money and peeled off two ten-dollar bills, which he placed in Tayshawn's hand. "Put that in your stash and buy yourself some candy or something when you go back outside. Don't let your moms and step-pops know I gave it to you, because you'll wake up and find that shit missing." Tango laughed. "I'm out. Stay up, young blood."

He rubbed Tayshawn's head and left.

Tayshawn walked into the apartment and found it exactly as he had expected to find it: a mess. The garbage can in the kitchen was packed to capacity, and instead of someone taking it out, they just hung plastic bags on the doorknob. Those were filled with garbage too. The dishes were overflowing in the sink, with roaches feasting on some old grits that had been drying on a plate for three days.

Tayshawn stuck his head in the refrigerator, looking for a snack, and came out with nothing but frost on the front of his nose. The milk was curdled, the bread was moldy, and the three roaches that had made their final resting places in the leftover spaghetti turned him off from that. Thankfully, Tango had given him a few dollars, so when his parents went to sleep or made their next drug run, he would slip out to the store to procure some food for Justice and himself.

Ignoring the hunger pains in his stomach, Tayshawn made his way into the living room.

Like the kitchen, it was mess. An empty wire cage with newspapers scattered across its floor dominated the middle of the living room. This was a grim reminder of the dog they'd once owned. That mongrel of a dog was one of the few things in the world that Tayshawn loved or felt loved him, but, like with everything else, it went to the crack man to support his parents' habit. Dirty clothes lay all over the floor, where his mother had thrown them when she had started the laundry three weeks prior. Ashtrays spilling over with cigarette butts littered the cracked glass coffee table. Between the ashtrays were empty soda bottles. The room looked every bit the crack den that it was, and in the center of the chaos were his mother and stepfather.

Marie sat on the tattered couch, eyes narrowed to slits and her mouth twisted slightly to the left. Her once full and beautiful head of thick black hair was now thin and streaked with white, pulled back into a tight ponytail. Marie was only thirty-four, but her years of drug abuse made her look like she was forty-four. The nails she had once kept manicured and painted were now chipped and scorched from epic battles with fifty-cent lighters. At one time, she had been the finest young thing on the block; now, she was just a smoker.

Next to her on the couch, looking just as smoked out as Marie, was Eddie, Tayshawn's stepfather. In his prime, Eddie had been a promising musician who played with a touring jazz band. Being a pretty, brown-skinned cat that was plugged in heavy on the music scene, Eddie attracted women like shit attracted flies. He loved pussy. It was like his god until he found something more powerful to worship . . . crack.

To Eddie, crack-cocaine was a gift sent straight from heaven. Chasing the drug made him neglect everything, including his band. Eddie began missing gigs, and when he did show up, he was always as high as a kite. It didn't take long before the band became frustrated with Eddie's antics and fired him. For a while, he floated around, playing gigs at various spots, but it was barely enough to keep the monkey off his back. Eddie began to rely more and more heavily on the women he bedded to support him, but with his physical and social decline, they became just as hard to keep as jobs. Eddie needed to find a new plan of attack, so he began using drugs to trap the women, which was how he had snagged Marie.

Marie was black and Hispanic. Her curvaceous body and thick lips made her appearance lean more toward her father's black side, but her fiery attitude was all her Dominican mother's. She was known to love a good time and could drink most men under the table, which made her the life of whatever party she was at. There were quite a few dudes who wanted to get next to the sassy party girl, but she was selective with whom she shared her goodies. Marie had had a few partners, but of them all, she had only loved three.

The first man she'd loved was a young Trinidadian who had a good job working for the MTA as a bus driver. He didn't like to party as much as she did, but he didn't judge her for it either. For Marie's nineteenth birthday, he had given her a son that they named Justice. For a while, they made a happy little life in their tiny apartment, with Justice's father working double and triple shifts to make enough money to buy them their first house.

Their happy life came to an abrupt end when, one night after his shift, somebody blew his brains out while trying to rob him. For their troubles, they got the twenty-one dollars he had in his wallet, and Marie and her son were left with nothing. Justice's father had a life insurance policy through his city job, but because he and Marie had never gotten a chance to get married, she was entitled to nothing. She was broke and left to make a way as best she could to keep her young son fed.

The second man she loved was an older man who claimed to speak the word of God, but behind closed doors, he did the devil's work. It was a fling that shouldn't have happened, but it did, and she had another son as a result of it. He promised Marie that he would be there for the kid, and in the early months of her pregnancy, he was. He had even managed to make it to a prenatal appointment or two. She thought that things were finally starting to look up for her and she might be getting a second chance at a full family, until she found out he already had one. Marie wasn't going to play herself and try to get him to leave his wife because, in her heart, she knew that he never would. The only proof Marie had that Tayshawn's father ever existed was a picture of the three of them they'd taken when Tayshawn was a few months old.

Years later, tragedy struck his family and sent him on a downward spiral. Marie had heard stories in the streets about the deeds of Tayshawn's father that made her happy he didn't stick around. She vowed that, no matter what, she would not allow that kind of evil around her two sons . . . and then came Eddie.

By the time Eddie came on the scene, Marie was already damaged goods. She had endured a great deal, and life was still shitting on her by the day. She was ripe for the picking. Marie had already started experimenting with harder drugs like LSD and cocaine, so when Eddie introduced her to crack, it was a wrap. In free basing, Marie found a way to fill the potholes in her soul. The more crack she smoked, the more of her respect for herself died. All she had left now was crack, and Eddie made sure she did whatever she had to so they could stay high. All her dreams, aspirations, and even her children were afterthoughts.

"Mama, I'm hungry," Tayshawn said from the entrance of the kitchen.

He knew she wasn't going to get up and cook, but he said it just so that he could have some kind of communication with his mother. Even though he was getting older, he still craved his mother's attention.

Marie looked at him with glassy eyes. "Go in there and heat up some of that spaghetti," she told him. She was so stuck off crack that she couldn't fully open her mouth, and it sounded like her jaw was wired.

"It's roaches in that spaghetti, Mama," Tayshawn told her.

"If you li'l niggas knew how to wrap shit back up when you went in it, maybe you wouldn't have to worry about the roaches getting it," Eddie said as he began to stir. He dug through the ashtrays until he found a cigarette clip sizable enough to get a few pulls from and lit it. "And why yo li'l ass always so hungry anyway? Don't they feed you in school?"

"It's still summer break. School doesn't start back until Monday," Tayshawn told him.

"Don't get smart, li'l nigga." Eddie jabbed his finger at him. "Y'all get too much time off from school as it is, and that's what's wrong with your generation."

Tayshawn didn't reply. He just sat on the floor and began taking his shoes off. He hoped that if he set them in the window to dry, he could salvage them before they completely lost their form from being wet.

"I know damn well that ain't them brand new sneakers we just bought you for school." Eddie squinted at the wet sneakers.

When he had made the positive ID on the sneakers, he got up and walked over to where Tayshawn was sitting. "What happened to them shoes?"

"They got wet," Tayshawn said, just above a whisper. Eddie, looming over him like that, filled him with such fear that he felt his bowels loosening. He expected it, but he still wasn't prepared for it when Eddie slapped fire out of him. Tayshawn's head bounced off the wall, and he could feel the knot instantly pop up.

"That's obvious to a muthafucking duck!" Eddie barked. "What I wanna know is how they managed to get wet when your monkey ass wasn't supposed to wear them outside anyway."

"I wore them because—"

Eddie slapped him again. "You wore them because you're a disrespectful little bitch who don't appreciate the sacrifices me and ya mama make so you can have nice shit." Eddie picked one of the shoes up and held it out for Marie to see. "You see this shit? Ruined!"

"Baby, stop yelling so much. You blowing mine." Marie moaned. She had just taken a blast and was still in the throes of it.

Eddie threw the shoe at Marie. "See, that's your fucking problem. You get faded and can't function, and that's why these damn kids of yours run all up and through here recklessly."

"Nigga, what the fuck is wrong with you? You in here throwing shoes and shit." Marie was sitting up now. The shoe had completely blown her high and put her in a nasty mood.

"Because I'm trying to tell you what the fuck your kid done and you acting like you don't hear me, as usual!" Eddie shouted. His high was now diluted too, and it only grew the chip on his shoulder.

"I'm sorry. Apple beat me up and pushed me in the water!" Tayshawn blurted. He had seen how nasty it could get between Eddie and Marie when they were both high, so he drew the fury on himself before it got there between them.

Eddie took the bait and spun on him. "Damn right you're sorry—the sorriest little bastard I ever seen. You let that little fat muthafucka whip your ass and ruin your sneakers? What kinda faggot am I raising under my roof?"

"I ain't no faggot," Tayshawn said, voice trembling.

"You must be a faggot if you keep getting punked in your ass by these neighborhood sissies. Where are your balls, kid?" Eddie glared down at Tayshawn, who was cowering against the door. When he reached for him, Tayshawn recoiled.

"Don't!" Tayshawn threw his hands up defensively.

"Oh, I get it." Eddie grabbed Tayshawn by his shirt and dragged the boy, kicking and screaming, into the living room. He snatched Tayshawn off the floor and held him in front of the mirror that lined the wall behind the couch where his mother was sitting. "Either you ain't got no balls or you just can't find them, so let me help you look." He tore off Tayshawn's T-shirt.

"No, no, no!" Tayshawn fought, but Eddie had him in a headlock, and he was no match for the grown man's strength.

After Eddie ripped off Tayshawn's T-shirt, he held him over his knee and tore away his denim shorts. When the money Tango had given Tayshawn fell out, Eddie and Marie knocked heads trying to pick it up off the floor.

"Bitch, watch out!" Eddie snatched the money up. Tayshawn tried to scramble away, but Eddie grabbed him by his underwear and pulled him back. "You holding out on us after all we done for you, li'l nigga?" He slapped Tayshawn viciously across the ass. "Ungrateful little bastard!"

"That's enough." Marie came over and tried to separate Eddie and Tayshawn.

Eddie tossed Tayshawn roughly to the ground and stood up to meet his new threat. "Oh, so now your crackhead ass wants to be the concerned parent?" Eddie palmed Marie's face and shoved her clear across the living room. "Bitch, please."

"Don't hit my mother." Tayshawn charged at Eddie.

He caught the older man off guard and managed to shove him into the china cabinet in the corner, shattering the glass. Eddie staggered from the mess of broken glass and 99 Cent Store dishes and took stock of the nicks and cuts on his arms.

"You gonna pay for that." He stalked toward Tayshawn.

Eddie tore into him and beat him until he lay on the floor like a wet noodle. Eddie opened the dog wire cage and looked at Tayshawn with a sinister smile. "Looks like I gotta remind you how old Eddie treats ungrateful-ass kids." He dragged Tayshawn toward the cage.

"No! I'm sorry! I won't fight you no more!" Tayshawn pleaded. He clawed at the carpet, trying to keep Eddie from tossing him into that cage.

"Too little, too fucking late." Eddie shoved him into the cage and slammed the door. "You wanna act like you ain't got no home training? Then I'm gonna treat you like you ain't got none." He put the combination lock on the cage. "That's in case anybody gets any bright ideas about a jail break for your li'l ass."

"Mommy, please help me!" Tayshawn clawed at the bars.

"Stop it, Eddie." Marie jumped on Eddie's back and clawed at his face from behind.

Eddie turned around and punched Marie in her face, dropping her.

"You must be crazy, putting yo muthafucking hands on me." He kicked Marie in the ribs. "I'm gonna teach you and this li'l nigga a lesson about who run shit in here." He grabbed Marie by her hair and punched her in the face.

"Mama!" Tayshawn raged. He worked himself into a fit, yelling until his throat was raw. Tayshawn threw himself against the cage over and over again until his bare shoulders were bloody from crashing into the wire cage.

Eddie turned his cruel eyes to the frantic little boy. "I see the little dog is hot around the collar, so let me see if I can cool you off." He grabbed a half-empty forty-ounce from the table and walked over to the cage. "See if this calms your ass down." He poured the beer on Tayshawn.

Eddie knelt down beside the cage and looked Tayshawn in the eyes. "Right now, I know you probably hate me, huh? Well, that's good, because I hate you too." Eddie kicked the cage. "Li'l muthafucka."

Tayshawn scrambled into the corner and tried to wipe the sting of the beer out of his eyes. Half naked, angry, and afraid, he glared up at Eddie with murderous thoughts dancing through his head. There was no doubt in his mind that, if the opportunity to kill Eddie ever arose, he would take it.

Chapter 3

Tayshawn was awakened by the sound of the front door opening. He wasn't sure how long he had been out, but from the hunger pangs in his stomach, it must've been a while. His body throbbed from the beating he'd taken earlier. There was the sound of sticky footsteps on the dirty living room floor, coming in his direction. It was dark, so he couldn't see much, but he could make out a shadow standing just outside the cage; it was likely Eddie coming to give him another beating.

The living room light came on, temporarily blinding him. He wanted to right himself and try to put up a fight, but he didn't have the strength. He lay there, preparing for whatever was to come, hoping it would be over quickly.

"Tay?"

Tayshawn looked up, expecting to see Eddie ready to administer more punishment, but to his relief, it wasn't his tormentor, but his older brother, Justice. He was a cinnamon-colored young man with broad shoulders and a square jaw. He was handsome, but in a rugged sort of way. All the girls liked him, and the boys feared him, because Justice was a known bruiser. It didn't take much to set him off.

Justice and Tayshawn had the same mother but different fathers. He and Tayshawn both had their respective fathers' facial features but shared their mother's beautiful dark hair. Tayshawn wore his wild, but Justice always wore his in braids. Justice was more than a big brother to Tayshawn; he was like a surrogate father and the only ray of sanity in his world of madness.

"Hey, Justice," Tayshawn said weakly. His lips were dry, and his throat was parched.

"Who did this to you? That nigga Eddie?" Justice knelt down beside the cage, tugging at the door, but it was secured by a padlock. "I'm gonna kill that muthafucka!"

"Wasn't his fault, Justice. I was talking smart, so he punished me," Tayshawn said. He knew Justice had a bad temper and didn't want him to get into it with Eddie. The last time they'd gotten into a fight, Justice had nearly killed Eddie. Had it not been for their mother threatening to turn him over to the police, he probably would have.

"This isn't punishment. This is Eddie being a dick like always." Justice set down the paper bag he was carrying and sat cross-legged on the floor in front of the cage.

Tayshawn's eyes went to the bag. He could smell whatever food was in the bag seeping out, and it made his stomach growl. Without even realizing he was doing it, Tayshawn licked his lips hungrily.

Justice noticed the look in his brother's eyes. "Did you eat today?"

"No. Tango gave me ten dollars to buy food, but Eddie took it," Tayshawn told him.

Justice shook his head sadly. "Fucking parasite." He dug into the bag and pulled out a piece of greasy fried chicken from the Chinese restaurant and pushed it through the bars. Within seconds, Tayshawn had mauled the chicken and was sucking on the bone. Justice took the remaining piece of chicken from the bag and gave him that one too, before crumpling the bag and tossing it into the corner.

Tayshawn was about to bite into the second piece of chicken but paused when he noticed that there was none left for Justice.

"Here, you eat this one." He tried to hand the chicken back, but Justice wouldn't accept it.

"Nah, you eat it. I'm not hungry," Justice lied. He was actually quite hungry, but he knew he could make it through the night on an empty stomach. Tayshawn looked like he was about to faint from hunger. "Let's see what we can do to bust you out of jail."

Tayshawn munched on the chicken while Justice studied the padlock on the cage. From his pocket, he pulled out what looked like a hairpin and began working on the padlock. Within a few minutes, he was opening the door and helping his little brother crawl out.

Tayshawn tried to stand, but being balled up inside the small cage for so long had stopped the blood from circulating properly in his legs, so they wouldn't support him. He stumbled forward, but his brother caught him before he could hit the floor.

The first thing Justice noticed was that his brother's skin was ice cold from being in the cage half-naked, and he reeked of urine.

"Damn, boy! Did you piss yourself?" Justice asked, holding Tayshawn at arm's length.

Tayshawn lowered his head in shame. "I had to use the bathroom, but Eddie wouldn't let me out. He told me I should pee on the newspaper like a good dog. I tried to hold it as long as I could, but—I'm sorry, Justice." Tears began to roll down his cheeks. He didn't want to cry in front of his brother, but he was embarrassed.

"Hey! What did I tell you about that crying shit?" Justice lifted Tayshawn's head so that he had to look him in the eye. "It's okay to cry over something you love, but if a man can make you cry, then you've given him the power to hurt you. Never give another man that kind of power over you, ever! Do you understand me, Tay?"

Tayshawn nodded.

"Good." Justice mussed his little brother's hair. "Now let's get your pissy ass in the bathroom and get you cleaned up."

Justice helped Tayshawn into the bathroom so he could clean him up. When he turned the light on, roaches scattered in every direction. Tayshawn sat on the toilet seat, while his brother rinsed the tub of any critters or debris before filling it with hot water. They didn't have any soap, but Justice found a box of laundry detergent under the sink, which he used to make the water sudsy.

"In you go." Justice helped Tayshawn into the tub.

"Ouch! That's hot!" Tayshawn yelped, trying to get out of the tub, but Justice wouldn't let him.

"You need it to be hot so your little ass can be clean." Justice forced him down into the water.

Eventually Tayshawn stopped complaining and went with it.

Tayshawn was glad Justice had spared him the embarrassment of trying to wash his body and let him do it himself. He could feel the grit of the laundry detergent scraping against his skin as he washed his arms and then his legs.

When Tayshawn had thoroughly soaped himself over, Justice drained the water and turned on the shower to wash away the film left behind by the abrasive soap. While Tayshawn dried himself with an old dish towel, Justice combed the tangles out of his hair. Justice was one of the only people who Tayshawn would let comb his hair because he was notoriously tender-headed. At first, it hurt because his hair was matted and tangled, but once the kinks were combed out, it was soothing. He could remember when his mother used to comb his hair that way, before she got strung out and when she still loved him.

He looked in the cracked mirror at the reflection of him and his brother. Tayshawn and Justice were like night and day. Justice was fair-skinned with straight hair, while he was dark with a mop of dry curls, which, most days, seemed to have a mind of their own. Justice was the darling of the neighborhood, while Tayshawn was the wretch, forever shunned for being everything that his brother was not. Maybe Apple and Eddie had been right in their assessments of him.

"Justice, am I an animal?" Tayshawn wasn't sure why he asked the question other than the fact that it was ringing in his head.

Justice stopped combing Tayshawn's hair. "What kind of question is that? Who told you that you were an animal?"

Tayshawn was silent.

Justice turned Tayshawn to face him. "Boy, don't go mute on me now. Who has been filling your head with bullshit?"

"Well, on television they always keep animals in cages," Tayshawn began. "When I do wrong, Eddie locks me in the cage."

"I told you to stop listening to what that junkie muthafucka Eddie says. Half of the time he's too high off crack to even know his own name, let alone pass judgment on someone. Fuck Eddie! And the next time he puts you in that cage, I'm going to put him in the ground," Justice promised.

"It isn't just Eddie," Tayshawn admitted. "I got into it with Apple earlier. He beat me up, then put me in the fire hydrant because he said I stank like an animal and needed a bath. Then he started calling me Animal and has all the other kids in the neighborhood calling me that too. It was his fault that I got in trouble for ruining my new sneakers, and that's how me and Eddie ended up getting into it." His voice was thick with emotion, but he didn't cry this time.

Justice's face immediately twisted into a hard mask. "You let that faggot-ass crack baby lay hands on you in the streets?"

"I fought him back, but he was stronger than me. Then, him and the other kids chased me into the building," Tayshawn told him.

"Well, it's good that you fought him back. Never let a nigga put his hands on you and not fight back. That's coward shit, and we ain't no cowards. Still, he put the beats on you in front of everybody and marked you as weak, and we can't have that." Justice shook his head. "He's gonna keep fucking with you for as long as he feels like he can, unless you do something to show him that he can't."

"I told you. I tried fighting him, and he beat me up. What else can I do?" Tayshawn asked.

"You show him," Justice said harshly. "Since he's seen fit to label you an animal, you show him what a *real* animal would do if backed into a corner. Embrace what that pussy used as an insult, and make it your strength. Tomorrow at four p.m., you're going to march up the block and make that boy bleed for disrespecting you."

"But what if his gang is there?"

Justice smirked. "You let me worry about that. You just make sure you're there at four, like I told you."

"And if I can't beat him?" Tayshawn asked.

Justice tenderly placed his hand on the back of Tayshawn's neck and pulled him toward him so that their foreheads were touching. "Little brother, you don't have a choice. You're going to beat Apple's ass, or I'm going to beat yours. Either way, a lesson will be taught tomorrow."

The bathroom door opened unexpectedly and in staggered Marie. From the spaced-out look in her eyes, the brothers knew that their mother was bombed, and from the skimpy skirt and heels she wore, they knew what she had been out doing to get her fix. Justice shook his head in disgust, while Tayshawn simply stared at her, not knowing quite what to make of the scene. There was an awkward silence, which Marie eventually broke.

"Y'all get the hell out of the way. I gotta pee." Marie half-stumbled into the bathroom, shoving her way past the two boys. She hiked her skirt up, showing that she wasn't wearing any panties and traumatizing her sons with the sight of her shaggy bush before plopping down on the bowl. Her eyes rolled back in her head as she released the stream of urine that she had been holding for only God knew how long. When she opened her eyes, she blinked and looked at her sons as if she was just noticing them standing there. "What the hell are y'all staring at?"

"I'm still trying to figure that out," Justice said sarcastically.

Marie rolled her eyes. "Don't be getting smart, Justice. You been smelling yourself a lot lately, especially since you and your little gang been running around terrorizing shit."

"I have no idea what you're talking about," Justice lied.

"You're a liar, and the truth ain't in you," Marie shot back. "All I know is that the police better not come around here looking for you and that little green-eyed monster you keep time with, because if they do, I'm gonna tell them exactly where to find y'all."

"Damn! You'd really turn your own kid in?" Justice didn't even know why he was surprised at the revelation.

"You're fucking right I would. I ain't letting you or this other little fucker draw no heat on me. If you commit a crime in the projects, they'll put me out, and I ain't about to be homeless over my kid's bullshit," Marie snapped.

"But, Ma, I haven't done anything," Tayshawn said.

"Not yet, but it's only a matter of time before your daddy's spirit shows itself in you, and I'll wind up cleaning up your messes too. I'll tell you this shit, though: The first time you lay a dead body at my feet, I'm turning you in, nigga."

"I ain't no killer, Mommy. Killing is wrong. I'm going to be a doctor like you want me to," Tayshawn said.

Marie shook her head. "My poor naïve baby."

"Don't talk to him like that," Justice interjected. He knew where the conversation was going and wanted to avoid it, so he drew the attention to himself.

"I'll talk to *my* son any way I damn well please. When you have kids of your own, you can talk to them however you want. This li'l nigga," she said, pointing at Tayshawn, "belongs to me." Marie got off the toilet without bothering to wipe herself or wash her hands, and she stormed out of the bathroom.

Tayshawn went to flush the toilet behind his mother and was horrified to see a used condom floating in it. It had fallen out of her when she used the bathroom.

Justice slammed the toilet seat down and flushed it.

"Well, at least, we know she's protecting herself." He meant it as a joke, but Tayshawn didn't laugh. He just looked sad. "Don't worry about Mama. She's gonna be okay. Now go get some rest, and I'll see you tomorrow."

"Where you going?" Tayshawn asked. He always slept better when Justice was in the room with him at night.

"I'll be back a little later. I'm gonna hook up with K-Dawg and take care of a few things," Justice told him.

"I thought they arrested him last month." Tayshawn recalled how the whole neighborhood had been talking about K-Dawg and the dude whose face he had cut for messing with one of his sisters.

"They did, but K-Dawg is still a minor, so they had to cut him loose after a while," Justice explained.

"Mama says he's got the devil in him."

Justice laughed. "Mama should worry about the devil she's got living in her house and let me worry about K-Dawg. Now off to bed, and make sure you have your ass on the block tomorrow at four like I told you." He mussed Tayshawn's hair and left.

Chapter 4

It seemed like Tayshawn had just gone to sleep when his mother was shaking him awake again. His brain was still heavy with the fog of sleep, but he immediately knew something was off. Marie had traded her streetwalker clothes for black jeans and a blouse. She had even taken the time to try to make her hair look presentable.

"What's the matter, Mama?" Tayshawn asked.

"Put your clothes on. I need you to come with me somewhere," Marie told him.

"Where?"

"Don't ask so many damn questions. Just put something decent on. You can pick from your new school clothes."

Now Tayshawn was really nervous. The day before, he had gotten an ass whipping and had been locked in a cage for wearing his new sneakers, and now she was telling him to wear an entire outfit. Something was definitely wrong.

"Okay," he agreed, afraid to say anything else.

"I'll meet you in front of the building. Don't take all day either, Tayshawn." Marie walked out.

Ten minutes later, Tayshawn emerged from his building, dressed in jeans, a short-sleeved button-up shirt, and the same sneakers over which he had gotten his ass beat the day before. He took a minute to scan the block, looking for Apple or any of the other kids who might give him trouble. Justice had made it clear that he would have to face Apple before the day was out, but he wasn't ready to do it just yet. At the curb, his mother tapped her foot impatiently, taking deep pulls off a cigarette.

"Boy, bring your ass on!" Marie called, waving her hand for him to hurry.

Mother and son walked the few short blocks to the train station. Marie purchased a Metro card. She swiped it at the turnstile and went through, leaving Tayshawn standing there, waiting for her to swipe for him to get through also.

"Duck under and come on. It ain't but two fares on this card, and I'm gonna need the other one to get back," she told him.

Tayshawn was skeptical because he didn't want to get in trouble for fare-beating, but the look on his mother's face said it was non-negotiable. He decided that he would rather risk the wrath of the transit police than Marie's, so he crawled under. The whole time they waited on the platform for the train, Tayshawn kept looking around nervously, as if he was expecting a cop to jump from behind one of the pillars and arrest him. It wasn't until they were on the train that he was able to relax.

The train car was so crowded that Tayshawn and Marie were forced to stand. He didn't mind, but she seemed irritated by it and cursed under her breath about people not having any home training.

Tayshawn stood near the door across from his mother, gripping the pole to keep his balance as the train started moving. As he swayed back and forth with the movement of the car, he imagined that it was what being on a rollercoaster would feel like, but he had never actually been on one to compare. It was rare that he ever left his neighborhood, so it was like an adventure for him.

He examined the different faces in the train car curiously. Sitting on the bench across from him were three men, speaking among themselves and passing a bottle in a brown paper bag between them. One of them looked especially intimidating because of the raised scar that ran cross his cheek. He had a hard face, which seemed to be locked in a permanent scowl.

Tayshawn tried to mimic the man's scowl so that he could look tough in front of the other kids on the block, but from the way the woman next to him was laughing, he gathered that he looked more silly than intimidating.

The train slowed to a stop, and the three men he had been watching got up to make their exit. As they moved toward the door he was standing in front of, the one with the scar looked down at him with cold eyes. Tayshawn's heart jumped in his throat, fearing the man had seen him mocking him and was going to kick his ass. To his surprise, the man opened his mouth and spoke.

"Too many teeth," the man with the scar said.

"Huh?" Tayshawn didn't understand the statement.

"You ain't gonna scare anybody if you're showing them all thirty-two of your teeth," he elaborated. "When you grill a nigga, show fewer teeth and make your eyes tighter," the man with the scar told him before stepping off the train. The man with the scar didn't know it, but his advice would stick with Tayshawn for many years.

For the rest of the ride, Tayshawn busied himself practicing his scowl and reading the small paperback he had brought along for the ride. It was an old book, written by some man named

Donald Goines, that Tayshawn had found in a box in the back of the hallway closet. According to the bio in the back of the book, the author had written several novels, but the one Tayshawn was reading told the story of a man named Kenyatta, who had waged war against corrupt politicians in the inner city. The story was told so vividly that Tayshawn could almost see himself at Kenyatta's compound, huddled with his men while they planned the execution of two dirty cops. He was so lost in the story that he didn't even realize they had reached their stop until Marie snatched him by the arm and dragged him off the train. This caused him to drop his book. He tried to go back for it, but the doors snapped closed in his face. Tayshawn was crushed because he really wanted to know how the story ended.

They emerged from the train station near a large park. It was Morningside Park, if Tayshawn remembered correctly. Marie and Eddie had brought him to a barbecue that one of their friends was throwing in the park once. The reason it stuck out was because they had gone off to get high and had forgotten about Tayshawn in the park. He had to call Justice to pick him up, and one of the people had told him the name of the park, so his brother knew where to find him.

They walked for a few blocks, passing some tenement buildings and a bodega that was littered with young men and women in front of it. Tayshawn saw a broken down–looking old man hand one of the guys in front of the store some folded money in exchange for a small package. Tayshawn wasn't a street kid, but he knew a drug deal when he saw one. The man who had been handed the package looked up and saw Marie. He smiled and waved. He looked like he wanted to talk, but Marie was a woman on a mission, so she just waved back and kept going.

Their journey carried them to the steps of an old church. Looking up at the church triggered something in Tayshawn and made him uneasy. He had never been to the church that he could recall, but it felt familiar. It reminded him of a recurring nightmare he'd had for a stretch of time. He had been a baby in the dream, wandering the halls of a dark and musty church, much like the one he was standing in front of now. In the dream, he would always cry out for his mother, but she would never come.

"What are we doing here?" Tayshawn asked.

"Just come on," she told him, making her way up the stairs and through the doors.

Tayshawn reluctantly followed his mother inside the church. The interior was dimly lit, but still bright enough for Tayshawn to take stock of his surroundings. A large picture window overlooked the empty worship hall. Covering the window was a stained glass mural of Jesus on a cross, surrounded by Roman soldiers. It was the only thing in the place that could've been called beautiful. The interior of the church needed work, but it was in better shape than the outside. On either side were worn-looking wooden benches that looked like they didn't get sat on much anymore. Dividing the two rows of benches was a stained red carpet that went from the entrance and down to the podium in front.

The church was nearly empty, save for a few worshipers and two men speaking in hushed tones at the foot of the aisle. One was a man who was clean cut, wearing a suit, and the other, a priest, but like no priest Tayshawn had ever seen. He wore his head bald, and one of his eyes was covered by a black patch. When he noticed Tayshawn and Marie, he stopped talking and stared in their direction.

"Wait right here for a minute, baby," Marie told Tayshawn. Taking a minute to fix her hair and try to look as presentable as possible, she marched down the aisle.

Tayshawn watched as the man in the suit and his mother passed each other on the aisle and stopped to exchange a few words. In the light, he could see him better. He was a tall, well-built man with long dreadlocks and a neat goatee. The man in the suit gave Marie a sad look before hugging her to him. There was a great sadness in his eyes when he did so. After whispering something into her ear, the man in the suit kissed her on the cheek and continued up the aisle toward Tayshawn.

"You're little Tayshawn, aren't you?" the man asked.

"Yes, sir," Tayshawn replied, looking at the carpet.

The man tipped his chin up and studied Tayshawn's eyes. "Yeah, I can see *him* all in your eyes. If you grow up to be anything like your father, you're gonna make a fine right hand for my Tommy Gunz. It'll be like me and your pappy all over again."

"Do I know you?"

The man in the suit smiled, showing off his incredibly white teeth. "It's been years since I've seen you, so it's no wonder you don't remember me."

The door to the church opened and a beefy man stepped in. He glanced at Tayshawn, then turned his eyes to the man in the suit. "Mr. Clark, your car is out front."

"Thanks, Butch. I'll be right there," the man who had been identified as Mr. Clark said. He dug into his pocket and pulled out a large bank-roll, peeling off a twenty-dollar bill, which he extended to Tayshawn. He was hesitant to take it. "It's okay to take it. I'm not a stranger. I told you, me and your daddy go way back."

Tayshawn was still leery, but not enough to turn down the money. "Thank you."

"No thanks necessary. Family should always look out for family," Mr. Clark told him.

"Mr. Clark, we have to go," Butch repeated, this time more urgently.

"Okay, okay," Mr. Clark said with an attitude. "It was good seeing you again, Tayshawn." He patted him on the shoulder and disappeared.

The sounds of shouting drew Tayshawn's attention to the front of the church. The priest and Marie were engaged in a heated exchange. The priest's body language was still and hostile, but he kept his voice at a decent decibel, which was more than could be said for Marie. She was yelling and cursing while pointing her fingers in the face of the priest. He looked like he wanted to slap fire out of her; instead, he pulled a stack of money from somewhere within the folds of his robe and held it out to Marie. She took the money, right before spitting on the ground where the priest was standing and storming back up the aisle.

"What's the matter, Mama?" Tayshawn asked, noticing the look of rage in his mother's eyes. Marie didn't answer. She continued out the door as if he weren't even standing there. Tayshawn turned to the priest and found him staring at him, smirking like he had a secret that he wasn't telling. After tearing his eyes away from the priest, Tayshawn went outside to catch up with his mother.

Tayshawn got outside in time to see that his mother had turned her aggression to Mr. Clark. He was leaning against a long black car, wearing a disinterested look on his face, while Marie pleaded her case. The man he had called Butch stood near the front of the car, looking at Marie as if she were a beggar, and shaking his head.

"Baby, you brought that shit on yourself, so don't try to pull me into it now," Tayshawn heard Mr. Clark telling his mother when he walked up. "Now if you'll excuse me, I have an appointment to keep." He slid into the back seat of the car. Taking that as his cue, Butch got behind the wheel.

"So, it's like that, Thomas? You and your partner are doing better than most now, so you forget about the people who were there for you during your rise to the top?" Marie's tone was indignant.

"It isn't me who forgot; it's you and that other nut-case ex-wife of mine, June, who forgot when you put powdering your noses over loyalty. I was there, so you can't feed me no fabricated truths," he shot back. "I've laid my demons with my ex-wife to rest, and you and Priest need to address yours. I won't intervene."

Marie took a step back with a look of hurt on her face. She couldn't believe that a man she had known for almost two decades was treating her like a complete stranger. "That's cold-blooded, Thomas."

He shrugged. "This is how you made it, baby. If you get yourself clean, maybe we can revisit this conversation, but for as long as you're fucking with that shit, I got no rap for you. And let this be the last time you walk up on me while you're high off that shit, ya dig?"

"Yeah, I dig," Marie said coldly, backing away from the car.

Tayshawn stood beside his mother and glared at Mr. Clark.

"Come here, Tayshawn," Mr. Clark called from the rear window. Tayshawn looked like he was rooted in place with fear. "It's okay. I ain't gonna hurt you," he promised. Tayshawn took a few timid steps toward the back window. "You over there eyeballing me like you're thinking about doing something."

"I don't like the way you talk to my mother," Tayshawn told him.

"And you shouldn't. Never let a nigga talk crazy to anybody you claim to love, but make sure you know your opponent and the circumstances before you react. Impulsive niggas are usually the first to die. A man who can control his impulses is always the one in charge of the situation, no matter how the situation may look to the naked eye. Do you understand?"

Tayshawn nodded.

"Good. Listen. Don't take that shit between me and your mama personal. That shit goes back to before you were born. Sometimes you have to be brutally honest with the ones you care about to really get it. I gotta go, kid, but if you ever need anything, you make sure that you come and find me. Just ask around about Poppa Clark."

Without waiting for a response, Poppa Clark gave Butch the signal and the car peeled off.

Tayshawn didn't know it at the time, but it was Poppa Clark's words to him that night that would plant the seed for what was to come. He would hear the name Poppa Clark quite a bit over the years, but the next time he laid eyes on him, it wouldn't be under the most pleasant of circumstances.

Chapter 5

Instead of taking the subway back to the hood, Marie sprang for a taxi. For the entire ride, she was eerily silent. The only sounds she made were when she was exhaling the smoke from one of the cigarettes she had been chain-smoking the whole way. Tayshawn had seen his mother in off moods before, but never like this. His mother was one of the meanest, toughest women he knew, but at that moment, she looked broken.

"You okay, Mama?" Tayshawn asked.

"I'm fine. Why the hell do you keep asking me that? You're getting on my damn nerves!" Maria snapped.

"I'm sorry, Mama. I didn't mean to make you mad. I'm just concerned. Are you still upset about what Mr. Clark said to you?"

"Who?" Marie was confused at first. "Oh, you mean Poppa Clark? Fuck him. He slings more poison than a little bit and wanna be acting all holy. He can go straight to hell as far as I'm concerned."

"He said he knew my dad and that he was there on the day I was born," Tayshawn recounted.

"He did. Poppa and your father were something else when they were out here heavy, but that was a long time ago. Poppa Clark used to take care of the neighborhood. He used to care what happened in the streets, but now all he cares about is making money."

"He seemed nice."

"They all do in the beginning, until their true colors come out," Marie said in disgust. "Just because someone puts a few dollars in your hand doesn't mean he cares about you. Men like Poppa Clark don't do anything out of the kindness of their hearts, because they don't have hearts. No handout is without a price, whether you pay it now or later."

"Is that what's going on between you and Priest?" Tayshawn asked.

Marie's head snapped around as if she had just been slapped. "What?"

"I heard Poppa say that you and that priest had to settle something, so I figured you owed him money. Is that priest going to try and hurt you over the money you owe him?"

Marie relaxed a bit, realizing her son was still unaware of the truth. "No, I don't owe Priest anything. He's gotten all he'll ever get from me. No need to worry, Tayshawn."

Tayshawn was silent for a few long moments, and Marie thought he was done until he spoke again. "I'd kill him."

"What kind of craziness you talking, boy? Kill who?"

"The priest," Tayshawn answered. "I saw the way he looked at you at the church, like he hated you, and how upset you were after you spoke to him. I know you said not to worry, but I know you were scared. You ain't gotta be scared over no nigga, Mama, because I'll protect you. Before I let that creepy, old priest or anybody else hurt you, I'd take Eddie's gun and shoot him dead!"

Marie was both surprised and saddened by the conviction in her youngest son's voice. He was so innocent and frail that his promise of murder seemed laughable, but the look in his eyes betrayed the seriousness of his statement. It was the same look his father would give her before he would leave the house at night, only to come home the next morning with his clothes covered in blood and no explanation. Marie held no illusions about her subpar parenting skills, but seeing that murderous look in her baby boy's eyes let her know just how deep her failures went, and it broke her heart.

"We're gonna be okay." Marie hugged Tayshawn to her chest so that he couldn't see her crying.

"One of these days, I'm going to get my shit together, and we ain't gonna never have to worry about another man hurting us."

Tayshawn felt good being nestled in his mother's arms. It was almost as if he were a toddler again and the family was still doing well, before the drugs. He could've stayed hugged to his mother's chest forever, but the moment of bliss was short-lived. As soon as they crossed into their neighborhood, Marie's demeanor changed. She released him from her embrace and began scanning the streets with a hungry glint in her eyes. It was a look Tayshawn was, sadly, too familiar with. He saw it every time Marie's monkey started clawing at her back.

The taxi had barely come to a full stop before Marie tossed a bunch of crumpled bills into the front seat and was getting out. Tayshawn made it out just in time to see his mother making a beeline for the building that Tango sold crack out of. He called after her, but she never so much as turned around. His small voice was drowned out by the roar of her addiction.

Tayshawn walked slowly back toward his building, lost in his own jumbled thoughts. He was a mix of emotions, ranging from love to confusion and rage. He'd always told himself that his mother's drug use was just a phase and that she would snap out of it soon, but as the years went by, it was becoming painfully obvious that she wouldn't. He loved his mother dearly, but he sometimes cursed her for the life she had condemned them to.

As Tayshawn's building came into view, he saw Noki and some of the other neighborhood girls jumping rope on the playground. When she spotted him, she smiled and waved. Tayshawn shyly waved back. He was going to go over and say something to her, until he noticed Apple and his gang shooting dice by the monkey bars. Tayshawn lowered his head and kept walking, hoping that he would be able to make it to his building unnoticed, but he would have no such luck.

"What did I tell you about walking through my neighborhood without a pass, Animal?" Apple started right in.

"Stop calling me that, Apple," Tayshawn snapped and kept walking.

Apple moved to block Tayshawn's path. "Oh, you must've gone to see the wizard this morning, because you came back talking like you got some heart," he taunted.

"Just leave me alone," Tayshawn growled.

Apple moved forward and stood nose-to-nose with Tayshawn. "And what are you gonna do if I don't, Animal?"

Tayshawn didn't have to look over his shoulder to know that the boys in Apple's gang had closed in behind him. He could feel them looming, waiting for the signal from Apple to pop off. His heart began to race in anticipation of the violence that he was sure would come, and a ball of heat settled in the pit of his stomach and began to grow. He didn't want to fight, but they weren't giving him another option.

By now, the kids who had been playing on the playground had gathered around to watch the brawl that was about to go down. In the crowd, Tayshawn spotted Noki. She had a worried expression on her face. Her eyes pleaded for him not to go through with it, but she didn't understand that they weren't giving him a choice.

Tayshawn's palms began to sweat to the point where he could feel the beads dripping from his fingertips. The day's stress over his mother and the mysterious encounter at the church had Tayshawn feeling like the walls were closing in on him. A part of him wanted to tear Apple's face off, and a part of him wanted to flee, so he could just be left alone. He had just opened his mouth to try to reason with Apple when pain exploded in the side of his face and he saw stars.

At first, Tayshawn wasn't sure what had happened to him. He was disoriented, and his ear was ringing. He looked up and saw Apple giving triumphant high fives to his boys. Tayshawn's nose dripped blood onto his brand new school shirt. Eddie was surely going to make him suffer for ruining it. He wasn't sure if he could take another beating or a night in the cage.

He scanned the crowd of kids as they laughed and pointed their fingers mockingly at him, and his eyes landed on Noki. When he saw the look of pity on her face, something inside him snapped. He would be the victim no longer.

Apple never saw Tayshawn coming, but he felt it when two blows crashed into the back of his head. Tayshawn probably hurt his fists more than he did Apple's thick skull, but he was too angry to care.

Apple managed to grab the smaller Tayshawn and use his weight to force him to the ground. After Apple straddled Tayshawn's chest, he pinned his arms and began raining blows on his exposed face.

The chants of the children shouting, "Apple, Apple, Apple!" rang in Tayshawn's ears while he took his ass-whipping. If he didn't do something, Apple was probably going to kill him, and he didn't want to die in front of Noki.

When Apple shifted his weight, it freed one of Tayshawn's arms, and he knew that this would be his one and only shot. When Apple drew back to deliver the knockout blow, Tayshawn sat up as far as he could and sank his teeth into the soft flesh of Apple's stomach. Then, in desperation, Tayshawn dug his teeth into Apple's thigh and bit down as hard as he could.

Apple sounded like a wounded water buffalo, instinctively throwing himself backward. He scrambled out of reach of the crazed young man. While clutching his stomach and breathing like he had just run a marathon, Apple looked over at Tayshawn. He was crouched on all fours, blood dripping from his chin, and he stared at Apple like a starved wolf. This was not the same mild-mannered young man he'd just given a beating to the day before.

Tayshawn was now moving more off rage than rational thought as he rushed in Apple's direction. From the corner of his eye, he saw one of Apple's boys stepping out to try to blind-side him, but he would never get the chance. A brown blur came out of the crowd of onlookers and hit Apple's minion with a powerful right hook. The force of the blow was so violent that it literally knocked Apple's friend out of his Nikes. Tayshawn didn't even stop to see who his benefactor was; he was too dead set on getting to Apple.

Tayshawn attacked Apple with the ferocity of a wild dog as he hit him with punches and kicks. What young Tayshawn lacked in technique, he made up for in determination to whip the local bully's ass. Apple tried to rush him again, but this time, Tayshawn was prepared. He moved at the last second, stuck out his foot, and tripped Apple up. The brute fell face first to the ground, skinning his chin. Tayshawn didn't give him a chance to recover this time. He climbed on Apple's back and grabbed a fistful of his nappy afro.

"All I wanted was to be left alone, and you couldn't do that, right?" Tayshawn whispered in his ear before slamming Apple's face into the concrete. Mentally he had checked out, and he no longer saw himself fighting Apple. He was fighting everyone who had ever hurt him in his life, and he wanted to hurt them all worse than they had hurt him. All he could see was red, but in his ears, he could still hear the crowd of kids chanting. This time, they weren't chants for Apple; they were chants of "Animal!"

Tayshawn would've surely killed Apple in front of the building had it not been for a pair of strong hands pulling him off the bully. Tayshawn didn't miss a beat when he turned around to attack whoever it was that had grabbed him. He was like a Tasmanian devil, lashing out with hands, feet, and teeth. It took a heavy slap across Tayshawn's face to bring him back from whatever dark place he was visiting. Slowly, the madness drained from Tayshawn's eyes, and he was able to recognize his older brother.

Justice held Tayshawn at arm's length, shaking him slightly to make sure he was fully aware. Seeing his little brother covered in blood, with a murderous look in his eyes, frightened Justice, not because he feared Tayshawn would attack him, but because, in that moment, he looked just like his father.

"Tayshawn, you in there?" Justice asked.

Tayshawn blinked as if he were waking from a deep sleep. It took a few seconds for him to survey the scene and recall everything that had just happened. When his eyes landed on the beaten and bloodied Apple, he tried to attack him again, but Justice held him back.

"Get the fuck off me so I can finish killing this nigga!" He struggled.

"Enough, little brother. You've proven your point," Justice whispered to him. He was holding Tayshawn in a reverse bear hug, keeping him from what was left of Apple.

Tayshawn stopped fighting, but his body still trembled with rage. "I fought him, just like you told me to, Justice."

"You did more than fight him; you beat him," Justice said proudly.

"Now this is a fine mess," a voice called from somewhere beyond the throng of children. The crowd parted like the Red Sea to let K-Dawg pass.

K-Dawg was the ringmaster of their circus of criminals called the Road Dawgz. He was the only guy Tayshawn had ever seen who was as black as tar but had the most beautiful jade-green eyes. K-Dawg was the kind of kid they warned you against becoming in those Scared Straight programs. He was the poster child for mayhem and had been voted by the neighborhood as most likely to grow up to be a serial killer. He was as feared as he was pitied in the neighborhood by those who knew the circumstances he'd come from.

The day K-Dawg's mother got pregnant marked the beginning of a dark time for his family. The violent way in which he was conceived—his mother was raped by a taxi driver—marked how he would go on to live his life in violence. From the day K-Dawg came into the world, tragedy walked with the members of his family. Some whispered that K-Dawg's birth was a curse put on their family, brought on by his mother bearing the seed of a man other than her husband.

Behind his back, the kids called K-Dawg "Devil Boy," and it was rumored that if you stared into his eyes for too long, he could take over your soul. Every member of his Road Dawgz crew was said to have been bound to him by black magic, including Tayshawn's brother, Justice.

Just behind him was the quiet kid that everyone called Demon. His pasty skin and lifeless eyes gave him a ghostly appearance. If K-Dawg was Satan, then Demon was the Devil's Advocate. His soulless eyes swept the crowd, causing some of the kids to turn away in fear. Demon looked at the bloodied and wild-eyed Tayshawn, and for the first time in as long as he'd known him, Tayshawn could've sworn he saw Demon crack a faint smile.

"So this is what we've come to, rat-packing on smaller kids?" K-Dawg asked, eyes burning holes in Apple, who was still on the ground, clutching his injured stomach.

Without provocation, the brown-skinned young man who had helped Tayshawn during the fight walked over and kicked Apple in the ribs. "Bitch-ass nigga, I should stomp you to death for trying to get at my fam." He raised his foot, causing Apple to cringe.

"Stand down, Brasco," K-Dawg ordered.

When Tayshawn heard the name, he realized that he knew the kid. Brasco was a young ruffian that Tayshawn had met a few times in the past. He was one of the young wannabes who hung around the Road Dawgz in hopes of one day becoming a member.

Brasco was two or three years older than Tayshawn, but he carried himself like a man almost twice his age. K-Dawg called him wise beyond his years, but he knew that Brasco still was not ready, so his membership was put on hold until their leader said otherwise. In the meantime, they kept Brasco around to handle what they liked to call "light work," which meant he was called on from time to time to throw a beating to those K-Dawg deemed "food." Even though he was very young, Brasco had the muscular frame of a grown man, and he loved to fight.

"Say the word, Dawg, and I'll knock all these niggas' heads off." Brasco's eyes swept over Apple's crew. His fists were balled in anticipation of violence.

K-Dawg stood, tapping his chin like he was pondering whether to let the young bulldog off the chain. "Nah, I don't think that'll be necessary. I'm guessing that this is the last time Tayshawn has to worry about being bullied by this lot. Isn't that right?" He directed the question at Apple.

"I don't want no problems with you, K-Dawg," Apple said, trying to hide the fear in his voice.

K-Dawg knelt beside him. "That's not what I asked you. Is this shit between you and Tayshawn over with?"

"Yeah, it's over." Apple assured him.

"Good. Now get the fuck up off the block before I let my little man slump you," K-Dawg ordered him. Apple didn't argue as he scrambled to his feet and hightailed it up the street with his crew in tow.

K-Dawg turned his attention to Tayshawn. "Damn, li'l bro! You handled yourself better than I'd have expected against somebody like Apple," he said proudly.

Tayshawn just shrugged. "Eventually the victim gets tired and decides to become the predator."

K-Dawg laughed at Tayshawn's wit. "Indeed he does. You was on that boy like a beast. As a matter of fact, that's what we need to start calling you—Young Beast."

"I like that for you, Tay," Justice said approvingly. "What do you think?"

Tayshawn looked at Apple's blood on the ground, and then over his shoulder at Noki, whose look of pity had turned into one of adoration.

"Nah," Tayshawn said softly. "Call me Animal."

PART II

—A History of Violence—

Chapter 6

The year went by quickly, and things changed in the hood. The transformation from Tayshawn to Animal was subtle, but anyone who had known him before and after felt the winds of change blowing. He was thirteen now, and though still a boy, life and circumstances were forcing him to grow up faster than he should have had to. Animal was still very shy and reserved, but the part of him that had tried to tear a chunk from Apple's flesh was still lingering just beneath the surface, and it didn't take much to bring it out. Animal became aggressive, and instead of shying away from confrontations, he met them head on. It was as if conquering his fear of Apple had opened a door in the back of his mind, and he now saw the world through different eyes.

K-Dawg had explained to him that it was the same as when a house dog got its first taste of blood. It could never be the same docile family pet again, because no matter how hard it tried to shake it, the craving for blood would always be there. Animal didn't know how much he appreciated being compared to a dog, but he got K-Dawg's meaning, and it made sense. He was no longer the docile house pet of the neighborhood.

Things got better for Animal as far as everyday life went, but at home, the situation was steadily getting worse. Marie hadn't been the same since their visit to the church to see the one-eyed priest. She spent most of her time in the house, getting high and staring off into space. Every so often Eddie was able to rouse her enough to hit the streets to do what needed to be done to get their next fix, but for the most part, Marie became more and more withdrawn. Animal tried to get through to his mother, but wherever she was, he couldn't reach her.

Marie's worsening condition didn't make Eddie any easier to deal with. She was his crutch, and with her not being in the best mental condition to hustle up money for them, he had to go in the streets and get it on his own. Eddie was a master con man, but the new age of hustlers on the streets weren't as forgiving as the marks on which he was used to preying. More than a few times, Eddie had come in bruised from an ass-whipping someone had treated him to for trying to play dirty. Those were the nights he would come in talking crazy to everyone else and taking his frustrations out on Marie and Animal. He didn't have the balls to go after those who had wronged him, so he went after those who feared him.

He never raised his hand to Animal or Marie when Justice was around, but Justice was spending more and more time out of the house. Animal feared that one day, Eddie would kill them, or he would kill Eddie. He started spending more time in the streets so he wouldn't have to deal with him.

Animal had also become somewhat of a local celebrity. Kids who had once shunned him now wanted to be associated with him. He didn't realize it at the time, but beating Apple had made him the new tough guy among the neighborhood kids. Animal didn't care for the attention though. He preferred to read quietly under the shade of a tree or hit the local arcades with Noki. The two of them had become very close. People often joked about them being a couple, but Noki would quickly shoot down the notion. She insisted that she and Animal were just friends, but it didn't stop her from trying to fight all the little girls who chased after him.

During their time together, Noki taught Animal about a variety of things, including fashion. Marie never gave Animal money for new clothes, so Noki showed him how to work with what he had. The young Japanese girl had a natural gift for style, and she was able to arrange the most off-the-rack looking pieces to make them not look so tacky. On more than a few occasions, they even went boosting in the clothing stores downtown. Animal wasn't very good at shoplifting, but Noki had some of the fastest hands he had ever seen. She could pull a shirt off a hanger and make it vanish in the blink of an eye.

Noki had also finally made heads or tails of his hair. Besides Justice and, occasionally, his mother, Noki was the only person he would let touch the curly mop. Noki would spend afternoons greasing Animal's scalp and braiding his hair into cornrows. He had inherited his mother's fine hair texture, so the braids would often come out after a few days, but Noki would just do them over. Her reason for fussing over his hair all the time, she said, was he needed to look presentable when standing next to her. She would tell Animal that, for as long as they were best friends, his hair would always be freshly braided.

Brasco also became a regular fixture in Animal's life. The two of them were always around the neighborhood getting into mischief. Brasco was a hustler to his heart and had hipped Animal to all kinds of petty schemes to score a few dollars in the streets. One of their favorite licks was buying water guns from the dollar store and painting them black with shoe polish. They would call in bogus orders to restaurants and rob the delivery guys when they showed up. It was always a pretty easy lick, until the time when they came across a deliveryman who wasn't so willing to give up his goods. He surprised them when he pulled out a Taser and lit Brasco's ass up. They managed to escape capture, but after that close call, they decided it was time to find a different hustle.

Sometimes, Justice would let Brasco and Animal tag along on some of their capers, but only the small ones. The big jobs were reserved for official members of the Road Dawgz crew. K-Dawg's name was ringing louder and louder in the streets, and he was pulling Justice and the others deeper in with him. They had gone from committing petty crimes to doing big-boy things. The streets were rumbling about the young crew, and Animal was scared for Justice. He was all that he had in the world and Animal didn't know what he would do if something happened to him. Justice always assured Animal that he and K-Dawg had things under control, but Animal didn't believe him. There was a black cloud hovering over K-Dawg, and Animal knew it would only be a matter of time before it rained.

Animal was still in school, but he didn't attend as regularly as he should. He was always running the streets with Brasco. The school sent notices home about Animal missing school, but Marie didn't care. Justice would get on him about the importance of going to school, but he was too busy with K-Dawg to enforce it. Animal was starting to march to the beat of his own drum, and he liked the way it felt.

He still kept time with Noki, but not as often as he would've liked. Unlike his drug-addicted mother, who could've cared less if he didn't go to school, Noki's parents would've killed her if she ditched. For all her hood girl antics, Noki's father paid a nice piece of change for her to attend a private school on the Upper West Side.

During the week, Noki's parents kept her under lock and key, so their time together was mostly spent on weekends or on those rare occasions when Noki was able to sneak out on a weekday. Animal missed seeing Noki more regularly, but Brasco kept him more than occupied with his bullshit.

One day, Animal and Brasco were sitting on the benches in front of Animal's building, scheming as usual. Brasco knew two sisters from 128th that had an apartment they could go hang out at and possibly get lucky. Their mother worked the day shift, so they were home alone a lot. The only catch was that Animal and Brasco had to bring weed and liquor if they wanted to hang out, and neither of them had any money.

Animal wasn't as thirsty to go see the girls as Brasco because he had Noki. Although they weren't an item, he didn't want to do anything to put himself out of favor with her, but he did want to smoke. Weed was something Brasco had recently introduced him to, and Animal found himself falling madly in love with Mary Jane.

"I can't believe this shit," Brasco said. "These bitches ready to fuck, and we sitting here like two clowns."

"Maybe they'll still be down to hang out even if we don't get the weed," Animal suggested.

Brasco gave him a look. "On what planet do they do that? These gutter rats ain't looking for nothing but a good time, and they'll jump off with anybody with a little smoke or drink, and I want that to be us!" He got up and began pacing. "Do you think you can get some weed from Justice?"

"Probably, but I don't know where he is," Animal said. Justice and K-Dawg had been moving at a million miles per minute lately, and it was hard to catch up with him. "What about if we go downtown and pick a few pockets?"

"Yeah, we could probably go downtown and make a couple of bucks, but by the time we do all that, then come back uptown to get the weed and drinks, some other niggas are gonna be up in the crib. We need a quick come-up."

Their conversation ended when the lobby door opened up and out stepped two local hard-heads known as Bump and Eddy. They weren't from the block; they were from Brooklyn, but Bump messed with a chick from their projects, so he and Eddy were always around. From time to time, you could catch them here and there, making crack sales when the big dealers weren't around, but their game was stick-ups. Bump and Eddy were too lazy to go out and hustle it up, so they lay in the cut while the next man made it and they could take it from him.

Animal had never cared for either of them, especially Eddy. He not only shared the name of his mother's boyfriend and his tormentor, but he was almost as big of an asshole as the elder Eddie. Every time he saw Animal, he had something slick to say out of his mouth, and that day was no different.

"Why does your dusty ass always seem to end up where I'm at?" Eddy started right in on Animal. "I'm starting to feel like you're following me."

"Ain't nobody following you, man. Unlike y'all, I live around here," Animal shot back.

"Watch your tone when you're speaking to grown folks," Bump interjected.

He was always short with Animal. Unlike Eddy, who didn't like Animal because he thought he was beneath him, the kid gave Bump the creeps. He would see him out at all hours of the night, tucked away in some shadowed corner, pretending to be reading but secretly watching everything and everybody. It was as if Animal was waiting for something to happen that only he was privy to. It made Bump uncomfortable, and he would have someone chase him away whenever he spotted him.

"Bitch-ass niggas," Brasco grumbled under his breath.

"Fuck did you just say, li'l nigga?" Eddy turned his attention to him.

"Nothing, man. I ain't said shit," Brasco said with a slight smirk.

"You think you funny?" Eddy opened his jacket, showing Brasco the butt of the .38 tucked in the waistband of his pants. His intent was to intimidate the young man, but Brasco showed no fear. He simply glared at Eddy, as if challenging him to shoot. "You don't think I'll pop you?" He reached for the gun, but Bump stopped him.

"Don't be stupid. There are too many people out here," Bump told his partner. "Leave these slum-ass niggas alone, and let's go take care of business." He pulled at Eddy's arm.

Eddy gave Brasco one last look before lowering his hand. "You lucky, real lucky," he warned, allowing his partner to pull him away. "Y'all better be careful. It's dangerous in these streets, and bullets ain't got no name." He followed his partner away from the building.

"Pussy," Brasco spat once they were out of earshot.

"I hate those two," Animal said seriously.

"You and me both. One of these days, somebody is gonna kill them for the way they're always out here doing wrong and harassing people."

"Probably sooner than later," Animal said, watching the two Brooklyn natives amble down the street.

The lobby door opened a second time, and out came Annie. She had been a looker once upon a time, with pretty dark skin, white teeth, and thick black hair, but hard living and drugs had caught up to her, and she was now a shell of the woman she once was. Her skin was ashen, and her hair was thinning. The pretty white teeth she had so proudly showed off were now yellow and rotting. She was another victim of the crack epidemic that had been ravaging the American ghetto for the last decade. Trailing her were her ever-present shadows, her two youngest kids, Ashanti and Angela. As usual, their clothes were dirty and their heads were unkempt.

Annie had five children. All of them had been taken away by the system over the years, except for the youngest two. Ashanti and Angela had remained with their mother, at least for the time being.

Angela was the older of the two. Her clothes were knock-offs, and her hair was hardly ever done, but she was a very pretty girl, with dark skin and thick black hair. She was the spitting image of her mother. Angela was eleven years old and just starting to blossom into a woman. Animal didn't miss the looks that dirty old men gave the girl when she wandered through the neighborhood by herself. Sometimes, when she was on the block at night, he would let her sit with him and read books. It wasn't that he enjoyed the girl's company, but by keeping her close, he could keep the predators away from her. On the outside, Angela looked like any other pre-teen girl, but mentally she was as fragile as glass. With Annie as a mother, Animal could understand why.

Ashanti was the soldier. He was only six or seven, but he carried himself like he had been born in the streets, which he had. When she was pregnant with him, Annie's water broke while she was in the park getting high with some of her friends. She wanted that last blast so bad that she pushed her child out on the concrete as opposed to going to a hospital. Being born in such a violent and cruel way made Ashanti different than the other kids his age. He feared little and respected less. It wasn't unusual to see him wandering the neighborhood in the middle of the night or vandalizing someone's property. When people would find him and take him home, he would simply sneak out again when Annie was getting high. After a while, people stopped trying to take him home and just made sure that he was okay while he was out. Ashanti was an accident waiting to happen, and if he didn't get some type of direction in his life other than the bullshit Annie fed him and his sister, it would happen sooner than later.

"Hey, y'all." Annie greeted Animal and Brasco.

Brasco only scowled, but Animal smiled and spoke. "How you doing, Annie?"

"Shit! I been better. I'm trying to get off empty. You got anything?" Annie asked in an almost pleading voice.

"You know I don't sell drugs," Animal reminded her.

Annie sucked her rotting teeth. "Then you need to start. These muthafuckas out here are unreliable as hell. Where's Justice?"

Animal shrugged. "Your guess is as good as mine."

"Damn. If I don't get right soon, I'm gonna be sick as a dog." Annie scratched her arm. "Is ya mom or Eddie home?"

"You sure do ask a lot of questions. You wired?" Brasco cut in.

"Damn! Why you gotta be so mean all the time, Brasco? You need to get you some pussy because you're too uptight."

"If you're selling, I ain't buying." Brasco laughed. His eyes landed on Ashanti, who was staring daggers at him. "Be cool, Ashanti. I was only joking with ya moms. What are y'all doing out of school at this time of day anyhow?"

"He ain't in school because he's too busy trying to get thrown in jail," Annie answered for him. "I was supposed to be taking Angela to get a checkup, but instead, I had to go all the way downtown to this little muthafucka's school this morning because his ass cut some boy with a pair of scissors." She pinched Ashanti to convey her anger.

"They lying on me. He ran into the scissors," Ashanti explained, rubbing his arm. One of his front teeth was missing, so when he used words containing the letter S, it came out sounding like a whistle.

"They said you cut him twice, so did he run into them twice?" Annie asked.

"Can't blame me because that nigga is clumsy," Ashanti said and was rewarded with a slap from Annie.

"I keep telling you about playing on my intelligence. You keep it up and I'm gonna have you put in the system with the rest of those ungrateful bitches and bastards I pushed out my womb," Annie barked.

"I don't give a fuck," Ashanti mumbled.

"See? That mouth is what got the shit slapped out of you a second ago. Keep it up and the next one is gonna be a fist!" Annie warned.

"Like I can't take a punch," Ashanti huffed.

Annie's eyes widened and her nostrils flared before she launched a vicious combination of slaps at young Ashanti. He hopped around, trying to protect his face as best he could while Annie tore into him, calling him everything but a child of God.

While Annie tightened Ashanti up, Animal watched Angela, who was silently observing them. The corners of her mouth were curled ever so slightly, as if she was amused by the sight of her little brother getting his ass kicked. Ashanti was bad as hell, so there was no telling what kind of torment he inflicted on Angela. She was probably glad to see him getting his medicine.

"See something you like?" Annie asked, startling Animal. He hadn't even realized she had stopped beating on Ashanti and had turned her attention to him.

"Huh?" he asked for lack of a better response.

"I see the way you're looking at my baby girl," Annie said slyly. "It's okay. She's young and fine like her mama, so I can't say that I blame you."

"Nah, it ain't like that, Annie. Angela is cute, but she's a little girl," Animal said, as if he were that much older than her.

"Yeah, but her little hot ass is out here playing grown woman games. Ain't that right?" Annie cast a resentful glance at Angela, to which she

responded by lowering her eyes out of embarrassment. "Tell you what." Annie turned back to
Animal. "Why don't you slide me a couple of dollars, and I'll go to the store and bring y'all back
some snacks? In the meantime, you and Angela
can go in the building and get acquainted. I'll
even have Ashanti stand watch."

Animal didn't immediately get Annie's meaning, but Brasco did.

"Bitch, are you really out here trying to pimp
your own fucking kid?" Brasco snarled.

Annie placed her hands on her hips. "Don't
act like I'm out here forcing her to do it. She's
already fucking for free, so why shouldn't I get a
few dollars out of it? Shit! I let the heifer lay up in
my house rent-free, so I don't see nothing wrong
with her kicking in a few dollars here and there,"
she said with conviction.

Animal's face went slack as the realization of
what Annie was suggesting finally kicked in. He
looked at Angela's sad eyes and thought of how
much they reflected his own that cold night years
ago, when his room door had squeaked open
and one of his mother's friends had had her
way with him. For a few dollars and some loose
crack rocks, Marie and Eddie turned a blind
eye while the older woman gave Animal a cruel
lesson about the birds and the bees, forcing him

to perform unimaginable acts for a child his age. It seemed like days before Animal was finally able to wash the stink of her unwashed pussy off his face, but the scars would be with him for all time.

Something in his head clicked, and he pounced on Annie. "You rank bitch, out here trying to sell your kids for a blast." Animal grabbed Annie by the throat, raining spittle on her face as he yelled. "You're supposed to protect them, not let them get hurt." He shook her like a rag doll.

"Get off my mama!" Angela yelled, leaping onto Animal's back and clawing at his face from behind. He was trying to protect her, but the child's brain was so twisted that her instincts told her to try to save the very person who was putting her in harm's way.

Ashanti just stood off to the side, looking like he wasn't sure whose side to jump in on.

Brasco let the scuffle go on for a few seconds, chuckling softly at the spectacle before intervening.

"Enough of this shit." He grabbed a fistful of Angela's hair and pulled her off Animal's back. She turned her wild eyes on him and tensed like she was about to pounce. "Angela, you know better than to test me," he said coldly. Once he was sure she got the message and would stay

put, he began the task of separating Animal and
Annie.

"Easy, killer." He pried Animal's hands from
Annie's throat.

Animal had scratches on his face from Angela's
sneak attack, and Annie had managed to pull
almost all of his braids loose. He looked like
a wild man standing there, eyes flashing hate,
breathing like he'd just run a marathon.

"They're your kids, Annie," he said emotionally. He wasn't sure if hate or sadness was the
dominating emotion at that moment.

Annie snapped the collar of her shirt, trying to
get it to lay correctly again. "Little boy, you got
some big balls out here trying to judge me and
mine like we're the only ones out here struggling to stay above the poverty line by any damn
means necessary. Your mama is a fiend, same as
I am, but she got you thinking y'all better than
everybody else because you got good hair and
connections. But them connections ain't seen fit
to pull y'all out of the slums, have they? Marie
spent years washing the blood out of that nigga's
shirts and ended up without a pot to piss in."

"What the hell are you talking about?" Animal
was confused by her ramblings.

When Annie realized that he might actually be
ignorant to the family shame, a cruel expression

crossed her face. "You busy out here trying to tell me about my family when you need to do a little digging into your own. The next time your mother has a lucid moment, ask her to tell you the story about the soldier and the fool," she snorted. "Let's go." She yanked Angela by the arm and started down the pathway, resuming her hunt for a fix.

Ashanti stood there for a few seconds longer, looking at Animal. His face was hard and expressionless, save for his lips being slightly twisted into a frown. Whatever he had been thinking, he decided it was best not to act on it, so he went to catch up with his mother and sister.

Animal stood there, just watching the unfortunate, dysfunctional family walk through the projects. Along the way, Annie stopped to talk to a slightly older man who lived in the next building. He saw her say something to him then motion toward little Angela. The man seemed to be contemplating her offer, but when he saw Animal glaring at him, he brushed Annie off and continued on his way.

Animal had always known Annie was fouler than most crackheads, but he never thought she would stoop as low as trying to pawn her child off just so she could get high. For as fucked up as Marie was, she'd never sell Animal . . . at least, he hoped she wouldn't. The one thing he had learned was that you couldn't put anything past a drug addict.

"What the fuck is wrong with you, Animal?" Brasco asked once Annie and her kids had gone.

"What you mean?" Animal asked.

"I mean you putting your hands on that bitch. I know Annie is a fiend, but she's still a woman, and they'll throw your ass in jail for hitting on her."

"Fuck that bitch. She's lucky I didn't kill her. What kind of person would try to sell off their kid?" Animal was still in disbelief.

"A crackhead," Brasco said simply. "When you're as far gone as Annie is, ain't no coming back. I know you were only trying to do right by those kids, but you can't help somebody who don't wanna be helped, or haven't those beauty marks on your face taught you that?"

Animal's hands subconsciously went to the side of his face. He could feel the raised welts Angela had left there.

Brasco placed his hand on Animal's shoulder comfortingly. "That bullshit Annie did hit me close to home too, but at the end of the day, there ain't a whole lot we can do about it. The best thing anybody can do for them kids is call child services to get them out of that house."

***

Thankfully, the rest of the day went on without a major incident. Animal and Brasco had finally managed to commit enough petty capers to scramble up some money for a meal and some weed. Brasco knew an older chick on the other side of town named Zena, who sold nickel bags of weed that she named Gangsta. It was a fifteen-block walk, but Zena had good weed and was always good to throw in something extra if you spent over a certain amount with her and were a regular customer.

It was during the walk with Brasco to get the weed from the East Side that Animal got his first real taste of Harlem. Animal rarely strayed more than a few blocks away from his projects. He had gone places with his mother on occasion, but that was always on the subway or in a taxi. He had never just taken a walk through Harlem and really gotten a chance to take it all in.

Harlem didn't look as dilapidated as it once had, but it still held an air of danger. Where there were once shooting galleries, brownstones now stood. The transformations were amazing, but the spirits of the old dope fiends who had taken their last hits on the stoops of the buildings remained.

It was a fairly nice night, so the gritty streets were alive with action. Pretty girls of all shapes and sizes occupied stoops and corners, and it seemed like they couldn't go more than a block without Brasco knowing someone. He was a young dude but seemed to be respected in the streets, even by some of the older dudes.

Zena lived in the East River Houses on 105th Street and First Avenue. When they entered the projects, Animal noticed Brasco's mood shift. He had gone from smiling and joking to stone-faced.

When Animal asked him what was wrong, Brasco simply said, "We're out of bounds, so be on point," meaning they were outside the comfort of their neighborhood where people knew them. They were in foreign territory.

Zena's building was located at the back of the projects, overlooking the F.D.R. Drive. There were a couple of young men loitering in the lobby, who gave them the once-over when they entered the building. Animal could feel the tension, and he knew Brasco could too, but they pretended not to.

It took less than ninety seconds for Brasco to make the transaction with Zena and for them to be on their way again. As promised, they spent twenty dollars, and she threw them an extra bag of weed. When they got back down to the lobby, the young men were still there, but they had been joined by a few more hard faces. They all turned their attention to Animal and Brasco, as if they had been waiting for them. When they tried to exit the building, the young men blocked their path.

"What's popping?" the biggest of the young men addressed them. He was a bulky lad with a wandering eye and pock-marked skin.

"Ain't nothing," Brasco said sternly, but not aggressively.

"What y'all doing in my building? Who y'all came to see?" Lazy Eye asked.

"A friend," Brasco replied, tucking his hands into his pocket and trying to step around him.

Lazy Eye cut him off. "You ain't from around here. What friends you got in my building? For all I know, y'all niggas could be trying to open up shop in my hood," Lazy Eye said.

"Listen, we don't want any trouble." Animal spoke up, trying to defuse the situation. They were outnumbered and a long way from home.

"That's too bad, because you've sure found it." A second young man stepped forward. He wasn't as big as Lazy Eye, but the knife in his hand made him twice as dangerous. "Y'all niggas empty your pockets."

Animal and Brasco looked at each other, and neither had to speak for the other to know what he was thinking. There were only two ways out of that situation: give up their goods or get beat down. They moved almost simultaneously, with Brasco landing a crushing blow on the chin of the kid who was holding the knife. Alone Brasco's punches were powerful, but the brass knuckles he had slipped onto his fist while his hand was in his pocket made it near critical. The kid with the knife flew backward, slamming his head into the mailboxes before pitching face-first onto the lobby floor and releasing the knife.

The rest of the kids in the lobby swarmed on Animal and Brasco. The two outsiders stood back to back, fighting their attackers off as best they could, but there were too many of them. In a matter of seconds, they were overrun.

Animal lay on the floor, while Lazy Eye kicked and stomped him. Through a haze of pain, he could see Brasco leaning against the wall, swinging wildly, trying to get the attackers off him. They had to do something, or they would surely get beat to death in the lobby. Animal felt something graze his fingertips and instinctively closed his hand around it. It was the knife. When Lazy Eye raised his foot to stomp him again, Animal lashed out with the object and drove the blade through his heel.

Lazy Eye's screams, coupled with the blood that now coated the lobby floor, gave the attackers pause, and gave Animal time to regroup. He now went on the offensive, slashing at the mob with the blade. When a hole opened up in the crowd, Animal grabbed Brasco and pulled him toward the exit. They burst from the lobby and took off running. Neither Animal nor Brasco ever looked back to see if the young men from the lobby were pursuing them. They just kept running and didn't dare slow down until they were safely back in their hood.

Later, they would laugh and joke about the near death experience, but at the time, Animal had been terrified. He had been in scuffles, but never before had he been that close to death. Had it not been for him having the good fortune to retrieve the discarded knife, things might've played out differently. He vowed, from that moment on, to always carry some type of protection with him so that he was never caught defenseless again.

Chapter 7

When Animal woke up the next morning, his whole body ached. Between the fight with the boys in the projects and his scuffle with Annie, he felt like he had been put through the wringer.

He looked at himself in the cracked bedroom mirror and saw a mess staring back at him. His face was bruised and his braids had come almost totally undone. He removed the last few braids from his hair and dressed for the day. At some point, Eddie or his mother had come into his room and stolen the new shirts Noki had boosted for him, so he was forced to put on the same shirt from the day before. There were splotches of blood on it, so he had to rock it inside out. Before leaving his bedroom, he reached under his mattress and retrieved the knife from the day before. Brasco had told him to get rid of it, because the knife could connect him to the stabbing, and Animal had promised that he would, but he didn't. It was the first weapon he'd ever owned, and he was reluctant to part with it.

There was no telling when he would have to rely on it to save his ass again.

When he walked into the living room, he was surprised to find his mother up and about. Marie sat on the couch, smoking a cigarette and drinking beer out of an old champagne glass. In the background, the sounds of Anita Baker's *Sweet Love* played softly on the radio. From the deep slant to Marie's eyes, Animal knew she was feeling nice, but she wasn't quite gone yet.

Animal had become extremely worried about his mother lately. She had lost a noticeable amount of weight over the past few months and always seemed to be sick. He had brought it up to Justice a few times, but his brother always brushed it off as the drugs wearing her out. Justice didn't seem too worried about it, but Animal was. He couldn't help but feel like something dark was looming.

"Why you ain't in school?" Marie asked.

"Had a half day," Animal lied. "Can I get two dollars, so I can go get a sausage, egg, and cheese on a roll?" He wasn't really hungry. He just wanted to change the subject.

"I ain't got it right now. I'm waiting on Eddie to come back. He's out making some moves," Marie told him, expelling smoke through her nose while stubbing her cigarette out in the ashtray. No sooner than the cherry burned out, she was firing up another one. "You hear what happened with your brother?"

"No. Is everything okay with him?" Animal asked nervously. His big brother was his heart, and he couldn't stand to hear it if something bad had happened to him.

"Got himself arrested last night." Marie exhaled a cloud of smoke.

"For what?"

Marie flicked the ash from her cigarette, only getting half the ash into the tray, with the rest hitting the table. "Questioning him about a shooting that happened out in the courtyard last night. You hear anything about it?"

"No." Animal shook his head. "Mama, Justice didn't shoot anybody."

"We know that and so do the police. They're saying he was there when somebody got shot, but he's refusing to cooperate. That bullshit code of the streets that he's such a fanatic about is about to land his ass in the slammer, and I sure as hell ain't got no money for no food packages or commissary. Your father was the first, last, and only nigga who can ever say I dropped a dime on their books, and even that was only twice. I don't do bids with niggas."

"Well, is there anything we can do to get him out? How much is his bail?" Animal asked, his young mind whirling, trying to think up schemes to earn some bread. If he had to, he was willing to rob a bank to free his big brother.

Marie laughed. "And what you gonna bail him out with, them scraps you and Brasco be out there ripping off?"

Animal was struck by the statement.

"Don't look surprised, Tayshawn. I'm in the streets every day, so I don't miss shit." She took a drag of her cigarette. "All I'm gonna tell your little ass is, if you get into some shit, don't go looking for Mama to get your ass out of it. I swear, every day you're becoming more and more like your brother, a damn follower. Y'all need to learn to think for your damn selves, instead of letting people like K-Dawg influence you. I warned your brother about being a damn follower. He didn't listen to me, and you see what that got him. That green-eyed monster is gonna bring the whole neighborhood down."

"Why do you hate K-Dawg so much, Mama?" Animal asked. To his knowledge, K-Dawg had never done anything to his mother, yet he was the only one of Justice's friends who she never had a kind word for.

"I don't hate him. *Hate* is a strong word, and he's just a child, but I know his heart. That boy is rotten inside and out, and everything he touches, he corrupts," Marie told her son. "It ain't all his fault, though. He came into the world wrong, so I can't expect a kid like him to live his life any other way. I just don't want him dragging my boys down with him."

"Justice is too smart for that, and so am I," Animal told her.

Marie snorted. "The fact that your brother is sitting in jail for some shit K-Dawg probably did means the jury is still out on how smart he is. I used to think he was smart, until I started seeing the way that he lets K-Dawg dangle him like a puppet on a string. It's like that boy has got more control over my child than I do. I know one thing: I better not catch your ass hanging around with that Road Dawgz gang, or I'm going to kick it for you. Do you understand me?"

"Yes, Mama," Animal said, but he didn't really mean it. He envied the way people respected K-Dawg and Justice, and he wanted the same respect for himself and Brasco. If the opportunity ever arose, he would jump at the chance to run with their gang.

As Animal stood there, watching his mother chain-smoke and slip in and out of a nod, he thought about what Annie had told him and was curious.

"Mama, what's the story of the soldier and the fool?"

Hearing her son's question, Marie's head snapped up, and for a minute, she looked completely sober. "Where did you hear that?"

Animal shrugged. "Just around."

So quick that it surprised Animal, Marie was on her feet and across the room. She grabbed two fistfuls of his shirt and shook him violently. "Bullshit! Somebody told you the story, and you're gonna tell me who, or as God is my witness, I'm gonna beat you to death!"

The look in Marie's eyes scared Animal. There was no doubt in his mind that she would attempt to make good on her threat if he didn't come clean, so he did. "Okay, okay. Me and crackhead Annie got into it, and she said some slick shit to me and told me to ask you to me tell the story."

Marie released Animal and gave him a light shove. "Should've known it came from some no-account muthafucka on the streets. That cock-worshiping whore Annie's mouth is only good for two things—taking in dick and spitting out bullshit!" She swung her hand and knocked her champagne glass over, spilling beer onto the dirty floor. "Shit!" she cursed, staring at the mess.

"Don't worry. I'll get it, Mama." Animal disappeared into the kitchen and came back holding a roll of paper towels. He got down on his hands and knees and began the task of cleaning up the beer.

"It happened a long time ago." Marie surprised him when she began speaking. She had fished another cigarette from her pack and lit it. "As with most tragic stories, this one starts with a woman. Flaca, as they called her back then, was a young Spanish girl from the bottom, trying to make her way to the top by any means necessary. Flaca had endured so much abuse at the hands of men that life had made her bitter toward the opposite sex. To her, a man was nothing more than a means to an end. So blinded was she by her hatred that she didn't know how to spot a good man when one came into her life.

"Joseph was not like the street guys Flaca was used to dating. He didn't sell drugs; he worked a city job and was saving up to buy his first house. He was a square in every sense of the word, which is what made him and Flaca such an awkward match. Those close to Joseph warned him about Flaca, but that didn't stop him from letting her into his home and his heart. That was the beginning of the end."

A look of great sadness crossed Marie's face. It was so powerful that Animal felt it in his chest. For a minute, he was about to reach out and comfort her, but just as suddenly as the sadness had come, it disappeared. She stubbed out her cigarette and reached for her pack. She shook it, frowning when she realized it was empty, and tossed it back onto the table.

"See, Joseph was head over heels for Flaca, but she didn't feel the same," Marie continued. "He was ready to settle down, but Flaca still longed for the streets. Joseph knew that he didn't totally have Flaca's heart, but he held onto the hope that one day she would come around and love him as he loved her."

"That Joseph sounds like a real sucka," Animal remarked.

In a rare display of affection, Marie ran her hand over his head. "Spoken like a man who has never loved a woman. Son, when your heart leads, the rest of you follows, whether you want it to or not. I don't expect you to understand now, but once you've loved and had your heart broken, this'll all make sense to you."

Animal nodded as if he understood, but it wouldn't be until years later that his mother's words would come back to him and he would truly get the lesson about the heart that she was trying to teach him.

"Early in their relationship, they had a son. Joseph thought Flaca becoming a mother would bring them closer together, but it only seemed to push them further apart. Flaca would take off at the drop of a hat, leaving their son with Joseph or anyone who was willing to keep him for the night. Joseph tried everything he could think of to try to get through to Flaca, from buying her gifts that he couldn't afford to proposing marriage, but none of it seemed to move her.

"For as much as Joseph tried to bring to her life, the young girl always felt like something was missing, so she set out to find it. Even before he started hearing the rumors about Flaca creeping with other men, Joseph knew that he was losing her. It all boiled to a nasty head when the soldier came back into her life."

"So, she knew the soldier?" Animal asked.

Marie nodded. "Flaca and the soldier had been lovers long before either of them understood what love was. It had been years since she'd seen him, but she had always been kept abreast of his exploits through the streets. Word had it that the soldier was making a name for himself and now served as the right arm of the man who was rumored to be the next King of Kings, Thomas Clark."

The name rang familiar to Animal, but he was too engrossed in the story to try to figure out where he'd heard it before.

"In the soldier, Flaca found everything that she couldn't find in Joseph. He was handsome, had money, and was well-known in the streets. When they went places, people treated them like celebrities. For the first time in a long time, Flaca felt alive and young again.

"For a while, Flaca and the soldier kept their romance a secret, but nothing stays a secret for long. The streets are always talking, and word was that Flaca planned to leave Joseph for the soldier and take their son with her. When Joseph confronted Flaca about it, he'd expected her to deny it and tell him that it had all been a nasty rumor, but she didn't. She told Joseph that she no longer loved him and that their time together had come to an end."

Animal released a faint gasp. Marie told the story so vividly that he felt like he was right there, living through the painful moment with Joseph.

"The revelation hit Joseph like a blow. He pleaded for Flaca to stay, but her mind was made up. When she left him, Joseph was on his knees, crying like a baby for her to stay, but his pleas fell on deaf ears. When the realization set in, Joseph snapped. The thought of losing the two people he loved the most was too much for him to bear.

"That night, when Flaca went to meet with the soldier, Joseph followed her. He watched them through the window as they partied in a neighborhood bar. Seeing the soldier touching his woman in the places that were supposed to be reserved for only him drove Joseph mad.

"He waited until they came out of the bar and were making their way to the soldier's car, which was parked on a dark block. Sticking to the shadows, he followed them, holding the .32 he had bought from a pawn shop that morning. When he'd purchased the gun, he wasn't sure what he was going to do with it, but when he peered into the car window and saw his woman with the soldier's dick in her mouth, it became abundantly clear. Without even realizing what he was doing, Joseph raised the gun and pointed it at the top of Flaca's head."

Animal's heart leapt into his chest. He wanted to know what would happen next, but he was almost afraid to find out. He had abandoned the task of cleaning up the beer long ago, and now the paper towels he had been using to clean it up were a soggy, dripping mess in his hands.

"Flaca must've felt something was wrong, because she looked up and saw Joseph holding the gun. The murderous look on his face froze her with fear, and she watched helplessly as his finger tightened around the trigger. Everything seemed to happen in slow motion. Flaca saw the muzzle flash, and the bullet seemed to drip from the barrel of the .32. She didn't think about screaming, or even trying to get out of the way. Her mind was fixed on her young son's face and how she would never see him again.

"While Flaca was too shocked to know what to do, the soldier was in motion, shielding her with his body as the shot shattered the window. Flaca lay pinned beneath the soldier as the sounds of gunfire and shattering glass filled her ears.

"The shooting had only gone on for a few seconds, but it seemed like hours. When she was finally able to crawl from beneath the soldier's prone body, Joseph was gone, but in his wake, he had left a gruesome scene that Flaca would never forget."

"So, Joseph killed the soldier?" Animal asked. He was slightly disappointed because he had come to like the soldier's character.

"No, the soldier took several bullets and shards of glass from the windshield blinded him in one eye, but he lived. Joseph might as well have killed him because the repercussions for the attempt would be just as severe," Marie said, with her voice taking on a serious edge.

"The soldier was a made man, so, within no time, minions of the streets were spreading the story of what happened and the parties responsible. When word reached Thomas Clark, he went ballistic. He had warned the soldier against getting too caught up with Flaca, because he never really trusted her. Thomas Clark was big on loyalty, and any woman who would sneak around on her man was not loyal. The soldier hadn't taken heed of his friend's advice, and it had almost cost him his life.

"Still, he was a made man, and to touch him was a death sentence on all parties involved, including Flaca and the child she was carrying. The soldier had been loyal to Thomas and never challenged an order until that moment. Flaca was the cause of his troubles, but his heart would not see her or his child harmed. So in love was he that the soldier was willing to stand against an army to protect her.

"As a favor to his friend, Thomas Clark gave Flaca a pass, but not before teaching her a lesson in loyalty. . . ." Her words trailed off as she visibly choked up.

"You okay, Mama?" Animal asked, genuinely concerned. He couldn't remember the last time he'd seen his mother cry, but at that moment, tears rolled freely down her cheeks.

Marie simply nodded. She took a few seconds to compose herself and continued her tale. "Thomas had some of his men bring Flaca to an auto repair shop on the outskirts of town. When she got inside, she saw a beaten and bruised Joseph with his hands cuffed to one of the car lifts and his feet shackled to the floor. His frightened eyes looked to her hopefully, as if Flaca might've come to save him, but she was powerless to stop what was certainly coming.

When Thomas activated the car lift, Joseph's body began to rise. Even when the shackles around his wrists and ankles had reached their limits and Joseph howled for mercy, Thomas showed him none. They made Flaca watch as Joseph's body was torn into quarters. He wanted her to see firsthand how he dealt with people who sought to bring harm to members of his family. It was a lesson that would stick with Flaca for all of her days."

"Did she ever tell the soldier what Thomas Clark had done?" Animal asked.

"No, she never spoke of it again to anyone until years later. With Joseph out of the way,

Flaca was free to be with the soldier. At long last, she was getting what she finally wanted: the high life that came with being a notorious gangster's girlfriend."

Animal nodded. "So Flaca and the soldier got to be together and Joseph got killed. I guess that makes him the fool in this story, right?"

"That all depends on who you ask. Flaca got what she finally wanted, but what she hadn't counted on was the price that came with being a gangster's girlfriend. The drugs, the other women, the murders . . . Flaca wasn't built to handle it, and within the first few years of their relationship, hard living and stress had reduced her to a shell of her former self. As the life took its toll on Flaca's mind and body, it also destroyed her relationship with the soldier. The soldier loved Flaca, true enough, but he loved the streets more, and it was she, the streets, to whom he had given his heart, and Flaca took a back seat to duty. Flaca abandoned a good man to ride off into the sunset with the devil and got burned. In the end, she was left with two kids to raise on her own and a drug habit to feed. So you see, Tayshawn, it was Flaca who was the real fool of the story."

By the end of Marie's story, she looked spent. Her shoulders sagged, and her face was stained with the tracks of the tears she'd shed during the telling of her tale.

Animal got off the floor and approached his mother timidly. When she looked up at him, her eyes were sadder than he'd ever seen them. His mother, who had always been so fierce and strong, now appeared weak and broken. Without even thinking about it, Animal wrapped his arms around his mother and hugged her. They had never been big on displays of affection, and he wasn't sure why he had done it, other than the fact that she seemed like she needed it. For the first time in a long time, they weren't the warring mother and the rebellious son at odds, but simply a mother and son trying to comfort each other during a rough time. The moment was beautiful, but it lasted only until the front door opened.

Chapter 8

Animal smelled him before he actually saw him. The stink of Wild Irish Rose and funk preceded him. Eddie half-walked, half-stumbled into the living room. Tucked under his arm like a football was a brown paper bag, which likely contained more alcohol. When he noticed Animal and Marie on the couch hugging, he frowned in disapproval. Before he even opened his mouth, Animal knew there was going to be trouble.

"Ain't this some cute shit." Eddie snickered. "What the fuck is going on, and why do the two of you look like somebody just died?"

"Ain't nothing. We was just in here talking." Marie downplayed it. "Did you score while you were out?" She was once again the hard junkie Animal had come to know her to be.

"Yeah, I managed to scratch something up." Eddie patted the breast pocket of his shirt. He saw the hungry look flash across Marie's face, and it made his dick hard. If she wanted a blast that day, he was going to make her work for it. He turned to Animal. "Why isn't your delinquent ass in school?"

"Half day." Animal repeated the lie he'd told his mother.

"Bullshit! Everybody else's kids are in school, except you," Eddie spat. "If you keep fucking around, they're gonna send the social worker here again, and you know I don't want them white folks all up in my shit. I'll let them take your ass up outta here before I run the risk of the law poking around my business because of some punk-ass kid who can't get right."

"Whatever, man," Animal mumbled under his breath. He was in no mood for Eddie's shit.

"What did you say, boy?"

"He didn't say anything, Eddie. Let the boy alone, and let's go in the room and get right," Marie interjected in an attempt to keep the peace.

"Shut your damn mouth, Marie. That's his problem now. You're always taking up for him instead of letting him take responsibility for his bullshit," Eddie snapped at her before turning his attention back to Animal. "Since you done kicked a few asses in the neighborhood, you've been getting real big for your britches. I see you 'round here, mumbling under your breath and cutting your eyes like a little bitch. Well, let me tell you something: I ain't one of these chump-ass neighborhood niggas. I been kicking asses since before you were born. So, when you get it in your mind that you got frog in you, by all means, leap."

Animal's fists tightened, and his heart began to beat faster. He wanted to punch Eddie in the face and finally get it over with, but the pleading look in his mother's eyes made him hesitant.

"You got it, Eddie," he said submissively.

"Muthafucking right I got it," Eddie boasted. "I keep telling you li'l niggas about playing with me, and that goes for your punk-ass brother too."

"Don't talk about my brother," Animal said. Peace be damned, he didn't allow people to talk about Justice.

Eddie set his bag on the floor so that his hands were free. "Oh, you mad because I'm calling it like I see it? Justice ain't no fucking gangsta. Now, K-Dawg, that little bastard is a gangster, but your brother ain't shit but a young punk trying to belong."

"That's better than being a fiend," Animal capped and started walking toward his bedroom. He had gotten maybe three feet before his head snapped back.

"I told you about that smart-ass mouth of yours, didn't I?" Eddie snarled in Animal's ear as he dragged him across the floor by his hair.

"Stop it, Eddie!" Marie yelled.

"Nah, I'm gonna close his smart-ass mouth for him once and for all," Eddie said, before delivering a sharp right hook to Animal's exposed ribs.

When Eddie hit him, it felt like all the wind had vacated Animal's body. He tried to twist himself in a way where he could get his footing and mount some kind of defense, but every time he did, it felt like every hair on his head was going to come out at the roots. Eddie pushed Animal against the wall and punched him in the face like he was a grown man.

"Eddie, stop it!"

As Marie rushed over and tried to keep him from landing another punch, she accidentally scratched his face. Eddie spun and slapped Marie so hard that she stumbled backward and fell into the glass coffee table, shattering it.

"Bitch, are you out of your rabbit-ass mind?" He stalked over to her and yanked her off the floor. "I'll kill you and your fucking kid!" he snarled and commenced to whipping Marie's ass.

Animal sat on the floor, slightly dazed. His lip throbbed so bad that he didn't have to see it to know that it was swollen. Across the room, he saw that Eddie had his mother pinned on the couch, punching and slapping her. Marie pleaded for him to stop, but her pleas only seemed to infuriate Eddie and make him hit her harder. Animal could feel the ball of anger building in the pit of his gut and spreading through his limbs. As if by magic, the knife he'd stolen appeared in his hand. The blade glistened in the sunlight, taunting Animal, mocking him for suffering the constant abuse. It was at that moment that he decided he was tired of Eddie's shit.

The sounds froze Eddie. It started as a low growl, then grew into a ferocious roar. When Eddie turned around and saw Animal hurling himself at him, he reflexively raised his hands, and that was probably the thing that saved his life. The knife slashed through Eddie's palm, instead of his throat where Animal had been aiming. Eddie took one look at Animal's face and knew, without question, that his intent was to kill him. Had Marie not thrown herself between them, he likely would have.

"Enough!" Marie shouted, covering Eddie's body with her own so that Animal wouldn't cut him again. Her face was bruised from where he had punched her, and seeing it only made Animal angrier.

"Get out of the way, Mama. I'm tired of this nigga putting his hands on us," Animal huffed. He was pacing back and forth, looking for an opening, so he could get at Eddie again.

"Tayshawn, I said enough! You had no right doing this to Eddie," Marie said, checking Eddie's wound, while he whimpered and bled.

Animal blinked as if he'd heard her wrong. "Mama, this nigga just tried to beat the breaks off both of us, and you're blaming it on me?"

"Sometimes Eddie can be hard, but it's only because he loves you and wants you to stay out of trouble," Marie told him.

"Fuck that! You ain't gotta explain, baby. He better hope I don't call the police on him," Eddie threatened.

Animal took a step toward Eddie, but Marie stopped him by raising her hand. "Tayshawn, you need to leave this house until you calm down."

Animal was stunned. "*I* need to leave? If anybody needs to leave, it's this nigga." He pointed at Eddie.

"You know what? He's right." Eddie pushed himself off the floor, leaving a bloody handprint.

"I don't have to put up with the bullshit your kids keep shoveling, Marie. I'm packing my shit." He stormed toward the bedroom.

"Wait, Eddie! Don't be like that." Marie grabbed his arm.

"Let him leave, Mama. He ain't did shit but bring you down anyway," Animal said.

"Tayshawn, shut up!" Marie snapped. "Eddie!" She continued to tug at her man. "Don't go, baby!"

"Fuck that, Marie. I'm supposed to be your man and the man of this house, and these kids got more say-so than I do. I got other places I can lay my head. I don't need you." Eddie was being overly dramatic for the effect. He really didn't have any other damn place where he could go and lay up rent-free.

"Then raise the fuck up and go, because we don't need you either." Animal called his bluff.

"See? That's the kind of shit I'm talking about. Zero respect." Eddie attempted to continue to the bedroom, but Marie stopped him again, as he knew she would.

"Baby, I'll handle it. I promise," Marie told Eddie. "Tayshawn!" She turned to her son. "Maybe you should go until everything calms down."

"You kicking me out over this nigga?" Animal asked.

"I'm not kicking you out, but whether you come back to this house or not is up to you. Eddie is the man of this house, and you need to be more respectful. Now, if you feel like you're too grown to respect my man and the rules of this house, then you're grown enough to put a roof over your own head."

Animal was crushed. He couldn't believe that his mother was siding with a man over him. Tears of hurt welled up in his eyes, but he wouldn't give Eddie the satisfaction of seeing him cry.

"Okay," he said softly. Without another word, Animal went into his room and packed a few books and a pair of underwear in his knapsack. When he came back out, his face was hard.

"Tayshawn—"

"Nah, don't stop him, Marie." Eddie cut her off. "He thinks he's a man, so let him go out and get a taste of the world. Just know that you'll never be welcomed back here until you learn to respect me."

"Then I guess this will be the last time we ever see each other, because I'll never respect you, nigga," Animal spat. "I'm sorry, Mama." He hugged her then headed for the door.

"Tayshawn, wait." Marie looked like she wanted to reach out to her son, to embrace him and tell him that he didn't have to go, but

Eddie's piercing gaze wouldn't let her finish her sentence.

"Goodbye, Mama," Animal said and walked out.

As he walked down the long project hallways toward the staircase, he could feel the tears welling up in his eyes again. This time, he didn't fight them back. He let them fall. He loved his mother, but he couldn't sit by and watch as she allowed herself to be abused. He reasoned that, in time, everything would settle down, fences would be mended, and his relationship with his mother would go back to normal. But, as the saying went, tomorrow wasn't promised to anyone. Animal didn't know it at the time, but the next time he laid eyes on his mother, nothing in his life would ever be the same.

PART III

—Blood Everywhere—

Chapter 9

The next couple of months were hard for Animal. During the first few weeks of his emancipation, he stayed with Brasco and his uncles. After spending a few days around them, he could see where Brasco got his criminal ways. There were four of them, all degenerate outlaws, who had spent most their lives either in prison, on their way to prison, or just coming home from prison. It was a miracle when all four of them were out of jail at the same time. During Animal's stay, three of the four uncles were home from prison, so the house was crowded. Animal had to sleep on the floor, but he didn't mind. After having slept in a dog cage on some nights at home, the floor was an upgrade.

The four uncles had varying personalities, with the second eldest of the uncles, Vernon, being the coolest. During his heyday, he had been a notorious heist man, rumored to have robbed nine banks by the time he was twenty-five. Several prison stints and a recurring crack habit had taken him out of the high stakes robbery game, but he was still a thief by nature and always had a plan for a lick.

Animal had spent countless nights sitting up with Uncle Vernon, while he told war stories and broke down the art of being an expert thief. A few times, Vernon had even let Animal tag along when he went out hustling. Watching Vernon steal was like poetry in motion. He could walk into just about any type of establishment and hit them for at least one thousand dollars in goods before they even realized he was in the store. Animal learned quite a bit from Uncle Vernon about the art of being a good thief, and it was the skills he picked up that allowed him to have something to contribute to the house every night. That was the rule established by Bizzle, who ran the house.

Bizzle was the second youngest uncle, but he was the one who always took charge when their oldest brother, Cliff, was in prison and somebody needed to step in to run the house. Bizzle didn't have the best relationship with his other brothers. In fact, they always seemed to be fighting about something or other, although they respected him. He was the most responsible and about his business.

Bizzle was quiet and not very approachable. He preferred to keep his own company, but for some reason, he took a liking to Animal. On nights when Animal came up short with his kick-in, Bizzle would float him. After a while, Bizzle had become comfortable enough with Animal to let him in on the source of the tension between him and his brothers.

Bizzle was the only one of the brothers who had a different mother from the rest. He was the product of a one night stand his father had had during a "business" trip to Portland. Bizzle had been the family secret until he was thirteen and his mother was killed, forcing his father to take him in. His brothers resented him because of all the attention their father gave him, and it often made Bizzle the odd man out. Over the years, the brothers learned to accept, if not love each other, and they made peace. As adults, all the brothers had fairly good relationships with Bizzle, except the youngest, Pop-Top.

Pop-Top and Bizzle were only two months apart and had never gotten along, but their beef wasn't over genes; it was over colors. Growing up in Portland, Bizzle had been raised by the North Side Mob Bloods and Pop-Top's loyalties were with the Harlem Crips. Bizzle was willing to put his gang ties aside to make his peace with his brother, but Pop-Top wasn't. He was fanatically loyal to his gang and decreed that the only way he and his brother would ever know peace was if he laid down his flag. Of course, Bizzle refused, and it drove a wedge between him and his baby brother from a different mother. Bizzle and Pop-Top had minimal interaction and only spoke to each other when it was absolutely necessary.

Watching the two brothers live under the same roof and go about their days without so much as a casual "Hello" was awkward for Animal, but it seemed normal for them. Vernon said that the longest they'd ever gone without speaking was a year.

Animal learned a little bit about this and that from each one of Brasco's uncles, and he used what he picked up on the streets to fill in the blanks. Living on his own was hard, but it was also educational. Animal had to grow up fast if he didn't want to get swallowed by the cold world.

Brasco's uncles were cool, but not a day went by that he didn't miss Justice. It had been almost two months since his arrest. Animal had tried to visit him on Rikers Island, but he was still a minor, so they wouldn't let him in. He'd thought about asking his mother to take him, but he quickly scratched that thought. She had proven she didn't give a fuck about anybody except Eddie, so reaching out to her would've been pointless.

He'd bumped into K-Dawg one day and inquired about his brother and what had happened. K-Dawg gave him a story that only sounded half-true about the events surrounding his arrest and assured him that he was already on the job of getting Justice out of jail. Animal wasn't sure what K-Dawg had up his sleeve, but the conviction in his voice made Animal believe him.

The original charge had been accessory to an attempted murder, and they were dangling hard time over Justice's head if he didn't cooperate, but Justice never uttered a word. When the victim had unexpectedly recanted his original account of what happened, he shot the DA's case full of holes. True to his word, K-Dawg had done his part. The current charge they were leveling against Justice was a probation violation for which the most he could get was eighteen months to two years. It was weak, but the DA had to take him down for something just to save face.

Animal's time staying with Brasco's uncles came to an end when the police raided the apartment. It seemed that Vernon had robbed someone in the building and had been dumb enough to stash the stolen goods in his bedroom. In his cracked-out haze, he forgot the number one rule of breaking any law: Never shit where you live. Not only had the police found the stolen merchandise, but they had also uncovered a stash of illegal guns. As it turned out, Bizzle had been getting guns from his homies in Portland and selling on the streets of New York. When it was all said and done, the raid made the nightly news, and everyone living in the house was taken into custody. It was Animal's first time being arrested, but it wouldn't be his last.

Chapter 10

When they walked Animal into the precinct for the first time, he felt like he had just stepped onto another planet. His palms sweated profusely, and his heart beat so fast that he felt like the oxygen was getting to his brain too quickly and he might pass out. He had never been arrested before, so he didn't know what to expect other than the war stories he had heard around the neighborhood from the self-proclaimed survivors of the prison system. Some of them glorified their time behind the wall and acted as if making it out had put them in a place of honor, but Animal couldn't see it. From the cold yellow walls to the rusted bars of the minority-filled cages, nothing about the place felt honorable. In fact, Animal was filled with great shame for even being there.

They tossed Vernon, Bizzle, and Pop-Top in one crowded cell and directed Animal and Brasco to another. When Animal saw the hard faces of the men in the cell, he thought there had to have been some sort of mistake. He was a kid, and they were adults. When he tried to bring this fact to the guard, he responded by kicking Animal in his ass and slamming the cell door behind him.

"You should've thought about that before you broke the law," the guard told him and walked away.

In addition to Animal and Brasco, there were five other men in the holding cell. What little space there was on the bench was taken by three inmates. Beneath the bench slept a man who smelled like he had seen better days, and the last man stood near the bars, staring out at the clock. Animal thought about sitting on the floor, but it was stained with dry urine and soot, so he opted to stand. Brasco, however, went straight to the business of making himself at home.

Brasco walked over to the bench where the three men were sitting and sized them up. The first two held eye contact with him, but the third looked away. He was the weak link in the chain.

"My man, you mind if I sit down for a minute?" Brasco asked in a less than friendly tone. The man looked up at Brasco as if he was weighing his chances before vacating the space on the bench for Brasco. "Good looking." Brasco plopped down on the bench. "Yo! It's enough room for you too," he told Animal, patting at the small sliver of bench that was left over between him and the wall.

"I'm good. Thanks," Animal told him and leaned against the bars.

After a while, the male officers who had raided the apartment started pulling men out of the cells for processing. An officer whose uniform looked one size too big took Animal into a room that was adjacent to the holding area. Inside, there were two more officers who looked like they would rather have been anywhere but there. One of them came to sit at the computer to take Animal's information, while the officer who'd brought him into the room slipped on a pair of latex gloves to begin fingerprinting him.

"Name?" the officer at the computer asked dryly.

"Tayshawn Torres," Animal said clearly. He figured if he cooperated he might be shown mercy and be cut loose.

"Date of birth?"

"September twenty-first, nineteen-eighty-eight."

The officer stopped his typing. "You're only fourteen?" he asked suspiciously. Animal had come in with a rough lot, and he found it hard to believe that someone so young could be involved with men so dangerous.

"Yes, sir," Animal answered.

"This your first time being arrested?"

"Yes."

"And you're sure you're only fourteen?"

"I'll be fifteen in a few months," Animal said honestly.

The officer shook his head. "Too bad. If you were a little older, we could've tossed you on the bus with the big boys. That would've made a real nice first time experience for you. Count yourself lucky, shithead." He went back to his typing.

The officer in the oversized uniform began the process of fingerprinting Animal. The ink roller felt cold across his fingertips and left a nasty black smear. The officer twisted and turned Animal's hands and wrists as he rolled his fingers over what looked like index cards, collecting his prints. When he was done, he took Animal back to the holding cell and handed him a paper towel to clean the ink from his fingers. The dry brown paper only seemed to smear it. Animal went to the small sink in the corner of the cell and attempted to wash his hands, but the water didn't work. The longer he sat in jail, the less he cared for it.

Animal couldn't have been there for more than a few hours, but it felt like days. The man who had been sleeping on the floor under the bench was now huddled in a corner, shivering. Brasco had said he was going through withdrawal. Living in a house with two drug addicts, Animal was no stranger to how ugly withdrawal could be, but he had never seen anything like a man being dope-sick. He watched pitifully as the man crawled over to the toilet and began to regurgitate everything he had in his stomach. When it was empty, he dry-heaved. The smell coming off him was so rancid that Animal had to cover his nose and mouth with his shirt. He needed to get out of that cell ASAP.

Just before dawn, the officers began rousing the prisoners from their cells. Brasco was asleep on the bench. At some point in the night, he had gotten rid of the other two squatters and was now stretched out on the bench as comfortably as if he were in his own bed. He didn't stir until one of the officers slammed his nightstick against the cage.

"What the fuck?" Brasco sat up. His eyes were heavy with sleep, and there was a dry line of saliva along the edge of his mouth.

"Your chariot has arrived." The officer opened the door. "If you're still here, that means you're going all the way through. You know the routine, so line up, and let's get this over with quick. We'll start with you, Sleeping Beauty." He waved Brasco forward.

"Man, you can't send me through. I'm a minor," Brasco told him.

The officer looked at the sheet in his hand. "According to your paperwork, you're sixteen, which means you're old enough for us to officially ship your ass out with the rest of the degenerates. Now move your ass before I come in there and get you."

"Fuck," Brasco said, shuffling toward the gate and extending his wrists to be cuffed.

"Brasco, where are they taking you?" Animal called after his friend. Brasco just looked over his shoulder and shook his head sadly, which made Animal nervous. "What's going on?" he asked one of the older cons who was lining up in the cell to be handcuffed and shipped.

"We're heading to The Bookings," the man said over his shoulder.

"Bookings? What's that?" Animal was unfamiliar with the place.

The man laughed. "You must be a first timer. Bookings is short for Central Bookings. They take you down there to get your day in court. Depending on how much of an asshole the judge feels like being, you'll either get cut loose or sent to the Island until your next court date. What're you in for?"

"I got caught up in that raid." Animal went on to give him the short version of how he'd ended up in custody.

The convict shook his head. "Stolen shit and guns? Unless you get damned lucky, you're sure to make the cut to get sent to Gladiator School today, youngster."

Animal's mouth went dry. *Gladiator School* was what he had heard Pop-Top refer to as Rikers Island, which was the city jail. They called it Gladiator School because when you passed through there, you had to be prepared to either do battle or get your ass kicked. Animal's night had gone from bad to worse. He wanted to blink his eyes, wake up, and see that it was a bad dream, but the cold shackles the officer had just placed on him said that it wasn't. Animal was being led through the rear door, in a line with other inmates, when one of the officers stopped them.

"Not him," he said, looking down at a list of names on a clipboard. "This one is under age."

Animal said a silent prayer as the officer released him from the chain gang. As he was being led back to the holding cell, he could hear the old convict calling out to him, "Looks like luck was on your side today, youngster!"

After securing Animal back in the holding cell, the officer looked through his paperwork. "Because of your age, you can't go play with the big boys, but your ass can't lay up in here either. The number you gave us for your house is disconnected. If we can't get somebody to come down here and pick you up, we'll have to send you to a group home until Social Services can get you all sorted out. Is there anyone else you can call?"

Animal racked his brain trying to think of someone he could call, but his mind fired nothing but blanks. Normally if he were in a jam, he'd call Justice; however, his brother had issues of his own, so he couldn't be of any help. Without much other choice, Animal took a gamble. It was a long shot, but he gave the officer the only other phone number he knew by heart.

Chapter 11

I'd be lying if I said I wasn't shocked to get your call, B," Tango said between puffs of the joint pinched between his fingers. He was riding low behind the wheel of his candy red BMW 325i. In the passenger seat was Animal.

He had taken a stab in the dark by having the police call Tango to get him out. He had no idea if the number was still good or if he would even bother to come for him, but it was the only card he had to play.

Animal almost hadn't recognized Tango when he walked into the precinct wearing a pair of cotton slacks, plain brown shoes, and a blazer over a button-up shirt. Tango looked every bit of the square he was impersonating. He spun the police a story about being Animal's uncle who had been looking after him. A few well-placed words later, Animal was being released into Tango's custody with a court date that was two months from then.

"Sorry about that, Tango. I didn't mean to drag you into this, but I didn't have anyone else to call," Animal said.

"No sweat, kid. I can dig it. Word around the neighborhood is that things ain't been so good between you and your mom since your brother got locked up," Tango said.

"Things ain't never been good between me and my mom. They've just gotten worse lately," Animal said, thinking of the argument they'd had.

"I can imagine, with an old parasite nigga like Eddie living up in your crib. I know a few cats that are looking for him now to knock his wig off behind some bullshit he did over drugs. That dude is bad news, man."

"I know, but my mother won't cut him loose. It's like he's got her under some kind of spell," Animal fumed.

"He does," Tango informed him. "Marie is a woman in love, and love will turn even the most sensible people into idiots, which is why I stay away from it. I'll lay with a bitch, but I'll never commit to one."

"That's cold, Tango."

"That ain't cold; that's facts! If you take the time to examine the fall of every great hustler, you'll likely find that a woman was the catalyst.

If they weren't the direct cause, they played a part in it. Love is more dangerous than a bullet, which is why it has no place in my world."

Animal thought on the story of the soldier and the fool. "If that's what love does to people, then it has no place in my world either. Fuck love," he declared.

Animal rode around with Tango for hours, listening to music and smoking weed while Tango conducted his business. Animal had always known Tango was about his business, but seeing him in action earned him a whole new level of respect. He had workers who moved his product and whores who worked his corners. All Tango really did was talk shit and collect money.

During one stop, Tango got out of the car and greeted his comrade with a complex handshake. A few more young men came over and greeted Tango in kind. The presence of the red-and-black beads around some of their necks told Animal that they were Bloods, like Tango. Animal knew Tango was supposed to be somebody important among the Bloods, but seeing his interaction firsthand was a whole different experience. Tango moved like a mob boss among the young soldiers, swapping stories and dap. He stood around for a few minutes and dropped some jewels on the young men. Animal couldn't hear what he was saying, but from the way they were hanging on his every word, it must've been powerful. When Tango got back in the car, Animal was looking at him curiously.

"What's good? You a'ight?" Tango asked, noticing the inquisitive look on Animal's face.

Animal hesitated. He was searching for the right words to ask what he wanted to know without running the risk of offending Tango. When he struggled to articulate it, he just spoke what was on his heart. "Why do you gang bang?"

The question caught Tango so off guard that his first reaction was to chuckle. "First off, li'l homie, I don't gang bang, not in the way you're thinking. I'm up there in years, so my days of spray-painting walls and shooting at niggas over colors are long over. I claim Lime Hood Piru because that's the neighborhood we lived in, and we were too poor to move. I grew up in this culture."

"So is that why most people get into gangs, because of where they live?" Animal asked innocently.

Tango measured him, trying to gauge his level of seriousness. "No, not quite. Some people are born into gangs, but most join up for one reason or another. Some do it for protection, and some do it because, with the gangs, they get that sense of family and belonging they ain't getting at home. We look out for each other when nobody else will."

Animal scratched his chin as he processed what Tango was telling him. "So is it true that you gotta kill somebody or get jumped in to join a gang?"

Tango laughed. "Nah, man. That's television and movies that got you all fucked up in the head about the life. Most hoods require some kind of show of fidelity before they put you on, but it isn't always through violence. Loyalty and respect is the glue that binds my hood. What's with the sudden fascination with gang life? You thinking about joining up?"

Animal shrugged. "Maybe."

Tango's words were almost poetic, and they tugged at something in him . . . that emptiness in him that seemed impossible to fill, the loneliness.

Tango gave him a serious look. "Check this out, Tayshawn."

"Animal," he corrected him.

"Say what now?"

"Animal. Everybody calls me Animal."

"Okay . . . Animal. Like I was saying, I'm not sure what your idea is of what this life is about, but I'm about to give it to you real. This life I live is held together by loyalty and respect, but it was built on blood. I know shit is rough for you at home, but you're a good kid who can still have a pretty bright future. When you join the movement, your path becomes predestined. Can you honestly say you're ready to give your life over like that?"

Animal looked Tango directly in the eyes for the first time since he'd gotten in the car. "Why not? Tango, I'm young, but I ain't no fool. My daddy is ghost; my moms is a fiend. I don't see no happy endings in my future. I'm out here lost in the world, man. Shit is bad for me, and I feel like I'm going to go crazy if I don't do something to change it. Whether you put me down with you or not, I'm gonna be out here in these streets. I just don't want to die before I've had a chance to live."

Animal's words touched Tango. He knew the void in Animal's soul all too well. He could remember being alone and lost in the streets, longing to belong to something or someone. "How old are you now, Tay—I mean, Animal?"

"Fourteen and a half," Animal told him proudly.

Tango nodded. "I was about your age when I was recruited. Look, I ain't saying I'm gonna put you on the set, but if you're really serious about getting down, you're gonna have to show me. If I smell any signs of you being a lame, I'm gonna kick you to the curb and act like I never knew you, understand?"

"You got that, Tango," Animal agreed.

"Cool. Now I'm about to drop you off at your building. I gotta go see one of my bitches, but I'll be back to get you tomorrow, so we can talk some more while I make my rounds."

"I can't go there anymore. Me and Eddie got into it a couple of weeks ago, so I been staying with Brasco and his uncles," Animal confessed.

"Well, all of them niggas are locked up and that apartment is padlocked, so that's not an option. Do you have any family I can drop you off with?"

"No, it's just me now. Don't worry about it though, Tango. I'll find somewhere to crash," Animal said. In truth, he had no idea where he was going to sleep that night or the next.

"Blood, I ain't 'bout to have you out here wandering the streets. I got a homegirl who stays out in Brooklyn that you can crash with for a few nights," Tango told him.

"Tango, you've done enough for me already. You don't have to go out of your way, man."

"It ain't about nothing, Animal. I told you, family looks out for each other, and we family now, ain't we?" Tango extended his hand.

Animal happily shook it. "Yeah, we family."

"My homegirl got a spot, and she lives by herself, so she shouldn't have a problem putting you up. I just gotta warn you: Kastro is a little *different*."

Chapter 12

It didn't take long for them to get from Harlem to Brooklyn. Rush hour was over, so traffic was light on the FDR. When Tango crossed the Brooklyn Bridge, instead of taking Atlantic Avenue, he turned off on Park. Taking the local streets to Bed-Stuy allowed Animal to take in the sights and sounds of Brooklyn. For the most part, it was much quieter than he'd expected. Animal had heard plenty of stories about how gritty the County of Kings was supposed to be, but the mix of renovated building and ongoing construction in the neighborhoods Tango drove through didn't reflect the stories. It looked almost chic. Animal's perception changed when they crossed Nostrand Avenue and entered Bedford-Stuyvesant.

Bodegas and variety stores selling everything from headphones to socks were on almost every corner, and the aroma and spices of the Caribbean could be smelled in the air from the restaurants that catered to the locals. The landscape changed considerably, with apartment buildings and squat houses giving way to tenements and brownstones in varying conditions of decay and reconstruction. It was as if, when they started beautifying Brooklyn, they neglected those few miles of neighborhoods.

Tango pushed further into Bed-Stuy, bringing them to a block lined with two- and three-story walk-up apartments, where he parked in front of a bodega. He retrieved his gun from the glove box, checked to make sure a round was chambered, and stuffed it down the front of his pants. "Stay close, kid, and don't speak unless I tell you to. Do you understand?"

Animal nodded.

"Good. Now let's go." Tango threw the door open and stepped out.

As Animal followed Tango down the street, he could feel eyes on him. It was as if the natives could smell foreigners in their territory. They walked to a building in the middle of the block that looked like it had seen far better days. Some of the windows were broken, while others were boarded up. Across the awning, where the numbers of the building had long worn away, the word "HELL" was spray-painted in red letters. The sight of it made Animal uneasy. The place gave him a bad vibe, and he wanted to turn around and wait in the car, but he didn't want to seem like a sucker in front of Tango. He just hoped that this wasn't the place where Tango was expecting him to stay. If so, he would rather take his chances sleeping in the streets.

Sitting on the chipped front steps of the building was an older man with long salt-and-pepper dreads that were thick and matted. Covering the entire lower half of his face was a shaggy beard that looked like it hadn't been groomed in ages. The brown sandals he wore were tattered and worn, like he had walked a million miles in them. Clutched between his index and middle fingers was a Red Stripe beer from which he took casual sips. The man looked like a borderline derelict, but everyone who passed him stopped and paid their respects, including Tango.

"Peace, Big Dread." Tango greeted him with a handshake and a hug.

"What go on, Tango?" Big Dread replied in a heavy Jamaican accent.

"Just trying to stay above the poverty line," Tango told him.

"From the looks of what you're driving, I'd say you're doing a fair job of it." Big Dread chuckled.

This surprised Animal. They had come into the block at the other end, so there was no way

Big Dread could've seen the car. He would learn later that Big Dread didn't miss much when it came to what went on in that neighborhood. He must've felt Animal's quizzical stare, because he turned to him.

"Who de youth?" Big Dread asked Tango, keeping his eyes on Animal.

"This is my protégé, Animal." Tango made the introductions.

Big Dread regarded him. "Ah, you a bad man in training?"

Animal wasn't sure what the proper response should be, so he simply shrugged.

"Nah, Animal is a good kid," Tango answered for him.

"Wit' a name like Animal, I can't believe that. And, if he isn't turned out already, he will be before long after hanging with you, Tango," Big Dread said half-jokingly. "So what brings you this far south of Midtown?"

"Nothing much. Just came to holla at baby sis right quick. Is she around?"

"Yeah, she's upstairs. Let me warn you. She been at the tables all night, and I hear she's down, so she's probably in a foul mood," Big Dread said seriously.

"That ain't nothing new. She's always in a foul mood. Let me go get with her, and I'll holla at you in a minute, Big Dread." Tango started to walk into the building, but Big Dread stopped him.

"You been up top so long that you forget how t'ings work in the slums? To enter hell, you must pay tribute to the gatekeeper." He extended an ashy palm.

Tango shook his head before digging into his pocket and producing his bankroll. He peeled off a few twenties and handed them to Big Dread.

"Bless, bless," Big Dread said without bothering to count the money before tucking it into the pocket of his tattered jeans. He gave Tango an approving nod and allowed him to pass into the building.

Animal stood there, somewhat unsure of what to do. He didn't have a dime to his name, so if the bum was looking for a handout, he was shit out of luck.

"Fret not, my youth. Your passage is on Big Dread today."

"Thanks," Animal said.

"No thanks needed. If you're willingly crossing into this place, you'll pay your marker at some point, and when the time comes, Big Dread will be here to collect it," Big Dread told him.

Animal wasn't sure what he meant and didn't care to stand around to try to figure it out.

Before he went into the building to catch up with Tango, he spared a glance over his shoulder and found Big Dread was still watching him, smirking like he knew a secret that he was dying to tell.

"What's good with that bum?" Animal asked Tango once they were inside the building and out of earshot of Big Dread.

"Who? Big Dread? He ain't no bum. Around here, he's like a landmark," Tango explained.

"Looks like a bum to me," Animal said sarcastically.

Tango stopped walking and turned to Animal. "Li'l nigga, you've got a lot to learn about the way shit works in the jungle. Nothing is ever as it seems. Big Dread is probably sitting on more money than half your favorite rappers. That old Jamaican has been at his post for more years than you been on earth, and nobody has ever breached the gates of hell uninvited and made it back out. Big Dread has been retired for years, so now, when we pay him the tribute, it's more out of respect to his post than him needing money."

Animal was surprised by the revelation. "I didn't know."

"There's a lot you don't know, Animal, which is why I'm here to teach you. The first rule is to know the players in the game. Misplaced disrespect, intentional or not, can get you murdered."

Tango led Animal up three flights of broken stairs to the top floor. Whereas each other level contained four apartment units, the top only had two, one at each end of the hallway. The smell of weed seeped through the walls, and the soft thump of reggae music played somewhere in the distance.

Their journey led them to an apartment at the far end of the hall, where four youths were shooting dice against the stairs leading to the rooftop. When they saw Tango, three of them stood and awkwardly tried to position themselves to look tough, but the fourth didn't seem rattled by his presence.

The boy was the smallest of the four and looked to be about Animal's age, if not younger, but he had the eyes of an old man who had seen the world twice. He was coal black, with a thick nose and keen eyes. His black Levi's sagged slightly off his ass, and the bottoms of his jeans were perfectly cuffed over his red Converse Chuck Taylors. Tucked in his right back pocket was a red bandana. He stood erect and, with his chest poked out, greeted Tango.

"O.G. on set," he said, saluting Tango.

"What's good, Outlaw?" Tango embraced him. "I'm surprised to see you out this way, but if you're here, then Tre can't be too far. Where that nigga at?"

"Inside playing cards with the rest of them old muthafuckas. Man, we was supposed to handle what we had to handle then dip, but once he sat down at the table, it was a wrap. I been waiting for going on two hours now." Outlaw filled him in.

"You know how Tre is when it comes to gambling. I doubt if y'all will be getting out of here anytime soon." Tango chuckled.

"Yo, Tango, I wanted to holla at you 'bout something, but it's kinda delicate." Outlaw glanced in Animal's direction. He was a new face, and Outlaw didn't trust new faces.

Tango caught on. "Oh, it's cool. This is my li'l man, Animal. Animal, this is Johnny Outlaw," he said, introducing them.

Animal had heard the name before while eavesdropping on one of Justice and K-Dawg's conversations. He was rumored to be a young gangster on the rise who didn't have a problem killing a man. He was only a teenager, but he was said to already have a half dozen murders under his belt. Meeting him in person, Animal thought he looked nothing like he had imagined. He was only a baby and hardly looked like he had it in him to kill a man. Then, Animal thought back to how angry he'd been with Eddie the last time they'd seen each other, and he reasoned that anything was possible if a person was pushed far enough.

"What up, Blood?" Outlaw extended his hand. When Animal took it, he tried to greet him as he would a comrade, but Animal's fingers were awkward and untrained. "My bad. I thought you were a homie."

Tango draped his arm around Animal reassuringly. "We're working on it. Animal is a solid young soldier."

"Well, if you're fucking with Tango, then you must be cool, but I'd still rather say what I have to say away from prying ears. No disrespect to you," Outlaw told him.

"None taken," Animal replied.

"If it's that important, give me a few minutes to go in here and holla at sis, and I'll get right with you," Tango suggested.

"Cool. You know where I'll be," Outlaw agreed. "Good meeting you, Animal," he said before returning to the dice game.

Tango rapped on the door in a pattern that Animal couldn't quite catch, and then he stepped back and waited. "Dig, Animal. I'm about to take you into the belly of the beast. Anything you see or hear in this apartment stays in this apartment, got it?"

"I got you," Animal said, now more than curious. The way Tango had been talking since they'd arrived made him feel like they were about to step into another world. When the door swung open, he realized they were.

Chapter 13

The cloud of weed smoke that spilled from the apartment was so thick that it stung Animal's eyes. He could hear the music clearly now as it bounced off the walls of the narrow foyer. Just beyond it, he could hear the rumbling of voices over the clanking of glasses and the flicking of lighters.

Looming in the doorway was an outstanding specimen of a man. He stood a hair over six feet, with broad shoulders that stretched against the fabric of the cashmere sweater he was wearing. He had a wide chest and thin waist, like he worked out regularly, and his clothes were neat and clean. His well-groomed attire didn't match his brutish face, which was marked with scars. His head and face were completely void of hair, like he suffered from alopecia. Scars marked his head, face, and arms, as if he had tried to win a knife fight with his bare hands. Two gold rings dangled from the skin just above his right eye, and a matching set looped through what was left of his right ear. It had been severed just at the lobe. When Tango greeted him by the name Gladiator, Animal wasn't surprised. Anyone with eyes could see that he had definitely been through some battles.

"So, this is him?" Gladiator asked, giving Animal the once over with eyes the color of tar. His voice was softer than Animal had imagined it would be, and it carried a hint of an English accent. When he spoke, it reminded Animal of an old movie he'd seen, starring Lawrence Olivier.

"Yeah, this is my newest protégé, Animal," Tango said proudly.

"Pleased to meet you." Animal extended his hand, but Gladiator just looked at it as if it were something vile.

"Based on your appearance, I'd say the name Animal is fitting," Gladiator said, not bothering to try to mask the insult. "You smell like you just got out of jail."

"I did," Animal said shamefully.

Gladiator shook his head sadly. "Tango, what is your fascination with strays? Didn't the fiasco with Li'l Red teach you anything?"

Li'l Red wasn't a name Animal was familiar with, but he stored it away in his head.

"Nah, he ain't like Li'l Red. Animal is a solid young soldier," Tango insisted.

"Did you break him in yet?" Gladiator asked.

"Nah, he ain't laid nothing down yet, at least not that I know of," Tango said.

"Then I think it's a bit premature to speak on how solid he is. When we walk him through the fire once or twice, we can revisit this conversation about his pedigree. Come on. Let's go into the drawing room where there's a bit more space to breathe. Standing in such close quarters with your little unwashed plaything is playing havoc on my nose." Gladiator fanned the air before turning to walk down the hall.

"What the fuck is his problem?" Animal asked a little too loudly for Tango's liking.

"Chill, Animal. Don't pay Gladiator no mind. He's like that with just about everybody," Tango explained.

"I don't care, Tango. For as grateful as I am that you're trying to help me out, I ain't gonna be talked to any kind of way, especially by some old, educated-sounding nigga in a tight sweater," Animal fumed.

Tango stopped short and took Animal by the shoulders. "You listen to me, and listen good. This isn't the block where that naïve-ass mouth of yours will get overlooked. This is Hell, and they play by a whole different set of rules, especially Gladiator. You think he got that name because he's a fan of Roman history? If he decided he wanted to break your skinny neck for slighting him, there wouldn't be a whole lot I could do about it, short of getting my neck broken with yours. Gladiator and his sister are doing me a solid, so unless you've got somewhere else to sleep tonight, I'd suggest you close your mouth and try to pretend to be grateful."

"I didn't mean any disrespect, Tango," Animal said apologetically.

"Sometimes what you mean and what you do conflict. Now, when we go in here, don't say anything stupid, especially in front of Kastro," he told him and walked into the living room.

Animal hesitated for a moment, making sure he looked as presentable as he could before following Tango. Further embarrassing himself wasn't going to help his situation, so he decided to err on the side of caution. There were men and women of varying ages all packed into the apartment. As Animal passed down the foyer toward the living room, he was greeted with a range of things from nods in greeting to scornful looks. If this was Hell, then the hard faces that eyed Animal were surely demons.

The living room looked far different than he had expected, considering the condition of the building. It looked very clean and sterile. The living room had been modified so that it opened up into the kitchen, allowing space for the pool table that dominated the center of it. The oak trim of the pool table had been dyed a red so deep that it looked like the wood was bleeding. From wall to wall, the floor was covered in thick amber carpet. Red seemed to be the theme of the whole house. Even the frames of the multiple televisions around the living room were red.

The men playing pool spared Animal a brief glance then went back to their game. He found Tango and a man he had never seen before, whom Animal assumed was Tre.

Tre was wearing a white sweat suit and a pair of red-and-white Nike Cortez. A neatly folded red bandana was sticking out of his back pocket. Tre didn't look to be a lot older than Tango, but Animal reasoned that he had to be because of the way he wore his hair. Outside of movies, he had never seen a real Jheri curl up close.

When Tango spotted Animal, he waved him over. "Animal, this is one of my oldest crime partners from the West Coast, Tre." Tango introduced him proudly.

"What it do, li'l homie?" Tre greeted him in a very easygoing drawl. He seemed personable and easy to like. Tre extended his fist to give Animal dap.

Animal raised his fist to return the gesture, and as soon as his skin made contact with Tre's, something passed over him. If he had to put it into words, it would be . . . a *sinister* feeling. He hadn't said or done anything to make Animal feel that way; his aura was just wrong.

Tre stared at Animal with his lips twisted into a half smirk. If Animal didn't know any better, he would've sworn Tre knew what he was thinking.

When Tre tired of watching Animal squirm under his gaze, he turned to Tango. "So what's up with it, Blood? You thinking about putting him on the hood? He looks kinda young."

"Not much younger than Johnny Outlaw was when you flipped him," Tango fired back.

"Outlaw was different. By the time he came to me, he was already on the path. That boy had been through some shit. What about you?" he asked Animal. "You been through anything?"

"I been through enough," Animal said.

Tre regarded him for a time. The boy who called himself Animal had the same dead look in his eyes that Johnny did at his age.

"Tragedy builds character," he told Animal. "When the world has tossed your ass to rock bottom, you'll be able to fully appreciate what it took to get back up."

"Spoken like a true O.G.," Tango said.

In truth, he had only spoken up to disrupt the connection Tre was trying to make with Animal. He wouldn't allow him to mind-fuck Animal like he had done with Outlaw. Tre was Tango's man, but he knew how he got down. "So what's going on over there that's so interesting?" He nodded toward the card table where everyone's attention seemed to be fixed.

"Shit! They been going at it for hours. You know how the lady of the house is when she's on a streak," Tre told him.

"Muthafucka!" a gravelly voice boomed throughout the room, followed by what sounded like something being slammed against the card table.

Tango shook his head, recognizing the voice. "I guess I don't have to ask which end of it she's on. I need to holla at her about something, but maybe I should wait."

"Yeah, you might want to. On another note, though, I hear you handling heavy in Harlem?" Tre changed the subject.

"You know me, Tre. I always keep some type of income coming in," Tango told him.

Tre gave a cautious look around before leaning in to whisper to Tango. "Listen, these Arab muthafuckas out here gave me a sweet hookup on that white lady. The prices get even better when I refer business to them, and I hear you're buying pretty heavy, which is why I'm bringing this to you. We could both stand to make a few dollars off this."

Tango shrugged. "Man, I ain't doing enough of anything to qualify for no discounts. I'm a local dealer, Tre."

Tre gave him a look of disbelief. "Tango, don't play that role with me. We both know you getting a few dollars in Harlem with that movement you got going. I don't want in on your operation, Blood. All I'm trying to do is break bread with my kinfolk."

"I know, and I respect that, but shit ain't like it used to be for me, Tre. Money has slowed up a bit, so I ain't moving as heavy as I was a few months ago."

"I can dig it," Tre said, sounding half-disappointed. "Well, I got the inside track with these dudes, so when you get up, if you decide you wanna put something together, I'm here to make it happen."

"Good looking out." Tango gave Tre dap. "I'll get with you on that in a minute, but for right now, let me see what's going on with my peeps," he said as he walked away.

Tango's departure was so abrupt and cold that it made for an awkward moment of silence. Animal looked at Tre, whose eyes were still locked on Tango as he made his way across the room. The look he was giving him wasn't a hateful one, nor was it pleasant. He was simply watching. Animal used the moment of distraction to slip away from Tre without saying goodbye.

There were quite a few people standing around the table watching the game. Tango was standing next to Gladiator. Their eyes, as well as everyone else's, were glued to the card table. Animal silently moved to stand between them so he could get a better view. He opened his mouth to say something to Tango, who motioned for him to be quiet and nodded toward the table.

There was a poker game in progress, and from the piles of money spread across the table, it looked to be for pretty high stakes. There were four people sitting at the table, but from sad looks and empty tabletops in front of two of them, Animal deduced they had tapped out already. This left the last two—an ugly man with an enormous head and gold teeth, and a female.

The female gambler couldn't have weighed more than one hundred and thirty pounds, give or take, and she had a youthful face. Fire engine red dreadlocks peeked from beneath the Rasta cap that sat slightly pushed back on her head. Dark sunglasses covered her eyes, making her face almost impossible to read. Pinched between her full lips was a blunt of something potent. The frail young woman looked completely out of place in this den of killers, but she seemed completely at ease.

"You know, your money is looking real nice over here on my side of the table," the big-head man said, taunting the woman. He shuffled his cards in his hands as if he couldn't wait to slap them down on the table.

The woman blew out the weed smoke and tipped the ash into the Hello Kitty ashtray sitting next to her. "I hear you talking, Mack, but let me pull your coat to something. Money is like an escort; that bitch might come over to keep you company and make you feel like a big man, but in the end, she ain't trying to spend the night. I think you're full of shit, and I call your bluff." She laid her cards down—four kings and a jack, four of a kind.

The onlookers erupted into cheers at the sight of her cards. Mack had been taking money from them all night, and they were happy that someone had finally turned the tables on him. She made to reach for the money, but Mack stopped her when he raised his hand.

"That's why I don't spend money on escorts. I like to fuck whores." Mack laid his cards on the table. He was holding four aces, which trumped her four of a kind. Smiling, he began collecting his money from the table. "I know getting your ass cracked is a tough pill to swallow, but I'm a good sport." He fished off a few hundreds from his winnings and tossed them across the table. When he did it, the room became deathly silent.

The woman sat there, shaking her head and taking slow tokes off her weed. For the amount of money she'd just lost, you'd have thought she'd be upset, but she was calm . . . too calm.

"Yeah, I have to give it to you. You're good, Mack. Maybe *too* good."

Mack took a pause from collecting the money. He looked up at the woman's face, and though he couldn't see her eyes behind the sunglasses, he could feel them on him.

"Come on, sis. Don't act like that over some light paper. You know the same way I win it in here, I'll lose it right back eventually." He gave her his best "slave grin," showing all his gold teeth.

The female shrugged. "Or either steal it, while you're in here scamming my establishment, you hustling muthafucka!"

Animal had been standing right next to Gladiator but still didn't see him move. He swooped in on Mack, producing a butterfly knife, which he drove through Mack's hand, pinning it to the table.

"My fucking hand!" Mack roared.

"It ain't your hand I'm concerned about; it's the sticky-ass fingers attached to it." She got up from her seat and walked around the table to confront him. "Knowing me as well as you do, do you really think you can come in here and steal from me and get away with it?"

"I swear I don't—"

Before he could finish his sentence, she drove her palm down on the blade in his hand. "It's bad enough that you're a fucking thief, but now you wanna lie too?" She grabbed his free hand and flipped it over, exposing the faint traces of red substance under his fingernails. He had been marking the cards by smearing it on the backs of them.

Mack opened his mouth to offer an explanation, but it was too late. The moment he'd decided to steal from Hell, he'd been tried and convicted already.

Animal watched the woman yank the knife from Mack's hand and, without breaking her motion, slash his throat. Mack fell off his chair, and just by chance landed mere inches from where Animal was standing, splashing a few drops of wayward blood onto his white sneakers. Blood spilled from Mack's neck and seeped into the carpet, seeming to make the red even deeper.

Animal's eyes were fixed on Mack's face. His lips moved uselessly, unable to produce any sound because his vocal cords had been severed. Animal watched Mack until the moment the light in his eyes went out. It was the first time he had ever seen death so close. Most boys his age would've been unnerved by the sight of a corpse at their feet, but it fascinated Animal. Until that moment, he had never realized how thin the veil between life and death was, and it made him curious to know more about it.

When Animal was finally able to tear his eyes from Mack's corpse, he looked up and found Gladiator staring at him, lips parted into a half grin, like he knew Animal's secret.

"Tighten up, kid." Tango nudged him out of his daze.

Animal turned and saw the woman who had cut Mack's throat coming in their direction. In her hand, she still held the bloody knife, leaving a trail from the table to where they were standing. She spared Animal a glance, but for the most part, she ignored him and turned her attention to Tango.

The woman hugged Tango with one arm, careful to keep the bloody knife away from his clothes. "What it do, Blood?"

"Came to see my favorite sister," Tango said, beaming.

"Bullshit. I'm an afterthought until you need something. You getting money uptown now, so you acting like you too good for the slums," she teased.

"Never that. You know it's family over everything," Tango said, shooting a glance at Animal.

The woman looked at Animal. "Is this him?" she asked Tango but kept her eyes on Animal.

"Yeah, this is my li'l homie, Animal. Animal, this is Kastro." Tango made the introductions.

The moment Tango identified the woman as Kastro, his earlier statement made sense. "Kastro is a little different," was what Tango had said. *Homicidal* would've been a more accurate description. Animal was surprised that a woman so small could have so much wrath in her.

"'Sup," he greeted her.

"I would shake your hand, but mine are a little messy," Kastro said, raising her blood-stained hands for him to see. "Tango says you need a place to stay for a couple of nights."

"Yeah, I had a little situation at home," Animal told her.

"It ain't my care or concern. Tango asked for a favor, and I'm doing it for him. I'll let you lay around my pad for a few nights, and maybe you'll learn a few things along the way, but what happens to you beyond that ain't my concern. I don't fuck with new niggas, and you're a new nigga. Don't go thinking we fam because I'm letting you crash. You got it?"

"Yeah, I got it," Animal told her.

"Good. Don't let me have to repeat it. Now here—" Kastro shoved the bloody blade in his hands. "Go clean this shit off in the bathroom. There's bleach under the sink. When you're done with that, help Gladiator get rid of that thief occupying space on my living room floor. If you ain't got the stomach for that, go in the kitchen and help the girls clean up and wash dishes. Either way, you're gonna clean up a mess tonight."

Kastro walked off, pulling Tango along with her. She didn't bother to wait for Animal to respond. She didn't have to because she already knew which road he'd take. Animal's eyes, when she killed Mack, told Kastro all she needed to know about the orphan Tango had dropped off on her doorstep.

Chapter 14

Animal's time living in the place which had been dubbed Hell could only be described as an experience. It seemed like every night, there was a party going on. Kastro was always in the center of it, barking orders, talking shit, or telling war stories. She always had a good story. Animal would sit quietly in corners for hours, soaking up game from the people who came to sit at Kastro's card table, especially the killers. Kastro seemed to know more killers than any other kind of people. It wasn't like they came in and announced their chosen professions, but after a while, Animal was able to tell which ones had murder in their hearts and which ones didn't. It was a trick he had picked up from Gladiator.

Initially, Gladiator didn't seem to care for Animal, and the feeling was mutual. He rarely said two words to Animal, unless it was to assign him some useless task or to insult him. Whenever he would catch Animal reading novels, he would take them, saying, "The only thing you can learn from a fairytale is how to dream about shit that'll never happen," and he would replace it with a book of his choosing.

One book in particular that stuck out was *Soledad Brother*. Animal had never heard of the Jackson brothers or their struggles, until Gladiator introduced him to them. It was way heavier reading than what Animal was used to, but he became quite fond of that particular book and had read it several times.

Gladiator taught Animal many things, mostly through unconventional methods and always under the guise of being some sort of punishment. One of Gladiator's favorite ways to irritate Animal was making him sit and watch countless hours of footage from Kastro's card games. There was an overhead camera in a light fixture that gave them a nice view of the table and everyone at it.

In the beginning, it bored Animal to no end, and he felt like Gladiator was just being an asshole, but he was actually teaching him a skill. Countless hours of observing people taught him the art of reading body language. Before long, Animal could tell what type of person a man was by the way he held his cards when he sat at the table. That first sip from the Well of

Knowledge made Animal thirsty, and he would secretly shadow Gladiator wherever he went, watching and learning.

Sometimes Animal would find himself standing in front of the mirror, trying to mimic Gladiator's mannerisms or even speaking proper like him when he met new people. Gladiator was well aware of Animal's antics, but he never brought it up to embarrass the younger man. Though neither of them would ever admit it, Gladiator liked Animal, and for Animal, Gladiator had become one of his unspoken heroes.

As Gladiator taught, Animal learned, and he had managed to learn quite a bit about his unofficial mentor. Gladiator and Kastro had the same father but different mothers. Gladiator's mother had been their father's first wife, a Jamaican college student from England who was doing continuing studies in the States. Their marriage was a short one, annulled in less than six months, but Gladiator was conceived during that time. His mother wanted to go back to England with her child, and his father made no attempt to try to sway her otherwise. Gladiator ended up being raised on the other side of the world, resulting in his only really knowing his father from the occasional birthday phone call or pictures.

Gladiator was raised in a working-class neighborhood in the Riverside section of Liverpool. He was known as a brawler in the streets, but he was also a good student. He attended the Defence Academy of United Kingdom and, from there, joined the British Armed Forces as a part of a Special Ops unit. After his tour, he came to the States to continue his education and look for a job in law.

It was around that time that he met his sister Kastro face-to-face for the first time. Kastro was already heavy in the streets and slowly building, but she hadn't gone major yet. Gladiator took one look at his sister's operation and immediately saw potential in it. He brought his resources from across the water, as well as his military experience, and within six months, he had paid off all his college loans.

Gladiator eventually finished his education and got his doctorate, but he decided to skip a career in law. Instead, he found new ways to break it. Dying young and rich was more appealing to him than growing old and waiting for a pension.

On the surface, one would've never realized that Gladiator's story was that deep, but Animal was learning that nothing in Hell could be taken at face value. Gladiator was a complex man, and though Animal was making progress, it would take time to really learn him.

Kastro was a bit easier to figure out. Animal quickly learned her likes and dislikes and went out of his way to please the mistress of the house. He made sure her glass of Hennessy was always fresh, made sure Kastro had freshly rolled blunts in the mornings when she woke up, and played on her love of sweets whenever possible. Kastro had a thing for junk food, so Animal would search stores far and wide for her favorite snacks.

Some of the other young boys who hung around called Animal an ass-kisser, but he was really just showing his appreciation for Kastro letting him stay with them. It was very rare that people showed Animal even the smallest kindness, and he was extremely grateful for Kastro and Gladiator.

When Animal wasn't in Hell, he was making the rounds with Tango. Tango would take him around for hours, giving him the game and showing him how his operation worked. He had a low-key network of hustlers and distributors who moved his product on the streets. Tango wasn't a major player in the game, but he had a good thing going.

In addition to teaching Animal about the hustle, he also taught him about gang culture. There was so much that Animal thought he had figured out, but when Tango broke down *Bs* and *Cs* to him, he realized that he really didn't know much about being in a gang. Tango told him stories about his early days as a recruit and about hood legends that he'd known and broken bread with in Los Angeles. He made being a Blood sound like something regal, and the more Animal listened, the more he wanted in. When he was around Tango, he would wear predominantly red and speak in slang terms he'd heard from Tango. Back then, he was a typical wannabe, but what he lacked in swag, he made up for in willingness to learn.

When Tango felt Animal was ready, he put him to work. Running errands for Gladiator and Kastro kept a few coins in his pocket, but Animal was alone in the streets, and it was time for him to learn to feed himself. Tango put him on a corner with a crew of young dudes that was run by a kid named Brimstone.

Brimstone was cool, but he made Animal nervous. He was loud, violent, and reckless. On more than one occasion, Animal had seen Brimstone brandish guns in broad daylight like they were legal. He was Tango's young gunner and enforcer. Brimstone and his goons were vicious, and nobody wanted problems with them, which was why Tango was able to conduct his business in the hood without too much trouble from the local dealers.

Being back on his old block was awkward at first for Animal. It had been so long since he'd come through for more than a brief drop-off or pick-up with Tango that it almost felt foreign to him. It was amazing to him how he could feel so far removed from a place where he had lived all of his life. Every night he was out there with Brimstone and his crew, he was constantly on high alert for his mother. She was an addict, and he was now a drug dealer, so it would only be a matter of time until their paths crossed.

It happened one rainy night. Animal had been on the block for about three weeks with Brimstone's crew, and he was learning the ropes very quickly. Brimstone had promoted him from hand-to-hand sales to the money man, which meant he collected the cash while someone served the fiend.

Animal had seen Eddie a few times, creeping for drugs. Whenever he saw Animal with Brimstone's crew, he would go and find someone else to buy crack from. Animal wasn't sure if Eddie had ever told his mother about him being out on the block, but since she had never come looking for him, Animal assumed that he hadn't. Then again, would Marie come looking for him even if she had known he was out there? Growing up, he sometimes found it hard to tell if Marie even liked him, let alone cared about what happened to him.

That night, things were slow because of the bad weather. It was as if the crackheads thought they were made of salt and would melt away if they came out in the rain. Brimstone was off somewhere doing God only knew what, leaving Animal and two of his underlings to handle the corner. He spotted Eddie first, looking like shit as usual with that thirsty look in his eyes. Following closely behind him was Marie.

Animal almost didn't recognize his own mother. She had lost a considerable amount of weight, and she looked pale. Eddie cast a glance his way, but Animal wasn't sure if he saw him or not. He pressed himself closer to the wall, waiting for Eddie to lead Marie off in search of their drugs from someone else, but to his surprise, they were heading in his direction. Even from where he was standing, he could see the shit-eating grin on Eddie's face. He was purposely trying to expose him.

"Hold me down. I gotta take a leak," Animal told the two boys he'd been left with.

He didn't wait for them to respond before walking to the next building and ducking inside the lobby. Through the cracked glass of the door, Animal watched his mother and Eddie approach his comrades. Eddie looked around as if he was trying to locate Animal, while Marie negotiated the purchase.

It was one thing to know that you had a drug-addicted parent, but something else altogether to see them buying drugs. The sight of it hit Animal like a physical blow. Part of him wanted to weep for his mother, and part of him wanted to pummel the boy who sold her the rock. But for what? No one had put a gun to his mother's head and told her to smoke her life away. Marie was an addict, and they sold drugs. It was the natural order of things.

Animal continued to watch until the transaction was completed. As Marie walked away, she suddenly stopped short and began looking around. Her eyes paused on the building where Animal was hiding. For a minute, Animal could've sworn she had seen through the wall and spotted him. Eddie barked something which drew her attention, and she went to catch up with him. Whether she'd seen him or not, Animal didn't know, but what he did know was that the sight of his mother buying crack sickened him to the point where he knew that he wasn't cut out to be a drug dealer. He would have to find another way to make his bones.

Chapter 15

Animal continued to play the block with Brimstone's crew, stacking his money while he tried to figure out where his next career path would take him. He didn't see his mother again, but he did see Eddie from time to time. On more than a few occasions, he'd thought about running up on Eddie and busting him in the head with a brick, but he reasoned it wasn't worth it. If Eddie's drug addiction didn't kill him, the streets would, saving Animal the trouble. He only hoped that Eddie didn't drag his mother to Hell with him.

The upside to being back on the block was seeing Noki. Every so often, Animal would see her coming from or going to school with her parents or one of her brothers escorting her. They would exchange winks or playful smiles but would never speak in front of her family. One day, Noki managed to have one of the neighborhood girls slip Animal a note saying that she wanted to meet in the hood that night.

Animal was as excited as a kid on Christmas Eve at the prospect of seeing Noki. It had been so long since they'd had a chance to talk, and there was so much he wanted to tell her. The entire day he had been on pins and needles, waiting for his meeting with Noki. Brimstone joked that Animal was sweating like a man on his way to the electric chair. It was true; he was a supercharged ball of nerves and felt like he would explode at any moment.

When he finally saw her come around the corner, he wanted to rush to her and sweep her off her feet, but he didn't want to look like a square in front of his boys. Instead, he ambled up to her as cool as he could and gave her a hug.

"What's up, stranger?" Animal asked in his coolest voice.

"You're the stranger. You got all Hollywood and moved out the ghetto." Noki squeezed him. "I've missed you, Tayshawn."

"I've missed you too, Noki," Animal said, smiling.

Noki ran her hand through his hair. It was tangled and matted from having not been properly combed in ages. "Looks like this wig of yours has missed me more. What did I tell you about walking around looking like a homeless person?"

"I'm out here getting money. I ain't got time to worry about my hair," Animal boasted. "I might just cut it."

"No the hell you're not!" Noki slapped him on the arm. "I know some chicks that would kill for what you're growing up there. Come sit down, so I can hook you up." She led him to a bench a few feet away from where Brimstone and his crew were posted up. Noki perched herself on the backrest of the bench and motioned for Animal to take the seat between her legs. She produced a comb from her back pocket and began the process of trying to make heads or tails out of Animal's hair.

"Did you hear what happened to Crack Head Annie?" she asked.

"No, I haven't seen her around in a while," Animal said.

He'd seen her once or twice when he first started selling drugs for Tango, but it had been a while since he'd bumped into her.

Noki shook her head. "You need to read the paper or watch the news so the world can stop passing you by. Everyone knows Annie is locked up for what she was doing with her kids. Somebody finally dropped a dime on her."

Animal couldn't say that he was surprised. Annie was foul, and he was glad that someone had put an end to her bullshit. He just hoped the kids were okay. "What about her little ones?"

"According to the newspaper, they found Ashanti at the apartment of one of the families she had sold her children off to. There was no sign of Angela or the man she sold her to. It's been about two weeks since either of them have been seen. They're planning to throw the book at Annie for what she's done."

"Serves her right. I feel no sympathy for that junkie bitch." Animal spat on the floor for emphasis. "I'm just sad that two kids had to get caught up in this bullshit, because it ain't their fault. We didn't ask to be born to junkies," he said, reflecting on his own childhood.

They were silent for a few moments. Noki combed through Animal's hair, braiding it into long cornrows as she went along. She laid her hand on his shoulder and could feel the tension in it like a knot. She knew her friend was going through some things, and she needed to let him know she would be there for him.

"I heard what happened between you and your mom. I'm sorry, Tayshawn."

Animal shrugged. "It's all good. Shit happens, I guess."

"Do you think you guys will ever be able to work it out?" Noki asked, parting his hair.

"I dunno. I hope so. I love my mom, but she's lost. I can't be lost with her. I gotta make my way in life," Animal said honestly.

"So, you're making your way in life by selling drugs for Tango?"

Animal tilted his head and looked up at her. "I don't see nobody else rushing to try and put no money in my pockets. What else should I be doing?"

"Going to school, maybe," Noki shot back. "Animal, you're a teenager. Your biggest concern should be graduating high school, not worrying about if the police are gonna come take you to jail."

"That's easy for someone who has two parents and comes from money to say," Animal said a bit sharper than he had intended to.

Noki popped him on his ear with the comb. "Don't even try that with me, *Tayshawn*, because we live in the hood just like everybody else. It takes more money to keep our family business going than it brings in, but it's all we have, and we all bust our asses to keep it."

"I didn't mean it like that, Noki. What I meant was that I don't have anything. You got your parents, your brothers, and your friends. What do I have?"

"You have me," Noki said sincerely. "Tayshawn, never forget that there are people in this world who genuinely care about you."

"And how much do you care?" Animal asked playfully, with his head tilted back so that he was looking up at her.

"Enough to risk getting my ass beat for sneaking out to see you," Noki replied, giggling.

As she looked down at his face, she got lost in Animal's sad eyes. She had always loved his eyes. Before she even realized what she was doing, Noki leaned in and kissed him. The kiss was awkward on both their parts, but passionate.

"That was nice," Animal said.

Noki smiled. "Yeah, it was. Should we do it again?"

Before Animal could answer, there were the sounds of screeching car tires followed by doors being thrown open and men shouting. At first, Animal thought it might've been the police running up on them, but when he saw men with their faces wrapped in blue bandanas, carrying automatic weapons, he knew they were not cops. An unspoken understanding passed between him and Noki, and they both took off running at the same time. They'd gone only a few feet before a man holding an assault rifle blocked their path.

"What's cracking, homie?" The man pointed the gun at them. He was tall, with smooth brown skin and thick black cornrows peeking from beneath the blue bandana, tied Aunt Jemima style around his head. "Where you from, Blood?"

Animal was stuck on stupid, staring into the face of what was surely his impending doom. Dark sunglasses covered the man's eyes, but Animal didn't need to see his eyes to know he was a killer. Animal knew he was being addressed, but he wasn't sure how to respond.

"Nigga, I said where you from?" The man was now pointing the gun at Noki but speaking to Animal.

"I . . . I'm from that building right over there," Animal blurted out, pointing to the building where he used to live.

The man holding the gun cocked his head as if he was confused. It was obvious that the young man had absolutely no idea what he was being asked. "Cuz, get yo' ass over there with yo' bitch-ass homeboys, before I bust on you just for being a lame." He motioned with the rifle, directing Animal and Noki over to where his blue-clad comrades had Brimstone and his boys rounded up.

Two dudes with their faces covered by bandanas relieved Brimstone and the others of their guns. One of them stood out to Animal because of his chain. A small gold hammer dangled from the end of it. There was a third man aiming what looked like a military-issued machine gun at Brimstone, daring him to move.

Unlike the others, the third man chose not to cover his face. He was dark-skinned and husky. He had a shaggy beard that looked like it hadn't seen a comb in quite some time. When he noticed Animal and Noki being escorted over at gunpoint, he briefly turned his attention to them.

"Looks like you snatched a few deserters, huh, Lou-Loc?" the man with the beard joked.

When Animal heard the name Lou-Loc, his blood ran cold. He had heard K-Dawg speak of him before. He was a founding member and assassin for the New York chapter of the Harlem Crips. Lou-Loc had killed dozens of men on the East and West Coast and had come out of every situation with barely a scratch. Some whispered that he had made a deal with the devil that made him nearly impossible to kill.

"Nah, these two ain't gangin', Gutter," Lou-Loc told him.

One of the boys who had helped to unarm Brimstone stepped up and removed the bandana from his face. It was Pop-Top. "I know that li'l dude. That's my nephew's homeboy, Animal."

Animal had never been so happy to see one of Brasco's uncles. Pop-Top would straighten everything out, and Animal and Noki would be given passes, or so he thought. His hopes became dimmer when Gutter took off his sunglasses and bore into his soul with his piercing hazel eyes.

Gutter looked Animal over from his red Converse to the red-and-white shirt he was wearing, and his lips twisted into a sneer. Without warning, Gutter pointed his machine gun at Animal. "I wouldn't care if it was your mama's best friend. This li'l nigga is flamed up like he from that side. You sure he ain't claiming?"

He pressed the gun against Animal's forehead. "What up, cuz? You ready to die 'bout that five? Or maybe we'll sponsor your bitch's trip to the afterlife." He turned the gun to Noki.

To everyone's shock, Animal stepped between Gutter's gun and Noki.

"Leave her alone," Animal said with his voice trembling. He wasn't sure what had made him do such a foolish thing, but he couldn't take it back now.

Gutter's face hardened. He adjusted his grip on the machine gun as if he was preparing to fire. "Would you die for her?"

Animal looked over his shoulder at Noki's terrified face. They were both afraid, but Noki hadn't signed up for what she was in the middle of; Animal had. He couldn't allow her to be hurt because of his choices. He looked back to Gutter, too nervous to open his mouth for fear of vomiting, and simply nodded his head. Yes, he would die to protect her.

Unexpectedly, Gutter lowered his gun and burst out laughing. "Damn! You were really ready to go all the way with it for her, huh? You should consider yourself lucky, young lady," he told Noki. "Man, it must be something in the water where all you niggas be ready to die over love. He kinda reminds me of you, Lou-Loc. Maybe we should make him flip Crip and have you take him under your wing. What you think, Loc?" Gutter teased his friend.

"Fuck you, G. Handle what you gotta handle and let's be done with this shit," Lou-Loc said, irritated. He hated when Gutter got like that, dragging the missions out for his own twisted pleasures.

"You out of bounds right now, Gutter," Brimstone spoke up. He had been so quiet until then that they'd almost forgotten about him.

When Gutter turned back to Brimstone, his face was hard and murderous again. "Nigga, wherever I walk is my hood. Or ain't them bodies I been leaving all over the city taught you niggas nothing yet?" Gutter asked cockily. "You dead-rag niggas on this side of Harlem exist because I allow it, and the moment you forget that, I'm gonna push you from this life. Luckily for you, I ain't here to kill nobody today. I want you to deliver a message to your big homies."

"I ain't no fucking messenger," Brimstone said boldly.

Gutter pressed his machine gun against Brimstone's chest. "You'll be a messenger or a fucking corpse. Pick your poison."

Brimstone sucked his teeth. "What is it?"

"It seems that you boys have allowed a weasel into your hen house, and it's fucking up business on both sides of the color line," Gutter told him.

A confused expression crossed Brimstone's face. "What the fuck does that mean?"

Gutter shook his head. "It means that one of your homeboys is a snitch, you dumb mutha-fucka."

"Bullshit," Brimstone spat. "All my comrades are solid Bloods."

Gutter raised his eyebrow. "You willing to bet your life on that?"

Brimstone remained silent.

"But fuck all that," Gutter continued. "Whether you deliver my message or not, I don't give a shit. The only reason I'm even bothering to give you a heads up is because your O.G. Tango and my uncle Big Gunn got history. It don't change the fact that a cat from your side is bumping his gums and got one of my homies twisted up, and somebody has got to answer for that."

"So what you saying?" Brimstone asked, as if he didn't already know.

"What I'm saying is that y'all can consider all operations you got going in my jurisdiction shut down, until y'all give us the rat."

"Man, we don't operate in Harlem Crip territory, so you ain't got that kind of authority," one of Brimstone's soldiers pointed out.

Gutter flipped his gun around, holding it by the barrel, and swung it like a baseball bat, breaking the soldier's jaw. He then flipped the gun back the correct way and pointed it at Brimstone. "He who holds the big-ass machine gun is the authority. This is your first and last warning. Until we get the informant, y'all better not try to move one stone in the hood. If we catch you out here slipping, we gonna gobble you the fuck up. End of story. Got it?"

"Yeah, I hear you," Brimstone said through clenched teeth.

"Don't just hear me; listen to me," Gutter said sternly. "We out." He motioned for his crew to head back to the car.

"Give me a sec," Pop-Top called after them and went to speak with Animal. "You straight?"

"Yeah." Animal nodded.

Pop-Top gave him the once over. "Listen, Animal, from the look of you and the company you're keeping, I'd say you either have already or are about to make a bad decision. Animal, this is a whole different side of the coin you're out here playing with. That snitch shit my homie Gutter was kicking is dead real, and a lot of folks are upset about it. Things are about to get real nasty in the streets for anybody claiming a color, red or blue. Don't let these Blood niggas you out here hustling with get you caught up in this madness. Take a vacation from your new friends," he told him then went to catch up with Lou-Loc and Gutter.

"Pop-Top," Animal called after him. Pop-Top stopped and looked back. "How's Brasco?"

Pop-Top shrugged. "He could be better; he could be worse. They hit him with one to three years."

"Sorry to hear that," Animal said.

"Don't be. Sitting on the sidelines for a while is what my nephew needs right now. Maybe when he comes home his head will be screwed on straight. Ain't nothing out here in these streets."

"Tell him I asked about him," Animal said.

"I'll do that, and you remember what I told you. This life ain't for you, Animal. Get out while the choice is still yours to make," Pop-Top said before departing.

"Muthafuckas!" Brimstone roared after the Crips had gone. He had been disarmed and disciplined like a child on his own corner by a rival gang. It was going to look bad on him when he tried to explain what happened to the big homie.

"What was that all about, Brimstone?" Animal asked.

"The fuck if I know, but I'm gonna find out. And when I do, bodies are gonna drop. They violated by coming over here with that shit. We going to war over this shit, bet that," Brimstone fumed and stormed off to report what had happened to Tango.

When Animal turned to check on Noki, he found her standing off to the side, hugging her arms around her and shivering like she was freezing.

"You okay?" Animal reached to touch her, but Noki pulled away.

"Hell no," Noki snapped. "I just had two machine guns pointed in my face twice within five minutes. What would make you think I'm even remotely okay?"

"Noki, I'm sorry. I didn't know that was going to happen, or else I'd have never had you meet me over here," Animal said.

"And that's just it, Tayshawn. With this life, you never know. Everybody playing this game is on borrowed time, including you. If something were to happen to you, Tayshawn, I don't know how I'd handle it. You have to promise me that you'll walk away from these corners before someone carries you away," Noki said emotionally.

"I will, Noki. I just need a little time," Animal said.

Noki shook her head sadly. "Didn't the four armed men who just threatened our lives show you that you don't have time? Men like Lou-Loc and Gutter don't make idle threats, Animal. If they say people are going to get hurt, it's only a matter of when and how many, but best believe that it's coming. If you want to play with your life, that's fine, but I can't let you play with mine."

"I feel you, Noki. I'll walk you home." He reached to take her hand, but she pulled away.

"Nah, I'll walk by myself. It's probably safer than being seen with you right now," Noki told him and walked away.

Noki's parting words hurt, but they were no less than what Animal deserved for putting her in harm's way. The experience had taught him a valuable lesson: love and dirt didn't mix. That would be the last time he brought someone he cared about to someplace where he did wrong.

Noki was upset, but she would get over it, or so he hoped. Aside from being on Noki's shit list, he had inadvertently stepped into the middle of a gang war. All Animal wanted to do was make a few dollars to feed himself and keep from getting swallowed by the ghetto, but it seemed like the harder he tried to pull himself out, the deeper he got sucked in. Animal wanted no parts of a gang war, but if one was indeed brewing, Tango would surely call on him to prove his worth. Whether he liked it or not, when that time came, he would have to shit or get off the pot.

Chapter 16

Since the altercation in Harlem, Animal had been spending more time in Brooklyn. He'd spoken to Tango about what had happened, and the O.G. assured him that he didn't have to worry, and it would be taken care of. Still, he suggested that Animal stay off the block until they got everything sorted out. That suited him fine.

He hadn't seen too much of Tango as of late. He would do the occasional ride through of the block, but other than that, he had been avoiding Hell like an ugly blind date. Animal had picked up on some type of tension between Tango, Gladiator, and Kastro, but he didn't know the source of it. When he tried to ask Tango about it, he always changed the subject, and Kastro looked at him like she wanted to slap his head off. Gladiator was tight-lipped about it too, but of the three, he was the only one willing to offer up some type of explanation.

"All families have infighting, some worse than others. Tango and Kastro and me . . . well, we just have some unresolved issues, but we're working through them," was all Gladiator would say.

Animal was afraid that whatever friction there was would present a problem with him living in Hell, but it didn't. They continued with business as usual and hadn't treated Animal any differently.

As he'd predicted, Noki eventually forgave him. She got a phone in her bedroom, so they were able to sneak and talk from time to time. She was ecstatic when Animal told him that he had decided to stop playing the block so close. Noki told him about how a few nights after the altercation, Brimstone and some of his boys led a mission into Harlem Crip territory and killed two of their soldiers. The Bloods and the Crips were on the warpath, and their neighborhood was becoming a free-fire zone.

Aside from the hood bullshit, Animal enjoyed his talks with Noki. Animal's life was sliding into a dark place, but Noki was his light. For as long as he had her, he knew that he would never fully give himself to the darkness invading his soul.

Animal spent more time in Hell than anywhere else. Gladiator was out of town, so Animal was with Kastro more often than normal. Unlike Gladiator, who was always sending Animal on random errands, Kastro was more content to let Animal kick it at the house and make himself useful when she needed him. During that time, he got to know Kastro better, and they wound up becoming very close. On occasion, she would sit down with him at the card table and teach him how to play different card games while talking about life.

"You sure are a strange one," Kastro said to him one day, as they were going over the basics of a card game called Casino.

"What do you mean by that?" Animal asked.

Kastro tapped the deck of cards on the table, looking for the right words.

"Animal, you've been crashing at my spot for a few months now, and with most people, that would be more than enough time for me to figure them out, but I still don't get you. This place is called Hell because, on each level of this building, you can indulge in damn near any vice you like from drugs to pussy. Most of the other young dudes who hang around here take full advantage of what we offer, but since you've been here, I have yet to see you even so much as tap the liquor stash or feel up one of the girls. What gives?"

Animal shrugged. "I'm just not into all that."

"Bullshit! All teenage boys love pussy and free drugs. I know you get high, because all you do is smoke weed and read books, and I'm pretty sure you ain't no fag, because I hear you on the phone giggling with that gal of yours at all times of the night. I see she even tightened that mess you call a hairstyle." She nodded at the braids Noki had put in his hair the last time he'd seen her. "She must be special if you let her touch that tender-ass head of yours, unless she's just a friend." Kastro made a limp-wristed motion, suggesting that she might've been wrong about his sexuality.

Animal shook his head. "No, Noki is definitely more than a friend."

Kastro frowned. "What the hell kinda name is Noki? She Chinese or something?"

"It's short for Anokia, and she's Japanese."

Kastro shook her head. "Most niggas wait until after they're rich and famous to start chasing women outside their race. I guess you're getting a head start, huh?" Kastro laughed, but Animal didn't. Seeing that he took offense at her joke, she got serious. "Listen, kid, I'm just giving you a hard time. The heart wants what the heart wants, and no matter what color she is, the only thing I'm worried about is whether she makes you happy or not. Does she make you happy?"

"Yes, very," Animal said.

"So what kind of stuff do you guys do when you're together?" Kastro asked.

The question stumped Animal. He had realized that outside of hanging on the block, he and Noki hadn't done much of anything together. He had never had a girlfriend to know what to do with one.

Kastro read the expression on his face. "Boy, you mean to say that you haven't even taken this girl you're so crazy about on a date? You're starting off on the wrong foot already. I ain't counting your pennies, Animal, but I know you make enough on them corners to at the very least take that girl out for a hamburger or to a movie. This is what I want you to do: Go tap into that stash you keep hidden away like leprechaun's gold, and you take this Anokia out. If you like her like you say you do, then you have to show her, and you can't do that hanging out on the block. Feel me?"

"Yeah, I feel you, Kastro."

"Good. Now get your ass up from this table and go handle your business."

Animal rose from the table and started for his bedroom to call Noki, but Kastro's hand on his arm stopped him.

"Take these." She shoved something in his palm.

Animal opened his hand and saw she had placed several condoms in his hand. "What are these for?"

"If you have to ask, then I doubt you'll need them, but better safe than sorry. Don't go bringing no babies in my house, because I damn sure can't feed another mouth. You kids are eating me out of house and home as it is. Now get your ass outta here and set up that date."

Chapter 17

The talk with Kastro had lit a fire under Animal's ass. He immediately went upstairs to call Noki. He was as nervous as a virgin girl on a prison cell block. Animal was still quite the novice with women and wasn't sure how to go about asking her out on a date, so he just suggested that they go catch a movie. To his surprise, Noki accepted.

They had to be very cloak and dagger about it. Noki's parents didn't allow her to date, and they would've especially gone through the roof to find out she was with a black guy. With the rash of shootings in their hood, sneaking out after dark was not an option. Noki's brothers had her on lockdown, and the only time she was permitted to leave the house was to go to school, and even then, one of her brothers always escorted her.

Animal and Noki bided their time and plotted until they came up with the perfect plan. When her brother dropped her off at school, she would

sneak out the side door and rendezvous with
Animal.

Their first date was on a Friday. It had been
raining off and on for two days. Animal had suggested that they reschedule, but Noki wouldn't
hear of it. She had put too much into her escape
plan not to execute it. The meeting spot was a
bodega two blocks away from Noki's building. It
wasn't far from where Animal had once hustled
with Brimstone. It was risky meeting in their
neighborhood, where someone who knew Noki's
family could spot them, but it was the only
mutual place that they both knew how to get
to. Neither one of them had much experience
traveling outside the neighborhood. Animal
even had to search the Internet for directions
to the movie theater where they were going.
They reasoned that they wouldn't be there long
enough to be spotted, so it was safe.

Animal had to pass K-Dawg's block to get to
the meeting spot with Noki. K-Dawg lived on a
strip of brownstones that were in varying stages
of dilapidation. Some were even abandoned. The
residents who cared did what they could to keep
their properties up, but it was a losing battle.
With the skyrocketing cost of living in New York
City, and the crackheads that were squatting
in the abandoned properties on the block, it

almost didn't seem worth it. It seemed like every time you turned around, families who had lived on the block for years were moving away.

Near the end of the block, Animal spotted several police cars and an ambulance. A few people from the neighborhood stood around, gossiping and watching. With his curiosity getting the best of him, Animal went over to see what had happened. As he neared the crowd, he realized that they were gathered in front of the building that K-Dawg lived in. Animal rushed over, bumping through the crowd, hoping that nothing bad had happened to K-Dawg or his family. K-Dawg was a sick and cruel bastard, but he was still Justice's best friend, and K-Dawg's family had always been good to them.

When Animal reached the front of the crowd, he saw two paramedics making their way down the stairs with a man's body on a gurney. At first, Animal thought it was K-Dawg, but upon closer inspection, he realized that it wasn't him, but his father. Animal wasn't sure how he had died, but the blood soaking through the sheets said that it hadn't been a pleasant death. The sight of Mr. Wilson being carried out hurt Animal's heart, but what he saw next nearly burst it.

A burly officer came out of the house, barking for the crowd to back up. Following closely behind him were two detectives wearing cheap-looking suits. Between them, wearing handcuffs, was K-Dawg. His face was hard and emotionless, and his strides broad and confident. His posture was that of a young man about to receive his high school diploma, as opposed to being escorted to a police car.

K-Dawg's green eyes took in the faces of each and every person standing around, as if he was committing them to memory. When he spotted Animal, a look between sadness and disappointment crossed his face. One of the officers shoved him forward, moving him along. As they lowered him into the police car, he gave Animal a nod and disappeared into the back seat.

Animal would find out later that K-Dawg had been charged with the murder of his father. It was revenge for what Mr. Wilson had done to K-Dawg's sister years prior. K-Dawg and his twin sister were the only children in the house who Mr. Wilson had not fathered. He wasn't very fond of either of them, but he was especially cruel to K-Dawg. Years prior, K-Dawg's sister had died due to what was initially called an accident. She'd drunk a cup of antifreeze that had been sitting out in the backyard of the house, where Mr. Wilson would work on his car. As it turned out, it wasn't an accident. Mr. Wilson had purposely poured the antifreeze into a cup and left it out in the hopes that K-Dawg would pick it up and drink it, but his sister had gotten ahold of it instead. Years later, when K-Dawg found out the truth of his sister's death, he killed his mother's husband.

It would be many years before Animal and K-Dawg would see each other again, and when their paths next crossed, neither of them would be the kids they remembered.

Seeing the police take K-Dawg away made Animal think of his brother Justice. It felt like forever since he'd seen him. The brothers kept in contact through letters but hadn't seen each other in the flesh since his arrest. Every so often, Tango would bring him word about his brother's well-being, so he knew Justice was okay, but he still longed to talk to him. There was so much he had to tell his brother, and he desperately needed his guidance at that point in his life. He knew that Justice was going to take what had happened to K-Dawg hard, and he was sad that he couldn't be there to comfort him. Justice had always been Animal's rock when he needed support, and he felt guilty that he wouldn't be able to return the favor. He was still too young to visit him on his own, and there was a shortage of adults he could call on to take him. Maybe if he caught Kastro on a good day, she'd agree to take him on a visit or, at least, assign someone else the task. He planned to ask her about it right after his date with Noki.

Animal was crossing the avenue, headed for the bodega where he was supposed to meet Noki, when a green Ford Explorer crossed his path. Animal probably wouldn't have even given it a second look had he not caught the driver staring at him while he idled at the crosswalk, waiting for the light to change. He had a hard face behind his dark sunglasses, and the gold hammer hanging at the end of the chain around his neck glistened in the sun.

Animal met his gaze but didn't hold eye contact. He stepped onto the curb, letting his hand slip inside his pocket and stroke his trusty knife. The light changed, and the driver drove through it slowly. As the Explorer rounded the corner, Animal thought he spotted someone in the back seat looking back at him. An eerie feeling settled in the pit of his gut, and he suddenly wanted to be as far away from that place as possible. The sooner he met up with Noki, the sooner they could be on their way.

Animal's heart was aflutter when he saw Noki coming down the street dressed in her school uniform, consisting of a navy blue-and-white plaid skirt and navy blue sweater over a white top. Her hair was pulled back into a ponytail with a plaid clip holding it in place. That was the first time Animal had seen her without her braids, and she was even more beautiful than he realized.

"I see your hair is holding up." Noki gently ran her hand over his braids. They had gotten a bit fuzzy but still looked neat.

Animal smiled. "Yeah, nobody braids like you, Noki."

"Of course not, and I'd kick your ass if I ever found out you ever let another girl braid your hair," Noki half-joked.

"Nah, you don't have to worry about another chick ever touching my hair, Noki. If you don't do it, then it won't get done," Animal assured her.

Noki held up her hand and extended her little finger. "Pinky promise?"

Animal locked fingers with her. "Pinky promise."

"Good, now let's seal the deal." Noki kissed him.

This time, Animal wasn't nervous. He pressed his lips against hers ever so softly. He was a bit surprised when she slipped her tongue in his mouth. Their tongues did a playful dance, as they explored the insides of each other's mouths. The kiss stopped time and washed away everything else in the world, except them. It was a near perfect moment, and they would've both been content to be suspended in it forever, but it was soon ruined.

"Aww. Ain't that cute?" Brimstone appeared. He had just come out of the bodega they were standing in front of, with a forty-ounce beer tucked under his arm.

Animal and Noki quickly separated and stood there, awkwardly squirming under Brimstone's gaze.

"I guess now I know why I haven't seen you on the block," Brimstone continued.

"Fall back with that shit, Blood. A nigga been busy," Animal said, falling back into his street corner slang. He'd found that his brain could turn it on and off automatically, depending on who he was talking to.

"Yeah, busy chasing pussy instead of out here trying to get this money," Brimstone quipped. "Let me tell you something, young blood. A nigga will lose money chasing a bitch every time, but he will never lose a bitch chasing money."

"I ain't no bitch." Noki rolled her neck.

"Take it easy, Chu-Li," Brimstone said, referencing the female character from the *Street Fighter* video game. "I didn't mean you in particular. I was speaking in general."

"Whatever." She rolled her eyes.

Brimstone chuckled at her irritation. "Dig this—" He turned to Animal. "We finally got to the bottom of that little piece of business from the other day."

Animal knew without him having to say so that he meant when the Crips rolled up on them. "What's the verdict?"

"They were right. One of ours was talking to the police," Brimstone told him. "Bitch-ass nigga been running his mouth, sending good people from both sides to the slammer."

"Damn! That's cold-blooded," Animal said.

"Nah, the cold part is that it ain't just some street-level nigga talking. It's O.G. Tre, the big homie."

Brimstone's words hit Animal like a slap. Of all the people he had expected him to name, Tre had never entered his mind. Animal didn't know him well, but from the stories Tango told, Tre was like a superhero in the Blood community. He represented everything they aspired to be. Until that point, getting initiated into the Bloods and standing in a circle forged of iron with men like Tango and Tre was what he was looking forward to. Brimstone's revelation showed Animal that even iron could be broken, and this took his thoughts to Tango. He'd always told Animal how he and Tre were like brothers and that he was the closest thing to family he had on the East Coast, so had his mentor been corrupted, too? Was that the cause of the tension between him and the siblings? All he could do was shake his head in disbelief as he now questioned everything he'd been taught.

"I was speechless when I heard it too," Brimstone continued. "Twenty years on the set as a recognized shot-caller, and he traded it all for a reduced sentence."

"So what now?" Animal asked, already knowing the answer.

"He dies," Brimstone said as if it should've been obvious.

"But he's one of ours . . . a *brother*. Shouldn't there at least be some kind of trial?" Animal asked, remembering the things Tango had told him about love for one's brother and fairness.

Brimstone laughed. "You got a noble heart, Animal, but not much understanding about the way this thing of ours works. Unless you're a civilian, talking to the police is never acceptable. Tre being put on a hit list ain't about Blood. This is about keeping it gangsta."

"So, what now? Does Tre get handed over to the Crips to stop the feud?" Animal asked.

"Fuck no! Tre is foul, but handing one of ours over to them would make us look weak. We administer our own discipline," Brimstone explained. "It don't much matter anyway at this point. Ever since Gutter and Lou-Loc showed up, them Harlem Crip niggas been on some Super Thug shit, and a few of us are tired of it. Maybe a good pat on the ass is what they need to let them know that our side still has a claim to Harlem too. If it's war, then let it be war."

"Tayshawn, are you about ready?" Noki appeared at Animal's side. "The movie is going to start soon."

Her face was impatient and Animal wasn't sure how long she'd been standing there or how much she'd heard. Animal held up one finger, signaling that he needed a minute. Noki sucked her teeth and mumbled something under her breath that didn't sound pleasant and walked away. She didn't go far enough to where she wouldn't be able to hear what they were saying, but she didn't crowd him either.

Animal turned his attention back to Brimstone. "If you need an extra shooter—"

"Thanks, but no thanks." Brimstone cut him off. "Animal, you're a righteous young soldier, but this ain't for you. It's obvious to a duck that murder don't fit in your heart, so no need to try and force it."

Animal felt slighted by Brimstone's words, but he didn't show it. "Whatever, Blood. Let me get with my lady."

As Animal was saying his good-byes to Brimstone, he saw the green Explorer bend the corner again. Something about it sent off a warning in his head. Slowly, the pieces began coming together, and he realized why it had looked so familiar to him. The hammer chain the driver was wearing was the same chain worn by one of the Crips who had run down on them. Animal opened his mouth to shout a warning, but it was too late.

The passenger window rolled down, and out came the barrel of a rifle. "Didn't we tell you slobs it was over for you?"

The world moved in slow motion as the rifle roared to life. The shooter swept the block with lethal fire, gunning for the rival gang members but cutting down anyone and everyone in their path. Animal watched in horror as Brimstone was nearly cut in half by the powerful slugs. He never had a chance.

Suddenly he remembered Noki. She was standing a few feet away from him, frozen with fear and in the line of fire. Throwing caution to the wind, Animal moved to dive for Noki, but he awkwardly tripped over his own feet and fell face first to the ground. He banged his head so hard on the concrete that the world swam, and he nearly blacked out.

Fighting the pain in his skull, Animal pushed himself into a crawling position and scrambled for Noki. Animal dove, grabbing her by the arm just before a hail of bullets tore through the storefront window she had been standing in front of. Animal covered Noki with his body and yelled for her to stay down, while the shooters continued firing. It went on for so long that Animal thought they had an endless amount of ammunition. He only hoped that one didn't find its way to him and Noki.

Finally, the shooting stopped. He heard the screeching of tires as the shooters peeled off, but he stayed down for a few moments more to make sure the coast was clear. Animal spared a glance around and was horrified by the carnage around him. Dead bodies and broken glass littered the streets. A few feet away, Brimstone was stretched out on his back. His stomach and the lower half of his face had gone missing. It had gone bad for Brimstone, and it could've gone just as bad for Animal.

Growing up, Animal used to say that God didn't care about him, but the fact that he had survived the onslaught told him otherwise. Moving forward, he would make it a point to be a bit more thankful.

He suddenly remembered Noki, who was being crushed under the weight of his body.

"You okay, Noki?" Animal asked, pushing himself off of her and to his knees.

It wasn't until he sat up that he noticed his shirt was covered in blood. He quickly checked his body to see if he had been hit. He seemed to be intact. There was only one other place the blood could've come from. Animal hurriedly turned Noki over on her back and began checking her for wounds. When he pushed up her sweater, his breath caught in his throat.

"God, no . . ."

A silver dollar–sized pool of blood sat over the left breast of her white shirt. He thought he'd been fast enough, but he hadn't. Animal pressed his hands over the wound and tried to stop the bleeding, but there was nothing he could do. The bullet had pierced Noki's heart and killed her on impact.

Animal cradled Noki's dead body in his arms and produced a wailing sound that should've been impossible coming from a human being.

"I'm sorry, Noki. I'm so sorry." He sobbed into her hair. Noki's death had broken him in a way that could not be repaired.

Animal was in a trance. He heard the sirens in the distance and knew how it would play out if the police found him there, but he didn't care. He was numb to everything except Noki.

When a strong pair of hands grabbed Animal under the arms and pulled him to his feet, he didn't resist. He wanted to, but he didn't have the strength. Animal continued to stare at Noki's face as he was carried away from the crime scene. As he was being pushed into a car, he burned the image of how she looked into his mind so that he would never forget it. Losing the first girl he'd ever loved, besides his mother, had broken Animal in a way that could never be repaired.

Chapter 18

For the next few days, Animal moved around in a trance. He wouldn't eat and would barely talk. All he wanted to do was sleep and try to forget what had happened, but every time he closed his eyes, he relived the shootout and his failure to save Noki.

From what he'd learned, it was Gladiator who had pulled Animal away from the crime scene. Kastro knew that Animal would be in the area to meet Noki for their date and potentially in harm's way, so she'd sent Gladiator to make sure they were good. Unfortunately, by the time Gladiator arrived, the shooting had already started. He had barely been able to pull Animal out and make their escape before the police arrived.

Word of Noki's death rocked the neighborhood. They called it a gang-related shooting and Noki a victim of circumstance, but people who knew her knew that it was bullshit. Noki was a good kid, and everybody loved her. Her parents had been respected business owners in the community for twenty years, and all of the kids in the household were straight-A students. With all this going for her, no one could figure out what Noki was doing on a high traffic corner with a reputed gang member in the middle of the day, instead of being in school. Only Animal knew the truth of that, and guilt rode him like a dark horse. Noki dying hurt him more than anything, because he felt as if he had put her in harm's way. Had she been in school instead of in the streets with him, she would still be alive.

Animal stayed in his room, huddled under his blanket, staring and staring at the wall. Kastro came in to check on him every now and again, but for the most part, she left him alone to grieve. Once she came in and attempted to braid his hair, but Animal almost bit her hand off when she tried to touch him. He had made a promise to Noki that no other woman would braid his hair, and he planned to keep to it for as long as he held her memory in his heart.

Tango had come to visit Animal once during his time of grief. The differences between Tango and the siblings were put to the side for a moment, so he could be there for his protégé. As Tango offered his condolences, he said, "I know you're in a lot of pain, kid. What happened to that girl wasn't right, and I'm sorry she got caught up in this madness. For what it's worth, I'm gonna make sure this gets made right."

Animal remained silent. Unless he was going to wave a magic wand and resurrect Noki, there was nothing he could do to make it right. It was all talk, and Animal wasn't trying to hear it.

"Animal, I know you might be feeling some type of way because I haven't been around lately, but there's a lot going on in the streets right now. This shit is one big mess, and I'm trying my best to clean it all up. I just need some time to sort it all out," Tango said.

Animal knew in his gut that he was talking about the situation with Tre, but what exactly was he saying? Ever since Brimstone had revealed that Tre was the snitch, Animal had been looking at Tango sideways. Were Tango's cryptic words an admission of guilt, or was he delivering some other message that Animal couldn't digest because he was still so blinded by his rage? He loved Tango like an uncle. He had always been good to him, so Animal wanted to trust him, but he was no longer sure that he could. One lesson that life had taught him was that the people closest to you were the ones who could hurt you the most.

At the end of Tango's visit, he left Animal a gift. Animal waited until he was gone to open the box. Inside, lying on a bed of soft velvet was a pair of gold grills. Tango knew how much Animal had always admired his gold teeth, so he'd bought him a set of his own. Animal ran his finger over the gold, and it was the first time since Noki's murder that he had even managed to muster up anything close to a smile. He promised himself that the next time he saw Tango, he would thank him for the gift and apologize for his behavior.

Over the course of the week Animal spent in his room, a few different people came and went, but Gladiator was the only regular visitor. Each day, Gladiator would come to his room to try to get him to eat or engage in conversation, but Animal wasn't receptive. From time to time, Gladiator would even sit and read him chapters from his favorite books, but Animal's expression never changed. He was in a dark place, and no one was sure what would bring him out of it.

One day, Gladiator came to Animal's room, intending to read him a few chapters from *War & Peace*. The room was dark, and when he went to flick on the light, nothing happened. He was just about to check the bulb in the ceiling, but Animal stopped him.

"Leave it." Animal's voice was a raspy whisper.

Gladiator turned to the sound of his voice. Animal was huddled in the dark near the window. He blended in almost perfectly with the darkness. The moon shone through the window, casting an eerie light on him. All Gladiator could make out was the silhouette of his wild hair and the faintest glint of gold in his mouth.

"What are you doing sitting in here with the lights off?" Gladiator asked.

"The darkness is soothing," Animal told him.

There was an edge to Animal's voice that made the hairs on the back of Gladiator's neck stand up. "Are you okay?"

"Tell me, if someone you loved was gunned down in front of you, would you be okay?"

"Animal, I feel your pain," Gladiator said compassionately.

Animal gave a sinister chuckle. "You couldn't possibly feel my pain, Gladiator. Nobody can feel my pain, but they will soon enough."

"Animal, those dudes who shot your lady will get theirs eventually," Gladiator assured him.

"Eventually isn't good enough. They should be dead now," Animal insisted.

"Animal, give yourself time to heal, and if you still feel that way, then—"

"I don't need time, Gladiator. I need blood." Animal slid off the bed and into the light, so

Gladiator could get a good look at his face. Animal looked like a ghost of his former self, and there was a maddened look in his eyes that Gladiator knew all too well. It was the look of a man who had nothing else to lose. "The Crips killed Noki, so I'm going to kill Crips." His tone was calm and lucid.

Gladiator shook his head. "Animal, right now you're speaking from a place of hurt and anger. You ain't no killer."

"Yes, and those are the only things that I have to hold onto right now—hurt and anger," Animal said emotionally. "They went and killed her, Gladiator . . . gunned her down right in front of me, and I'm supposed to let that go?"

Gladiator didn't have an answer.

"You're right. I ain't no killer, but *you* are. Now I can go at this half-assed and maybe get away with it, or you can teach me how to do it the right way."

Gladiator studied Animal. He searched his eyes for any signs of the innocent kid that Tango had dropped on their doorstep, but he found none. "Animal, you're a kid asking me to teach him how to commit murder."

"No, I'm a young man asking you to teach him how to survive. Don't deny me this," Animal pleaded.

Reluctantly, Gladiator agreed. "Okay, Animal. I'll grant you your revenge, but there's one condition."

"Anything," Animal assured him.

"When it's done, I'm casting you out of Hell," Gladiator informed him.

Animal was stunned. "But why? You don't have to worry about me ever telling anyone you helped me."

"You don't get it, do you? I'm a soldier, but not a monster, and a monster is what you're asking me to become by knowingly putting blood on the hands of a child. If I'm not damned already, I surely will be after this. Every time I look at you, I'll either want to kill you or myself from the guilt of it, and that isn't good for either of us. Your exile from Hell is the price for my help."

This was an unexpected twist. Hell was the only place that had ever really felt like home to Animal, and the misfits who lived there had become his family. Kastro and Gladiator had become like his surrogate parents, and, had it not been for them, he wouldn't have made it as far as he had. The thought of leaving behind his home and family for a second time broke his heart, and he wanted to call the whole thing off, but his need for revenge overrode everything else. "I accept your terms. Let's do this shit."

Chapter 19

Animal didn't expect to go after his targets right away, but he didn't expect Gladiator to make him wait weeks either. Each day, Gladiator would wake Animal up at the crack of dawn and make him exercise until his limbs hurt, and after that, he would make him spend the rest of the day reading books on the human anatomy. It pissed Animal off to no end that Gladiator was wasting precious time making him do seemingly pointless things. He didn't need to be in shape to pull a trigger. Animal wasn't trying to hear all that; he wanted his revenge, and he wanted it immediately.

More than once, Animal tried to sneak out of Hell and go after Noki's killers on his own, but each time, Gladiator would track him down, kick his ass, and drag him, kicking and screaming, back to Hell. Whenever he questioned Gladiator about it, he would simply say, "You aren't ready. Murder is an art that requires your body and mind to be in sync."

Animal hated being Gladiator's captive and thought he was just stalling in hopes that Animal would change his mind, but he didn't realize that he was being conditioned for what was to come. His weight was starting to come back, and he knew almost as much about the human body as a first year medical student. By the end of the second week, Gladiator deemed him ready.

For several days, they rode through known Crip neighborhoods, getting familiar with the comings and goings of the men they were stalking. The shooter with the chain was a boy called Hammer, who was older than Animal. For what he had done to Brimstone and Noki, he had gained street credibility and had taken to strutting around like a peacock flaunting his new status as a shooter. His superiors had also given him a block to call his own and several underlings to move their drugs. They sold crack out of a project building in West Harlem.

When Animal saw him for the first time since the shooting, he wanted to hop out of the car and take him down immediately, but Gladiator insisted they wait until the time was right. The right time came sooner than later.

One night, Gladiator had awakened Animal from his sleep and instructed him to get dressed. Animal jumped into a pair of black jeans, a black hoodie, and red Converse. He was dressed combat appropriate, but, to his surprise, Gladiator wasn't. He was wearing a white shirt, wool slacks, and a blazer with a pair of wire-framed glasses sitting on the bridge of his nose. Gladiator looked more prepared for a business meeting than a mission of murder. Animal started to ask him about his choice in clothing, but Gladiator motioned for him to be quiet and follow him.

They crept past Kastro's bedroom like two thieves. She was sound asleep, and they doubted she would be stirring anytime soon. Kastro had been up running back and forth to court or jail every day, checking on different homies who had been caught up in the web of Tre's bullshit. He was telling all he knew and making up other things as he went along. It seemed like homies were getting knocked or spots were getting rushed on the regular. The only thing that stopped the police from running up in Hell was Gladiator. He had several detectives in his pocket. Still, at the rate things were going, there was no way to tell how long the peace would be kept. To be on the safe side, Gladiator had forbidden anyone to bring drugs into Hell and stopped the girls from turning tricks in the apartments. They still hosted the card games, but that wouldn't get them more than a slap on the wrist if they were ever raided.

Animal asked if Kastro knew what they were up to. Gladiator told him that she didn't, and he must never tell her. When it came to murder, the fewer people who knew about it, the better your chances were of not getting caught.

Animal had butterflies in his stomach. He didn't know if it was fear or the anxieties of knowing he was finally about to avenge Noki's death. He couldn't put his finger on it, but something was making him anxious. He was a ball of nerves and needed something or someone to calm him down before he fell apart. When Gladiator went to get the car, Animal went to the pay phone on the corner and called Tango. He wasn't sure why he did it, other than wanting to hear a familiar voice. The phone rang several times, and Animal was about to hang up when Tango's voice came over the line.

"Who this?"

Animal was silent.

"Whoever the fuck this is, I ain't got time for you to be playing on my phone, Blood," Tango said, sounding irritated.

"Don't hang up," Animal blurted out.

"Young Blood, is that you?" Tango recognized Animal's voice. "How you be, soldier?"

"I'm okay," Animal said, trying to hide the nervousness in his voice.

"You sure? You sound like something is wrong. And why are you out at this time of night? I thought Kastro had you on restriction."

"She did, but I needed some air," Animal lied. "I just came to the store to get a soda, and I'm going right back upstairs, but you were on my mind for some reason."

"I'm cool, man, just handling business. Listen, I know I been moving kinda creepy lately, but there's a good reason for it. I can't speak on it over the phone, but I promise I'll let you in on it as soon as I can. As a matter of fact, I gotta come down that way tomorrow to take care of some business with Kastro."

"You and Kastro got business?" Animal hadn't meant it the way it sounded, but he was surprised.

"Yeah. She didn't tell you? Me and Kastro are opening a social club a few blocks from Hell called Blood Orchid," he informed Animal.

This both surprised and relieved Animal. For over a month, Kastro and Tango had been acting as if they were on the outs. That and Tango's closeness with Tre were the main reasons Animal had begun to question his loyalty.

"Glad to hear it."

"Yeah, it isn't done yet, but I'll take you around to see it tomorrow when I come down," Tango said.

"Sounds good to me. Oh! And before I forget, thanks for the grills," Animal said, subconsciously running his tongue over his new gold grills.

"It's all good, li'l homie. Shit! Them golds against that black-ass skin of yours, them grills probably look better on you than they do on me. Maybe when you get your weight up, I'll take you to get some diamonds thrown in them."

"I'm gonna hold you to it," Animal said.

"Fo' sho. Now let me get off this line and handle business. I'll see you tomorrow," Tango said and ended the call.

Animal felt better after talking to Tango. He still wasn't sure what to make of the situation with Tre, but his suspicions were eased a bit. Before he could ponder it further, he heard Gladiator's voice.

"Who were you talking to?" Gladiator asked suspiciously.

"Nobody. I was calling K-Dawg's sister to see if they had any word on him," Animal lied.

Gladiator gave him a disbelieving look but didn't press it. "Whatever, man. Stop yanking your dick and get in the car. We've got killing to do."

***

They rode to Harlem in relative silence, making small talk here and there. Animal asked Gladiator if he was sure they'd be able to catch Hammer slipping. It had been two days since their last surveillance mission, and there were no guarantees that Hammer would be out there. Gladiator explained to Animal that people like Hammer were creatures of habit that never strayed too far from what they were familiar with. Sure enough, Hammer and his boys were in front of the building. Gladiator parked the car a half block away, killed the lights, but left the engine running.

Gladiator lowered his head and offered up a prayer. "We are the damned, and the damned are we. This is the role you've given us to play in life, and we accept it as the way of things. If we are to die here tonight, then let it be a soldier's death so that we may look into the eyes of our killers in our final moments."

"What the hell kind of prayer was that?" Animal asked.

"It was a warrior's prayer. I learned it while serving in Her Majesty's army," Gladiator explained. "As soldiers, every time we were deployed, we knew it could potentially be our last day on earth, and we accepted that fact. We killed and died in the name of the queen with pride, but we also did so with honor. If a man is to die, then, at the very least, he should see it coming. Shooting someone in the back is cowardice. If I am to die, let me face it with dignity and pride, knowing I died for what I believed in. Give me a clean death, a soldier's death."

It was a deep philosophy. Though Animal was too young and not yet battle hardened enough to grasp it at the time, it would be a code he would come to live by later in life.

From the floor of the back seat, Gladiator produced two guns, a black Tech-Nine and a Glock. He checked both guns to make sure they were loaded and operational before handing Animal the Tech Nine. Animal stared at the gun for a while, as if he were waiting for it to speak to him. He had seen plenty of guns in his day, but this was his first time he'd ever held one.

As Animal's moment of truth approached, he found that he was nervous. He had replayed the scene over and over in his head, but now that they were there, he was unsure. Killing a man in the heat of the moment was one thing, but cold and calculated murder was something else.

"It isn't too late to turn back," Gladiator told Animal, noticing the look of uncertainty on his face.

"Nah, I'm not turning back. I'm ready," Animal assured him.

Gladiator nodded. "This is the plan. I'm going to go in through the front, and you'll wait around back until—"

Animal cut him off. "Wait a second. This is supposed to be my kill."

"Nobody is trying to steal your glory, Animal, but because of the way you're dressed, they'll spot you before you make it within spitting distance. Don't worry. You'll get your fill of blood before it's all said and done, but we do this my way, or we won't do it. Do you understand?"

"Fine," Animal reluctantly agreed.

"As I was saying, you'll wait around back near the fire exit. When you get my signal, handle your business."

"No problem." Animal got out of the car. "Wait. How will I know what your signal is?"

Gladiator smiled. "Trust me. You'll know it. Now go take your position." Animal started for the back of the building, but Gladiator called after him. "Animal, show no mercy. Anybody who isn't one of us dies. You got it?"

Animal nodded that he understood and disappeared around the back of the building to wait for Gladiator's signal.

***

When Animal arrived at the exit, he found that it was dark. Someone had taken the liberty of busting out all the lights on that side of the building. Either one of the dope boys who hustled out of it, or Gladiator had done it. He was always planning in advance. Either way, Animal welcomed the shadows. They helped to conceal him and the gun he was toting.

The glass window in the fire door gave Animal a near perfect view of the lobby. There were five Crips inside, drinking, smoking, and hustling. Standing in the center of them, giving orders, was Hammer. Animal's blood boiled when he spotted him. He wanted to kill him so bad he could almost taste it, but he wouldn't act on his impulse. He would stick to Gladiator's plan.

Speaking of Gladiator, he had just sauntered into the building. The Crips took one look at the seemingly square man with the face full of scars and started right in, harassing him. They were laughing and pointing as if someone had just told a joke, but the laughter stopped when Gladiator pulled the Glock from his blazer and blew one of the boys' heads off. The Crips scattered like roaches when their comrade dropped.

Gladiator fired round after round but didn't hit anyone else. Animal knew from watching Gladiator train that he was a crack shot, especially at such close range, but he seemed to be missing them on purpose. He was herding them like cattle toward the back door and their impending doom.

Animal took a few steps back and leveled the Tech Nine. His hands were sweating so bad that he feared he might drop the gun, but seeing Noki's face in his mind secured his grip. When the fire exit swung open, Animal squeezed the trigger. The Tech Nine had more kick than he expected, so his shots were uncoordinated, but the spray of bullets found their marks. Two of the young men crumbled under the bullets and met their ends in the shadow of the same building they had sold poison out of, while one of them took a slug to the leg and fell to the floor. This left only Animal and Hammer, who was frozen by terror.

"Remember me, Blood?" Animal asked in a low growl.

Hammer looked confused at first, but as he stared at the young man holding the smoking gun, he realized where he'd seen him before and knew why he had come.

"It wasn't supposed to go like that," he said just above a whisper. "We came for Brimstone. Those bullets weren't for you."

"That's too bad, because these are surely for you," Animal sneered and pulled the trigger.

Animal saw Hammer's mouth appear to scream something, but he couldn't hear him over the roar of gunfire. Hammer fell after the first few bullets hit him, but that didn't stop Animal from standing over him, still firing. The gun clicked empty, and Hammer was long dead, but Animal's thirst wasn't yet sated. Discarding the gun, he picked up a broken bottle from the ground and straddled Hammer's corpse. Tears for his dead lover stung Animal's eyes.

"She was the only girl who ever loved me, and you took her," he sobbed before stabbing Hammer in the throat.

Animal drove the bottle into Hammer's flesh over and over while babbling like a mad man. With every cut he gave Hammer, he envisioned himself stabbing someone who had wronged him—Apple, Eddie, the boys who had jumped him and Brasco in the projects. He was settling all old scores. Animal would've cut Hammer's head from his body with the broken bottle had Gladiator not pulled him away.

"Get the fuck off me, Gladiator! I have to finish it! They all have to die!" Animal struggled.

Gladiator spun him around and forced him to look at the collection of corpses. "It's over. There's no one left to kill!"

Animal looked around at the dead bodies. . . bodies he'd dropped. He'd often wondered what it would feel like to kill the man who had murdered Noki. He thought he would feel some sort of satisfaction, or at least guilt, from taking a life, but there was nothing. Animal had taken his revenge, but he still felt empty. There was a gaping hole in his soul, and only more violence would fill it.

The sounds of moans drew their attention. A young man crawled on his stomach, trying to get away from the scene. He was bleeding badly but still alive. Animal broke free of Gladiator's grip.

"There's always someone left to kill." He stalked over to the crawling man.

Animal flipped him over, glass bottle raised and ready to deliver the death stroke, but froze when he realized that he knew the young man.

"If you gonna kill me, get it over with, muthafucka," Pop-Top rasped. He was bleeding badly from his side where a bullet had struck him, and the blood in his eyes made it hard for him to see. Even on the brink of death, he was still a gangsta.

"Pop-Top?" Animal asked, shocked.

Pop-Top immediately recognized the voice. "Animal?" He was shocked to find it out was Brasco's friend behind the trigger. He knew Animal as a shy neighborhood kid, not a killer.

Animal grabbed Pop-Top by the back of his neck and put the broken bottle to his throat. "Were you there?"

"Where?" Pop-Top asked, genuinely not knowing what Animal was talking about.

Animal pressed the glass deeper into Pop-Top's throat. "Pop-Top, don't play with me. Were you one of the Crips who shot at me and killed my girl?"

It all began to make sense. Pop-Top wasn't there, but he had heard about the botched mission and the little girl who got hit in the crossfire. He'd had no idea it was Animal and his friend. "Animal, on everything I love, that child's blood isn't on my hands. I'm a lot of things, but I ain't no baby killer."

"C'mon, kid. Stop playing with your food and eat it," Gladiator urged him.

Animal ignored him and searched Pop-Top's eyes for signs of a lie. He was Brasco's uncle, but neither relation nor friendship mattered at that moment. Only when he was sure that Pop-Top was telling the truth did he release him. He got to his feet, turned to Gladiator, and said, "Not him. Let's go."

He tried to walk away, but Gladiator blocked his path.

"What do you mean *let's go*? You aren't done. I told you before we created this mess that there would be no mercy shown." He tried to shove his gun into Animal's hand to finish the job, but Animal wouldn't take it.

"That man was kind to me and gave me a place to stay when I was ass-out in the streets. I won't repay him by taking his life, not tonight."

Gladiator was angry, but he didn't force the issue. "Fuck it! If it comes back to bite you in the ass, you can't say I didn't warn you." He tucked his gun and stormed off. "Dumb kid," he mumbled and walked away.

"Thank you, Animal," Pop-Top said, happy to still be alive.

"You can thank me by staying the fuck away from me," Animal said to Pop-Top's surprise.

Pop-Top looked stunned. "I thought we were family."

"At one time, maybe, but not anymore," Animal said. "I don't recognize nothing but Blood. That's my family now, and everything that ain't Blood is food," Animal told him. "I spared your life today on the strength of Brasco, but don't look for any more passes. The next time you see me, you better have a gun on you, because I'm sure gonna have one, and it ain't gonna matter who you're related to, *Blood*,"

Animal warned before disappearing into the night.

Gladiator didn't say much on the ride back to Brooklyn; he simply stared at Animal, waiting for some type of reaction, but it never came. The first time Gladiator had taken a life, he was sick, but Animal seemed unmoved. If Gladiator hadn't known better, he could've sworn he saw Animal smile. Part of Gladiator was proud that Animal had performed a successful hit on his first time out, but another part of him was filled with great sadness. He knew that no matter what happened next, there would be no turning back. Animal was now walking a dark road, and Gladiator was the one who had put him on it.

Chapter 20

By the time they made it back to Brooklyn, the sun was almost up. They had been out all night. To their surprise, the block was teeming with activity, especially Hell. A bunch of the young homies and homegirls were gathered on the stoop. Some of them were crying, and some were making threats. Even Big Dread, who was normally calm and easygoing, seemed agitated. Something was wrong.

"What in the bloody hell is going on?" Gladiator asked when he approached the stoop.

"All bad, my youth, all bad." He shook his head. "They kill him . . . shoot him down like a dog, and I gwan kill dem. A curse on all Babylon until them bleed like me li'l burdda!" Big Dread staggered away. He looked like he was on the verge of tears.

It was obvious Gladiator wasn't going to get a straight answer from Big Dread, so he snatched one of the young girls off the stoop. Her eyes were red and swollen from crying.

"What the fuck is that old kook talking about?"

"They killed Tango!" The girl sobbed.

Animal felt like someone had punched him in the chest. He had just spoken to him the night before, and they promised to meet up that day. There was no way he could be dead.

"Tango? That's impossible. I just spoke to him a few hours ago," Animal admitted, exposing the fact that he had lied to Gladiator.

"I'm telling you. He's dead," the young girl insisted. "Kastro got the call about an hour ago."

Animal's knees felt weak. She was wrong. She had to be. Animal pushed past the girl and bounded up the stairs. Gladiator lingered to gather some last-minute pieces of information before following him.

The floor their apartment was on was packed with young men congregating, smoking weed, and passing around bottles. Some of them tried to offer Animal their condolences, but he wouldn't hear them. His brain wouldn't accept the fact that Tango was dead.

He threw open the apartment door and found it surprisingly empty. Even though Kastro had cut back on most of the extracurricular activities, you could still find at least a dozen people in the apartment, either gambling or just taking up space. That morning, it was empty, save for Kastro and a few trusted homies. She was sitting at the card table, drinking Hennessy out of the bottle and smoking a blunt. When she saw Animal, she almost knocked the table over getting up to greet him. Animal and Kastro met in the middle of the living room and embraced.

"Thank God. I thought I had lost you too," Kastro said, fighting back the tears.

"I'm good, Kastro," Animal told her before breaking her embrace. "Is it true? Is my friend dead?"

Kastro's eyes said what her mouth couldn't.

"Damn!" Animal collapsed in the chair.

He felt like someone had sucked all of the breath from his lungs. He tried to hold back the tears to save face in front of the crew, but he couldn't. Tango had been his friend, mentor, and big brother, and now he was gone, just like his real brother. Animal wasn't sure what he had done to offend God, but it must've been truly heinous. He was snatching everyone Animal loved and leaving him to watch helplessly.

"It's okay, baby." Kastro rubbed his back. It was an extremely rare show of compassion for her, but she really cared about the boy.

When Gladiator walked in the room and saw Kastro comforting Animal, he didn't have to ask if the rumor was true. "What happened?"

"That bitch-ass nigga Tre happened," Kastro spat.

At the mention of the traitor's name as the one responsible for Tango's death, Animal turned to Kastro. "That rat muthafucka killed my nigga?"

"He didn't pull the trigger, but he might as well have, because Tango's death was still his fault," Kastro told him. "When word got out that Tre was moving foul, the big homies had a meeting and voted that he had to go. They wanted to send pros at him, but Tango didn't wanna go that route. Tre was foul as shit, but he and Tango had history, so he wanted him to at least have a clean death."

Animal remembered Gladiator's words to him in the car about a soldier's death.

"Tango had been playing Tre close for months, which is why he kept his distance from all our operations, so as not to give that rat fuck more ammunition to hurt us, which is why you haven't seen him around here lately," Kastro explained. "He was rocking Tre to sleep and waiting for the proper time to kill him, but somehow, Tre got hip to what he was planning. Tre let Tango lead him to a deserted block, where Tango was to kill him, but the police were waiting for him. Tango, being a gangsta to his heart, felt that it was better to hold court in the streets than be locked in a cage. He died like he lived—with a gun in his hand."

"And what happened to Tre?" Animal asked.

"That's the only good thing that came out of this. Before the police took Tango out, he treated Tre's bitch ass to a permanent nap. That rat fuck will never bump his gums in a court of law about a real nigga again. Tango is gone, but we ain't gonna mourn his passing. We're gonna celebrate what he's done for the set. Him sacrificing himself for the good of our thing is the ultimate display of Blood Love." Kastro raised her bottle.

"Blood Love!" The homies who were gathered raised their glasses in salute.

Kastro was about to say something to Animal when she noticed the blood on his clothes for the first time. "Animal, where have you been, and whose blood is that?"

Animal got quiet.

Kastro looked from Animal to Gladiator, who couldn't meet her gaze. Calmly, she placed her bottle on the table, walked up to her brother, and slapped him hard enough to draw blood from his lip. Kastro's eyes filled with tears, and her voice trembled with rage when she spoke. "Gladiator, I knew you were a cold man, but I'd have never taken you for cruel too. He's only a boy. How could you steal his innocence?"

Gladiator wiped the blood from his lip with the back of his hand. "You can't steal something that is given freely, sister dear. He was already determined to walk the road. I just showed him the best path."

Animal moved to stand with them. "Kastro, don't blame Gladiator. I was the one who—"

Animal's words were cut off when Kastro punched him in the chest hard enough to knock him to the ground.

Kastro grabbed him by the front of his shirt and snatched him to his feet. "You were just going to what? Dig a hole deep enough for these crackers to bury you in? Animal, do you understand what you've done?"

Animal pulled free of her grip. "Yes, I did what needed to be done!" he shot back. "Kastro, I know you're mad, but I had to do it. They killed Brimstone and Noki and tried to kill me. I couldn't let that ride. I did it for the set."

Kastro was taken aback by Animal's tone. "You couldn't let it ride? You did it for the set? Li'l nigga, who the fuck died and made you a gangsta? Two months ago, you were a snot-nosed fucker without a pot to piss in, and now you're in here telling me what you did for the set?" She grabbed two fistfuls of his hair and pulled hard enough to where he felt the pinch in his scalp. "Little boy, I'd advise you to get away from me, and don't let me see you anymore tonight, because I'm having serious thoughts about putting my hands on you."

"Kastro, you need to lighten up." Gladiator intervened.

"No, what I need to do is cut your throat while you're sleeping and put this little dummy back out on the streets. All this shit is falling apart, and instead of being here trying to help me hold it together, you two idiots are in the streets killing people and bringing more heat down on us! You know what? I don't even have time for this right now. There's too much going on. Gladiator, I think you need to stay at your place tonight. Just get your package and go."

"What package?" Gladiator asked. He hadn't been expecting anything.

"The package you had Li'l Harv leave here for you." Kastro nodded to the small box on the table.

Gladiator knew the name Li'l Harv. He was one of the soldiers who attended his combat training classes and sometimes worked as muscle in Hell. He used Li'l Harv as an errand boy sometimes but hadn't had him deliver any packages.

Gladiator moved past his sister and examined the parcel, which was wrapped in brown paper.

The first thing he did was put his ear to it to see if it was ticking or beeping. When he was sure it wasn't a bomb, he tore it open, and his eyes widened in shock when he unveiled two neatly packed kilos of cocaine inside.

"Kastro, this isn't mine," Gladiator said.

"Then why the fuck would he bring it here?" Kastro thought out loud. Her question was answered when the front door came crashing in.

"Police, everybody on the fucking ground!"

Animal stood there, wide-eyed and in shock, as the apartment was flooded by New York City police officers wearing body armor and carrying automatic weapons. Anyone within arm's reach was getting handcuffed, no questions asked, and those who resisted were met with near deadly force. There were at least a half dozen inside the apartment, and just beyond, he could see more of them in the hallway. The unthinkable had happened—Hell had finally been invaded.

From the amount of cocaine on the table, Animal doubted he'd get off with a slap on the wrist like the last time. His life was slowly but gradually going from bad to worse.

Two detectives moved to the forefront of the blue wall that had been erected between them and the exit. Animal knew they were detectives and not regular police officers because of how they were dressed. One was a short, brown-skinned dude, who wore his hair in a neat afro. The wrinkled suit he wore looked like it had come straight off a rack in some bargain basement. His counterpart, a tall Hispanic detective, was dressed a bit sharper. He wore crisp blue jeans and a white shirt under his blazer.

When the tall Hispanic detective brandished his gun and repeated the order for everyone to get on the ground, Kastro instinctively pulled Animal to the floor. This wasn't her first raid, and she knew how trigger happy police could get if they felt like they were being challenged. It was their world, and poor black kids just prayed to survive in it.

One by one, everyone in the apartment was forced to the ground, except Gladiator. He stood defiantly between the police and his people.

The black detective in the wrinkled suit stood nose to nose with Gladiator. "I told you I'd nab your murdering ass one day, Gladiator," he said gleefully.

Gladiator's jaw hardened. Then, unexpectedly, he chuckled. "Detective Brown, one thing I can give you Yankees credit for is your consistency. You consistently fuck up by trying to cut corners when building cases, and when your shenanigans bottom out, you create cases. In your own words, I'm a murderer, so what use do I have for cocaine? This case is weak and fabricated, and you know it."

"All I know is facts, and the fact is that you've been caught with your hand in the cookie jar." Detective Brown spared a glance at the cocaine on the table. "Or should I say the sugar jar in this case?" He laughed. "Gladiator, I don't care how the fuck I get you, so long as I get you. Now button that limey mouth of yours and get on your knees."

Gladiator shook his head. "This is low, even by your standards."

"If I have to tell you to get on your knees again, this is going to get nasty," the black detective told him, sliding his gun from the holster on his hip.

He was trying to intimidate Gladiator, but the Englishman was without fear. Gladiator looked at the gun and locked eyes with the detective. When he spoke, his voice was as cold as the grave. "The only time I'll ever kneel before a man is when I finally meet my maker, and you don't look like him." He spat on the ground near Detective Brown's feet. "Stop tossing my cock and do what you gotta do."

Detective Brown happily honored his request and slammed his gun into the side of Gladiator's head. Gladiator stumbled backward, and a kick to the gut for good measure from Detective Brown sent him crashing through the card table, raining broken dishes and abandoned liquor glasses on him.

"You didn't wanna get on your knees, but your back works too," Detective Brown taunted him.

Gladiator attempted to get up, but when one of the officers pressed his machine gun to the back of Gladiator's head, it gave him second thoughts. He wisely lay on his belly and didn't resist further.

From Animal's vantage point, he could see Gladiator's eyes and saw that the very fires of hell burned in them. He looked like he was thinking about taking his chances anyhow, but Kastro's hand on his arm gave him pause.

The tall Hispanic cop squatted down and picked up the bag of cocaine that had fallen over with the table. Keeping his eyes on Animal and Kastro, he dipped his finger in the bag and ran it across his gums. Looking over his shoulder at his partner, he gave him a knowing nod that said it was the real deal.

"Well, looks like everybody is going on a little ride," he told the suspects.

"Alvarez, this is bullshit, and you know it!" Kastro yelled at the Hispanic detective.

Detective Alvarez nodded. "I know it, and you know it, but the jury don't know it, and I plan to keep it that way. Round these shit birds up and roll 'em out," he ordered the uniformed officers.

Animal watched from his position on the floor as the cops rounded everyone up and prepared to usher them out. He turned to Gladiator and Kastro and noticed a look pass between them. Kastro's eyes pleaded for him not to do whatever it was that he was thinking, but Gladiator's mind was made up. It was then that Animal saw a dagger-sized shard from a broken glass plate in Gladiator's hand.

"I can't go to jail, Kastro." Gladiator's voice was pained. "If my prints pop up on Interpol's radar, it's a wrap for me. I'll take my chances."

"Don't," Kastro whispered, but the decision had already been made.

The homies had just been led from the apartment when two uniformed officers came over to handcuff the remaining three. They started off with Gladiator, which was the beginning of the end. When one of the officers reached down to put the handcuffs on Gladiator, he made his move. Gladiator rolled, bringing the broken plate around and cutting the officer's throat.

Before he'd even hit the ground, Gladiator was on his feet and moving in on his next target.

The second officer at least got to put up a fight. He fired a round that hit Gladiator in the stomach, slowing him but not stopping him. He struck twice with the broken glass, opening the officer's wrist and relieving him of his pistol, before the death blow, a clean cut across his stomach, spilling his entrails onto the floor. His fellow officers watched in horror as their comrade expired in a messy pool at their feet. Arresting Gladiator was now out of the question. He had to die.

Wounded, armed, and determined, Gladiator stood to defend his home against impossible odds. He looked back at Animal and smiled, mouthing the words *If I am to die, let it be a soldier's death,* before opening fire on the police.

Until that moment, Animal thought that the way Brimstone was gunned down was the worst he'd ever seen, but Gladiator's death topped it. They hit Gladiator with more bullets than Animal could count, and even when he was down, they kept firing.

Kastro snapped her eyes shut, refusing to watch as the police murdered her brother, but not Animal. His eyes absorbed every detail, every bullet, every drop of blood, every scream.

Animal would remember it all, and the scene would only make his heart harder. Gladiator died horribly that morning, but he'd gotten to look into the eyes of his killers before he went. It was a soldier's death.

One by one, the members of Hell's fallen army were led from the building in shackles. There were so many of them that the police had run out of handcuffs, so some of them had to be bound with plastic restraints, including Animal. The whole neighborhood had gathered around to see what was going on, and when they saw who the police had arrested, there were angry shouts of "No justice, no peace!" and "Fuck the police!" Animal kept his eyes on the ground and shuffled with the others to the awaiting paddy wagons.

Things took a turn for the worst when they brought Gladiator's body out. Gladiator had been a hero to the locals, and they were outraged to discover that the police had murdered him. People began spitting on the police and hurling bottles. There were a lot of police, but the residents outnumbered them, and the police were getting agitated, aiming their guns at the locals and ordering them to stay back. If the crowd attacked, they would be overrun. They needed to get their prisoners loaded and cleared out before the volatile situation erupted.

The homies and homegirls were loaded in first, cursing the police the whole time. Kastro was loaded in next. Normally, she would've been right along with everyone else, cursing and carrying on, but she was silent, except for the occasional sob. Losing Gladiator had zapped her spirit, and it was doubtful that she would ever be the same again.

She wasn't moving fast enough, so one of the officer's shoved her forward, almost making Kastro fall.

"You touch her again, and you're going to die," Animal told the officer in a low growl.

"Is that right?" The officer looked at Animal.

Animal nodded. "Yeah, that sounds about right."

Without warning, the officer slapped fire out of Animal. "You ain't gonna do shit but get your bitch ass in the back of this van with the rest of your co-defendants."

Animal could taste the metallic blood on his tongue. With hate in his eyes, he looked up at the officer and told him, "You're going to regret that."

"You threatening me?"

"Nah, karma is gonna settle your tab, pussy," Animal sneered.

As if the universe had heeded Animal's command, a beat-up van came to an abrupt stop on the other side of the paddy wagon. The side door of the van slid open, and out spilled several heavily armed Jamaicans, with Big Dread leading the charge, holding an AK-47.

"Let them who invade Hell be cleansed by its fire!" Big Dread roared before opening fire on the NYPD.

The police were caught totally by surprise and unprepared for the revolt. The Jamaicans' bullets cut down several cops before they were able to collect themselves and return fire. For a second, it looked like Big Dread's crew was going to succeed in liberating the captives, but the tide turned when reinforcements arrived. The additional cruisers boxed the Jamaicans in and, from them, poured more cops with more guns.

The Jamaicans put up a good fight, but they were no match for the police. It was a massacre. Before Big Dread fell, he put two slugs into the cop who had slapped Animal. As Animal had predicted, karma had settled his tab.

Because the police had to divert their attention to the attack, the police never got a chance to load Animal in the van with the others, so he was left unattended. This was the perfect opportunity to escape, but he couldn't leave without Kastro. With his hands bound in front of him, Animal ran to the van and tried to get the door open. He had just managed to open it when one of the officers, ducking gunfire, had come around the side of the van and saw Animal trying to free the prisoners. He raised his gun, intending to kill Animal, but the van door flew open and hit him in the face.

Kastro was kneeling in the doorway of the van and chained to the prisoner next to her. "They got us shackled together, so we can't all get away, but you can. This is your only chance, so you gotta take it."

Animal wanted to stay and try to help her get away too, but he knew she was right. This was his only chance. With his heart heavy, Animal took off running down the street. He heard voices behind him screaming for him to stop, but he kept going.

Animal ran and ran until he could no longer hear the gunshots or the sirens or the screams. He ran until his lungs burned and he found himself in a section of Brooklyn he had never been in before.

It didn't take Animal long to find a bodega and borrow a pair of scissors to liberate himself from the restraints. He was free, but for how long?

There was no doubt that there would be a search initiated for the escaped fugitive, but they didn't have any information on Animal. He hadn't made it to the precinct to be identified, and he was sure Kastro wouldn't tell, so finding him would be tough. Still, he wasn't going to make it easy on them. He had to get low.

Disappearing would be easier said than done. He had no money, no friends, and nowhere to turn. He could've taken his chances and lingered in Brooklyn until he got word back about what was going to happen to Kastro, but sticking around was too much like tempting fate. Though he knew Kastro was solid and would never speak his name, the same couldn't be said about some of her co-defendants. There was no telling what a desperate man would do for a reduced sentence. Tre had shown him that. His time in Brooklyn had come to an end. With nowhere else to turn, he had to go back to the only other place that he had ever called home: Harlem.

Chapter 21

After the fall of Hell, Animal found himself back on hard times. He had no money, no friends, and very few options, but he still had his wits. For food, he would steal from supermarkets or grocery stores. When he couldn't boost from the stores, he would go hungry.

Being back in the old neighborhood felt good because it was familiar, but with familiarity came contempt. With neither Justice nor Tango around to back him, some of their old rivals sought retribution against Animal for things that they had done. They came seeking a victim, but what they found was a hardened youth who was willing to go where most were not in the name of survival.

Animal took on all comers, big and small. Sometimes he would lose, but, more often, he won his street fights. Animal hadn't realized how much his fighting skills had increased since he started training with Gladiator, until that point.

He could knock a man out who was almost twice his size, if he hit him in the right spot. Being the smallest dog on the yard made him the most picked on, but not necessarily the victim. That was something else he had picked up from Gladiator.

Thinking about Gladiator and the way he'd died made Animal's heart bleed. He was a criminal, but he was also a good dude who had done a lot for all the misguided youths who had passed through Hell. It was Justice who had set Animal on the path of teaching him how to be a man, but it was Gladiator who had taught him to be honorable.

He reflected on Gladiator's last stand and wondered, *When my time comes, will I be that brave? Will I receive a soldier's death?* He hoped it would be many years before he ever had to find out, but Animal vowed on the soul of his dead friend that he would always stand tall against any and all odds, just as Gladiator had.

Animal missed his friend, but he didn't have time to grieve. He was too busy trying to survive. Animal had considered seeking out some of Tango's old crew and seeing if one of them would let him make a few dollars, but he learned quickly that things in the hood had changed since the last time he'd been in Harlem. Lou-Loc and Gutter had murdered most of the old crew, and the ones who weren't dead were either on the run or had become Crips out of fear. The sight of dudes he'd once thought were solid, now working for the same people who had killed their boss, disgusted him. Animal would rather starve than try to get a dollar with the traitors and tarnish Tango's memory. And, with this in mind, starve was exactly what he did.

Most nights, he slept on park benches or, when it was too cold, he slept in the stairwells in the projects. The stairwells were warm, but they were also dangerous. It was very easy to get trapped off by police or other predators. Sleep never came easily, because every time he heard even the slightest noise, he would be on his feet, prepared to fight or flee, depending on the situation. He was doing worse than he ever had in life and didn't see any light at the end of the tunnel. When he thought things couldn't get any worse, they did, and the bottom fell out of his life.

After about a month of living on the streets, Animal had finally hit rock bottom. He was broke, dirty, and hungry. One night, Animal was casing a strip of local restaurants, as he generally did when he couldn't hit a lick for a meal.

He was too proud to beg but wasn't too proud to snatch an unfinished meal that may have been abandoned on a table that the busboy hadn't had a chance to clear yet. He'd gotten very good at moving unseen and could usually snatch the plate and be out the door before anyone had even noticed him. It shamed him to no end to have been reduced to such an existence, but pride had taken a back seat to starvation.

He was coming out of a Chinese restaurant, devouring a container of pork fried rice that someone hadn't finished, when he heard someone calling his government name. It had been so long since he'd gone by Tayshawn that he didn't even realize he was being addressed until someone walked up behind him and touched his arm.

Animal spun—eyes feral, lips drawn back into a sneer—and was ready to pounce. When he saw who was trying to get his attention, he had to blink to make sure his eyes weren't playing tricks on him. When he took in the heavyset Spanish woman standing before him, for a minute he thought his mother had finally cleaned up her act, but it wasn't his mother. It was his aunt Rosa.

Rosa was Marie's older sister and the matriarch of the family. In the right light, Rosa and

Marie could've passed for twins, except Rosa was chubby and her hair had begun to gray. When their mother, Animal's grandmother, had died, it was Rosa who was left to raise her siblings. Rosa was one of the few people in his mother's family who didn't treat him like an outsider because he had a black father.

As a kid, he and Justice would often visit with Aunt Rosa and her husband, Juan, at their West Harlem apartment, but the deeper Marie got into drugs, the less frequent the visits became. It eventually got to the point where Rosa could no longer bear to watch her sister destroy herself, so she cut her off, and by extension, her kids too. She would send Christmas gifts to the house for Animal and Justice, or birthday cards with money in them. The toys they got, but the money went to the crack man.

It had been years since Animal had seen his estranged aunt, and he wondered what had brought her to the slums that night.

For a long while, Rosa just stood there, looking at her estranged nephew in disbelief. He looked every bit of a savage in his tattered clothes, mouthful of food, and his hands covered in rice and grease. Rosa had heard stories that her sister and her children weren't doing well, but she had no idea it had come to this. Unable to find her voice, she pulled her nephew in for a much-needed hug.

"Thank the Lord I found you." Rosa embraced Animal, trying her best to ignore the heavy scent of musk and mold that clung to him. "Everybody's been so worried about you since we heard you'd run away."

"Really? Then how come nobody came to look for me?" Animal asked. He wasn't trying to be sarcastic; he was just speaking from his heart.

There was a momentary pause.

"Tayshawn, I know there's been some distance between us as a family because of my differences with your mother, but right now, we have to put those to the side. We've been combing the streets looking for you for days and weren't sure we'd find you in time. I need you to come with me," Rosa said with a sense of urgency in her voice.

Animal felt a cold knot develop in his stomach, and for a minute, he thought he would regurgitate his stolen rice. "Aunt Rosa, what's wrong?"

"I'll explain on the way to the hospital."

Animal lay awake some nights, thinking of his mother, what she was doing and how she was holding up. They'd had their differences, but she was still the woman who had brought him into the world, and he would always love her for that. He knew that one day he would see her again, but he never imagined that it would be in the intensive care unit at Mt. Sinai Hospital.

Rosa led Animal into the sterile room where his mother was being kept. Outside the room hung a wooden crucifix that reminded him of the one he'd seen at the church, when they had gone to visit the one-eyed priest.

Animal barely recognized the woman lying in the hospital bed, hooked to tubes and wires. Timidly, he moved forward to get a closer look. Marie had lost so much weight that Animal could see just about every bone in her body. The thick black mane of silky hair she had always been so proud of was gone, and in its place were a few thin strands of gray. An uncomfortable looking tube was run down her throat, helping her to breathe, as she was having trouble doing it on her own. Animal stood there in disbelief. The person lying in that bed wasn't his mother . . . it couldn't be.

"What's wrong with her?" Animal asked Aunt Rosa.

"Acquired immune deficiency syndrome," she said sadly.

"AIDS?" Animal reflexively took a cautionary step back. He didn't know much about the disease, outside of what he'd seen on the news and heard on the streets. "But how? I thought only dope fiends and fags got AIDS. My mother didn't shoot up. She was a smoker."

Rosa looked at her nephew and shook her head at his ignorance. "AIDS and HIV don't just affect homosexuals and people who use needles. You can also get it from having unprotected sex with someone who is infected, which is how I suspect your mother got it."

"Eddie," Animal said in a low growl.

"The first time I laid eyes on that snake I knew he wasn't going to do nothing but bring my sister down. I tried to warn her against him, but she wouldn't listen, and now that bastard is taking my sister from me."

"Where is he?" Animal asked. He was already making plans to track his mother's boyfriend down and murder him.

Rosa shrugged. "Your guess is as good as mine. Nobody has seen him in weeks. The only reason I found out Marie was in the hospital is because they called me when her condition got worse. I'm listed as her next of kin. Don't you fret over Eddie. Karma will settle up with him. Right now, you make peace with your mother while you still can." She nudged him forward.

Animal stood at the edge of the hospital bed awkwardly, not quite sure what to say or do. It was difficult for him to even look at his mother in her weakened condition. From the looks of things, this may have been his last chance to say what he needed to his mother, so he found the words.

"Mama." He took her hand in his. Marie's skin was dry, and her bones felt as brittle as twigs, like he would break it if he squeezed too hard. "I don't know if you can hear me or not, but it's Animal—I mean, Tayshawn." At the sound of his voice, he thought he saw Marie's eyelids flutter. "Mama, I'm sorry about everything that happened between us," he said with a shaky voice. He had been trying to hold his tears back, but they were now falling freely down his face. "I know you did what you could under the circumstances, and I should've done more to try and help you hold it together instead of running off, but Mama, if you could just live for a while longer, I promise to change. I swear to God that I'll be a better son. Just don't die, Mama!"

Animal dropped to his knees and began praying as hard as he could. "God, please don't do this. You've taken everything else from me, but let my mama live. I'm begging you."

He sobbed uncontrollably. He touched her hand to his face, wetting it with his tears.

As if in answer to his prayers, Marie's eyes fluttered open. She looked at her son, kneeling by her bedside, and when their eyes locked, something passed between them. She was letting him know that she forgave him and that she was at peace before closing her eyes for the final time.

Everything that happened next was a blur. He stood in the hallway, leaning against the wall, while the doctors went to work trying to resuscitate his mother. When the doctors and nurses came out of the room, all wearing somber faces, they didn't have to say a word. Animal knew she was gone. They offered condolences to Animal and Rosa, but Animal barely heard them. He was in a dreamlike state, staring blankly at the crucifix hanging outside his mother's hospital room.

"Are you okay?" Rosa asked. He looked at her as if she was speaking a different language. "I know you're hurting, but your mother isn't suffering anymore. She is with God now."

"God?" Animal turned his eyes to her, madness dancing behind them. "You mean the God that has been taking shit from me all my life and giving me his ass to kiss in return." He chuckled.

"There ain't no God, and if there is, he surely don't give a shit about niggers in the ghetto."

Rosa gasped. "Tayshawn Torres, how dare you spew that blasphemy!"

Animal laughed maniacally. "I'll give you blasphemy." He marched over to the wall and snatched the crucifix down. He brandished the wooden cross for his aunt and the horrified doctors and nurses to see. "Any God who turns a blind eye to the suffering of the creations he's supposed to love ain't 'bout shit." He broke the cross over his knee. "He might be your God, but he ain't mine." He tossed the splintered wood at his aunt's feet and stormed off.

Rosa shouted after Animal, but he was too far gone to hear what she was saying or to care. There was only one thing on his mind at the time: murder.

Chapter 22

Animal hit the streets in a numb state. For days, he wandered around, trying to come to grips with what had happened. He had lost the woman who had given him life, and with her, he felt like the last of his humanity had died too. He was a beast now more than ever.

Rosa came around looking for him to go to Marie's funeral, but Animal avoided her. He couldn't take seeing his mother in a box. The sight would've made it too real to him, too final. Instead, he trolled the streets, looking for his prey, the man who had been the source of his grief for as long as he could remember.

Animal was a man on a mission. He combed the entire neighborhood, searching all the drug houses and haunts Eddie was known to frequent, but no one had seen him. This didn't deter Animal in the least. If he had to search to the ends of the earth, he was going to find Eddie and kill him. He didn't have any weapons, but he had his hate, and that would be enough. He couldn't wait to wrap his hands around Eddie's neck and take him from the world, as he had taken his mother.

He was heading back toward his old building, to see if he could get a clue as to where Eddie might be hiding, when he spotted Bump and Eddy. Those were the last two people he wanted to see because of the way he was feeling. Animal tried to alter his course to avoid bumping into them and dealing with their bullshit, but it was too late. They'd spotted him.

"Fuck is this little dirty nigga doing back in the hood? Didn't we tell you not to come around here anymore?" Eddy approached him.

"Not now, man. I'm going through something," Animal told him, trying to contain his anger.

"You act like I give a fuck about what you're going through. I told you if you came back to my hood, I was gonna beat your ass." Eddy shoved him to the ground, drawing laughter from the spectators.

Animal got up, brushed his clothes off, and tried to step around Eddy, but he blocked his path.

"Please don't make me do this," Animal said just above a whisper.

Eddy laughed. "You ain't gonna do shit but get fucked up for not following my rules," he told him before taking a swing at Animal.

Animal had been expecting it. He ducked under Eddy's punch and countered with two of his own to Eddy's stomach. When he tried to protect his stomach, Animal went to work on his face. The smaller boy was throwing punches and moving so fast that Eddy felt like he was getting jumped by more than one person.

Animal managed to get Eddy on the ground and began choking him. Eddy tried to break his grip, but Animal was far stronger than he expected. The only thing that stopped Animal from putting Eddy's lights out was Bump hitting him in the back of his head with a gun.

The blow from the gun dazed Animal, but the kick to the mouth Bump delivered was what put him on his back. Eddy and Bump jumped on Animal and gave him a fierce beating. Animal thought they were going to kill him, but thankfully a woman who had been watching from the window called the police. When Bump and Eddy saw the boys in blue rushing toward the scene, they took flight.

The police asked Animal a series of questions, most of which he wouldn't answer. Bump and Eddy were locals, so the cops knew them on

sight, but Animal refused to confirm that it was
them who had beaten him. When the police saw
that they weren't going to get any cooperation
from Animal, they opted to let it go rather than
waste the time filing the paperwork.

Animal limped through the projects, nursing
his wounds. His lip was busted, and his ribs
throbbed every time he breathed. They had
beaten him terribly, but their mistake was letting him live, because Animal now had a new
agenda. His mother's boyfriend was still going to
lose his life, but only after Animal killed Bump
and Eddy. They would be the first to fall during
the bloody reign of terror he was planning to
unleash on the unsuspecting world, but they
wouldn't be his last.

Regardless of what he did, death seemed to
be the only constant in his life, so he decided
to embrace it. Anything and everyone he'd ever
cared about had been taken from him, so he had
nothing left to drive him except revenge.

Animal had been on Bump and Eddy for two
days, tracking them and becoming familiar with
their habits, like Gladiator had taught him.
Animal still didn't have a weapon, so he had
to be smart about his approach. Gladiator was

probably rolling over in his grave, watching Animal attempt to go at the two men unarmed, but Animal had a plan. He'd learned that, while they sometimes both carried weapons, it was Bump who was always in charge of the guns. He would have to take him down first and try to get his gun if he was going to successfully pull it off. It was a shot in the dark, but that and the element of surprise were all he had.

He followed Bump and Eddy to a local bar on the West Side. Animal posted up across the street, in the shadows of an electronics store, which had already closed its doors for the night. There was no telling how long Bump and Eddy would be inside drinking, but Animal was a patient man. Their pit stop at the bar might even work in his favor. If they came out of the joint drunk, they wouldn't be on point, and that would make easier pickings.

About twenty minutes went by and the bar door swung open again. Out staggered a young dude who wore his hair in long braids that hung almost to his shoulders. From his uncertain steps, Animal could tell that he was drunk. He continued watching the man until he staggered off up the street. About a half minute later, Bump and Eddy came out of the bar. They scanned the streets until they spotted the drunk young man, then fell in step behind him. It appeared that they were doing some stalking of their own.

Animal trailed them by about a half block, staying just close enough not to lose sight of them. Bump produced a gun from somewhere and closed in on the drunk from the rear. He barked something at him, causing the drunk to turn around and slowly raise his hands in surrender. Animal couldn't believe that Bump and Eddy were thirsty enough to rob a man out in the open like that, but their folly would be his edge. They would be so focused on relieving the drunk of his goods and watching for the police that they would never see Animal coming.

The drunk must've said something to get under Bump's skin, because he suddenly became agitated and pointed his gun in the drunk's face. Eddy nervously rummaged through his pockets while Bump screamed at the drunk. Things took a turn for the worse when Bump slammed his gun into the side of the drunk's face, knocking him to the ground. When the drunk tried to get to his feet, Bump kicked him down again.

Bump was out of control, and Animal knew that it was only a matter of time before he did something stupid and had the police crawling all over the block. If that happened, Animal would be denied his vengeance, and he couldn't have that. He didn't know the drunk from a hole in the wall, but circumstances were forcing Animal to either be his benefactor or fellow corpse to be picked up by the meat wagon. Either way, he had to make a move.

Scooping a stray beer bottle from the trash can, Animal hurled it at Bump like a missile and prayed that it hit its mark. The bottle made impact with Bump's face at the same time he pulled the trigger. Glass shredding his face threw his aim off, so when he fired, the shot went wild and hit a window behind the drunk, instead of connecting with his melon. Before Bump could recover, Animal was on him, throwing a flurry of punches and kicks.

From his peripheral view, Animal saw Eddy rushing him, but the drunk he'd just rescued tripped him up, leaving Animal and Bump to square off.

Bump tried to turn the gun on Animal, but Animal grabbed him by the wrist and they struggled. Bump was stronger, but Animal's will to live was greater. In desperation, he sank his gold teeth into Bump's shooting arm and held on for dear life. Bump was eventually able to shake loose of Animal's jaws, knocking Animal into a wall and dropping him, but not without sacrificing a chunk of meat from his forearm.

Looking up at the barrel of Bump's gun, knowing he was about to die, Animal expected to be afraid, but he wasn't. He was tired: tired of life constantly dealing him a bad hand, and tired of losing. If this was to be his end, then he would meet it with honor and have a soldier's death, just like Gladiator.

"What you waiting for, nigga? Pull the fucking trigger!" He spread his arms, inviting death. "I ain't long for this world anyhow. Go ahead and set me free!"

Before Bump could grant the boy's death wish, his head exploded in a mass of crimson, splashing Animal with blood. Animal wiped the blood from his eyes and looked down at Bump, whose ruined skull was now oozing onto the concrete. A few feet away, Eddy's body lay in a heap. His head was twisted almost all the way around, and his neck broken. Standing in the center of the carnage, still holding Eddy's smoking gun, was the drunken young man Animal had rescued.

The young drunk looked at the blood-stained teenager, and a light of recognition went off in his eyes.

"Ain't you Justice's little brother?" he asked. He'd recalled seeing the boy a few times when he'd come through the hood to do business with Justice and K-Dawg. "What's ya name again?"

Animal pondered the question before answering. "These days, they call me Animal." He wiped Bump's blood from his mouth with his sleeve. It had begun drying and made his face feel sticky.

"They call me Tech," the young drunk introduced himself. He was about to shake Animal's hand, but seeing it covered with blood, he thought better of it and instead bumped fists with him. He looked down at Bump's body and thought about how ferociously he'd attacked him, even though he was unarmed. Tech had been around some cold cats in his lifetime, but he'd never met one with as much heart as the boy who called himself Animal.

"I appreciate what you did, helping me out, but I gotta ask you something. What in the hell would make you risk getting blasted to save a dude you hardly know?"

Animal looked at Tech. "I didn't do this to save you. I've been plotting on killing these muthafuckas for a while now."

"Why?" Tech asked curiously.

"Because they kept fucking with me. They were always talking about how I dress, how I live. Those two have been ridiculing me almost all my life."

"So you wanted them dead because they cracked a few jokes on you?" Tech was trying to figure out Animal's logic. He was guilty of killing over small things too, but never over something as small as a joke.

"It wasn't just the jokes or the bullying. They were without honor and needed killing," Animal said heatedly. "To most of y'all, the concrete jungle is a playground, but to me, it's the only place I've ever had to call home. I was literally born and raised in the streets. When you live in the jungle, you have to live by its rules. The strong get to make it to tomorrow, while the weak become food. I can't be nobody's food." His voice was shaky, and his eyes glassy, as if he would burst into tears at any moment. "Do you know what it's like to live your life as a victim?"

Tech's mind momentarily took him back to a place he had long tried to forget. "Yes, I do," he said solemnly.

The world wasn't kind to children like Tech and Animal. They were both the runts of the litter of wolves they were born into, and they had to fight twice as hard for everything they wanted. In Animal, he saw what his own mentor, Jah, must've seen in him all those years ago when he plucked him from the streets. Had Jah not taken Tech in and shown him the game, it could've very well been Tech roaming the streets, looking for a place to call home, instead of Animal. Jah had done him a kindness, and now this was Tech's opportunity to pay it forward.

"Don't worry about it, my nigga." He draped his arm around Animal's frail shoulders. "You ain't never gonna have to worry about being nobody's food again."

PART IV

—Resurrection—

Chapter 23

Animal and Tech's relationship grew quickly. Tech took an instant liking to him because he reminded him so much of himself when he was that age. When he found out that Animal didn't have anywhere to stay, he invited him to move into his apartment. It was only a one bedroom, and Animal had to sleep on floor pallets, but he didn't mind. The hard floor was way more comfortable than sleeping with one eye open in various stairwells. People criticized Tech for letting a stranger stay with him, especially a vagabond like Animal, but Tech didn't let their opinions influence him. Jah had given him a chance to prove himself, and he would do the same for Animal.

Having the teen around proved to be a blessing in disguise. Animal was very helpful around the house, cleaning up behind himself and Tech. He even cooked. Tech was impressed by the youngster's skill in the kitchen, and when he

asked where he'd learned to cook, he told him he
had learned from his mother and then changed
the subject. Tech knew that Animal's mother
was a sensitive subject. From what Animal was
willing to tell him, his mother had recently died,
but he had yet to open up and say how or why.
Tech never pressed him for more details; he figured Animal would tell him when he was ready.

While Animal kept his secrets, Tech was a bit
more forthcoming about his life story. Tech had
been running the streets since before he was
old enough to wipe his ass and had started out
as somewhat of an errand boy to some of the
older and more hardened killers in Harlem. You
could always find him in some back alley or trap
house, sitting with the old heads, soaking up
their deepest and darkest secrets.

When he was slightly younger than Animal,
he had been taken under the wing of a cat named
Jah, who was heavy in the streets. From the way
Tech talked about Jah, it reminded him of how
he'd looked up to Gladiator. They were both
warriors.

Jah could have been a legend in the streets
had a hail of bullets not ended his career far too
early. Jah's murder had left a huge void in Tech,
a void which he had tried to fill with chaos.

It didn't take long for Animal to figure out
that Tech was deep in the game. He was eighteen

years old, with his own apartment, expensive jewelry, and he always carried a gun with him. He initially thought that Tech was a drug dealer, and from time to time, Tech did sell drugs, but that wasn't his main hustle. Tech was a goon, and he made his bread by taking it from other people. Tech was known in the streets as a wild young cat who had no problem letting his gun fly. He would go at anybody if the risk was worth the reward.

Tech claimed allegiance to none other than his Blood set, but he was affiliated with a powerful crime family through a friend named Swann. Tech had known Swann from the streets, so when Swann was promoted, he showed love to Tech by letting him do freelance jobs for the crime family he worked for. Tech had major love for Swann, but he couldn't say the same for the boss of the Clark family. Tech never came out and said that he disliked Shai, but the tone he took when he spoke about him told Animal that there were underlying tensions.

When Tech wasn't out doing dirt, he would play the block with other members of his small crew, drinking or smoking weed. He tried to get Animal to come hang out, but the boy had little to no interest in social activities. For the most part, Animal kept to himself. He spent most of his time with his nose tucked in a book or working out. In the wee hours of the night, Tech could hear Animal in the living room, shadow boxing and cursing at some imaginary foe. Animal was like a machine when it came to his daily regimen, and he never missed a day of training. It was as if he was preparing for something that only he was privy to.

In the time they'd been together, Tech developed a love for Animal, as if he were the brother he never had. From the time he'd met him on that dark Harlem street until that point, Animal had always proven reliable and loyal. He was the prefect protégé, but still not battle-tested in Tech's eyes. If he was going to truly let Animal in, he had to see how he would hold up in the field. One afternoon, Tech decided to put his new tenant to the test.

"Yo! How long you been staying with me, Animal?" Tech asked one day, while they were in the local pizza shop enjoying a few slices.

Animal thought about it. "About three months."

"Three months and thirteen days," Tech calculated.

"Wow, I didn't realize it had been that long. I guess time flies sometimes," Animal said, sounding a bit uncomfortable.

He had been living rent free with Tech for months and thought Tech liked him well enough.

Animal knew that nothing in life came without a price. If you couldn't pull your weight, then you couldn't eat. He knew Tech was about to tell him he had to go, so he took the initiative.

"Listen, Tech. I wanna tell you how much I appreciate everything you've done for me. If it hadn't been for you, I can only imagine where I'd be today. I don't have a dime to my name, but you've opened your home and your heart to me. You'll always be my favorite nigga for that, but I also understand if I've worn out my welcome, and you're ready for me to move on. No ride lasts forever, especially not a free one."

Tech threw his head back and laughed. "Damn! You must think I'm one cold-blooded dude. Animal, for as much as I looked out for you, you've looked out for me. You saved my life, homie, and I think that outweighs the few meals I've tricked off on. We're family, and you're welcome to stay with me for as long as you need to, but you were right about one thing—free rides don't last forever."

Animal was glad Tech wasn't putting him out. "Thanks, Tech. Look, I've got a birthday coming up in a few months, and I'll be old enough to get a part-time job, or at least a decent hustle. The minute I can get some constant income coming in, I'll start kicking in on the bills."

"You don't have to wait until your birthday, kid. I got some work for you now, if you're up to it," Tech said slyly.

"What kind of work?" Animal asked suspiciously. He didn't like the tone that Tech's voice had taken on.

Tech leaned forward on his elbows and smiled. "You ever pulled a lick?"

Tech sat behind the wheel of the turquoise Honda Accord, taking deep pulls from a blunt of 'dro and listening to the quiet night. His hair was freshly done, parted in neat squares with a jungle of long braids that hung down the side of his face.

In the passenger seat was a homie of Tech's who they called Jibs because of his oversized pink lips. Jibs was a jokester who was more into making people laugh than making people bleed, but occasionally he would go on capers with Tech and his crew. Jibs wasn't the hardest cat in the streets, but he was a good and loyal dude who would bust his gun if his back was against the wall.

In the back seat was the third member of the group and the most unusual suspect in the car—Animal. That day at the pizza shop, Tech had presented him with an opportunity to ride along on the caper with him. It would put some money in Animal's pockets from his split of the lick, and it would also solidify the bond between him and Tech. In Tech's line of work, you couldn't trust a man whose hands weren't as dirty as yours. Animal had never done anything like what they were about to attempt, so he was reluctant, but he knew it meant something to Tech, so he went along.

"Can I smoke wit' you, my nigga?" Jibs broke the silence.

Tech cut his eyes at him, taking another deep drag off the blunt. "Nah, roll yo' own shit, Blood. Me and this bitch here are having an intimate love affair." He went back to smoking.

Jibs twisted his big lips. "Tech, why you always gotta go to the face on the blunt?"

"Because I'm always the nigga buying the weed," Tech shot back.

"That's a valid point," Animal said from the back seat. He had been so quiet they'd almost forgotten he was there.

Jibs looked back at Animal and gasped dramatically. "It speaks!" he said sarcastically.

"Don't mock me, Jibs," Animal said seriously. People had mocked him and his strange ways all his young life, and he hated it.

"C'mon. I was just playing with you."

"Playing is for kids, and I ain't no kid." Animal poked out his frail chest. It was important for him to impress Tech that night, so he wasn't going to take shit from Jibs or anyone else. He had too much riding on the opportunity.

Jibs laughed. "Shorty, fall back. You ain't spooking nobody with that psycho shit. Personally, I ain't buying that tortured child shit you sell to the rest of these niggas. Crazy li'l muthafucka," Jibs snorted and turned back around in his seat.

Tech felt it coming before it happened but could do nothing to stop it. With a guttural growl, Animal sprang from the back seat and locked his skinny arms around Jibs' neck, pinning him against the headrest. "I told you not to mock me," Animal whispered in Jibs' ear, strangling him.

Jibs was taken off guard and thoroughly surprised by Animal's strength. He tried to break the grip, but Animal had him at a disadvantage in the cramped Honda.

"Li'l nigga, you better turn me loose before I—" Jibs gasped but couldn't finish his sentence because he was on the verge of blacking out.

"Before you what? Fall over and die?" Animal braced his knees against the back of the passenger seat, applying more pressure.

"Knock it off," Tech said from the driver's seat.

If Animal heard him, he gave no indication as he applied more pressure to Jibs' throat. By then, Jibs' eyes were going wide and saliva was running down one side of his mouth. He knew if he didn't do something, Animal would kill Jibs, and the mission would have to be aborted to address the new problem, a dead body in the stolen car. Cautiously, Tech placed his hand on Animal's forearm.

"Enough," he whispered.

Animal glared at Tech as if he were seeing him for the first time. The hateful little boy, who was still scarred from the loss of his mother, screamed for Animal to finish Jibs off, but the part of him that lived to please Tech begged for him to show mercy. Reluctantly, Animal let Jibs go, giving him a shove for good measure.

Jibs made to climb over the seat and retaliate, but Tech grabbed him by the arm. "Don't do it, Jibs," Tech warned.

Jibs glared at Tech. "You siding with this li'l nigga?"

"It ain't about siding, Jibs. This is about focus. We're here with a purpose, not to fight among each other like bitches. Now, if y'all wanna scrap, y'all can do it after we get this money and get back to the hood."

Jibs weighed it out then slid back into the passenger seat. He glared at Animal in the back seat, through the rearview mirror. "This is far from over, li'l nigga. I'ma see you for this."

"Or you might get seen," Animal taunted him.

"Animal, leave it alone," Tech said sternly.

After making sure that his henchmen weren't going to attack each other again, Tech turned his attention back to the block. He was just in time to see the mark they had been waiting for getting out of a taxi in front of the spot. "Showtime." Tech withdrew his gun from under the seat. "Y'all niggas ready?"

"Let's do this." Jibs cocked the slide on the shotgun he was carrying.

"Animal, you ready for this?" Tech asked. When he didn't get a response, he turned around and discovered Animal was no longer in the car. He looked around frantically and spotted his protégé moving in the darkness, creeping up on their mark. "This nigga here," Tech sighed. "Let's go, Jibs, before he fucks everything up." Tech slid from the car.

"I told you not to bring that li'l crazy nigga." Jibs followed him.

Chapter 24

Animal's heart beat in his chest as he crept up on their mark. He was a cat named Suave who had the misfortune of having his name land on a piece of paper. He was a good-looking and well-groomed dude, draped in lots of jewelry. Animal could probably eat for a month off just what he'd get for the bracelet, but he wasn't there for jewelry. He had an agenda and planned to stick to it.

Animal fell back a bit when he saw Suave stop in front of a building and begin undoing the locks on the faded green door. He waited until he'd heard the last tumbler fall before making his move. Suave must've felt him, because he turned just as Animal was raising the big .357. At first, his eyes were wide and nervous, but when he saw the skinny little boy behind the trigger, he wasn't as afraid.

"Shorty, be easy with that ratchet. You don't want it to go off by accident and make this situation worse than it already is," Suave told him.

"If this ratty ring off, you can bet yo' ass that it ain't gonna be no accident," Animal said, sounding like a person who had done that sort of thing a million times, instead of the novice that he was. "Get that door open, so we can take what we need and be gone, or I can kill you, and we take the shit anyway. Make your choice, Blood."

Suave looked like he was considering testing his luck, but when Tech and Jibs joined Animal, he had second thoughts.

"Fuck," he cursed before opening the door.

Suave led them through a small, foyer which led to another door, which led to the count room. This one had a keypad on it, which required a combination to unlock. Suave nervously punched in the code, but the screen flashed INVALID. He tried it again with the same results.

"Stop stalling and open it." Jibs shoved the barrel of his gun into Suave's back.

"I'm not stalling. The system is new, and it don't help with you shoving that gun in my back," Suave said.

Tech stepped up and pressed the nozzle of his gun to Suave's temple. "You either pop this door, or I'm gonna pop you."

Suave finally composed himself enough to enter the right code, and the door opened with a click.

"Take what you're gonna take and go." Suave stepped to the side for the men to enter.

Jibs stepped forward and cracked Suave in the jaw with the butt of the shotgun. Suave crumbled into a heap and lay against the door, clutching his jaw. "Bitch-ass nigga, I should kill you for playing with us. You're lucky I want this money more than I want your life." He stepped over Suave and headed for the count room. "Last one in has to count the singles," he teased his partners.

"Thirsty-ass nigga." Tech went after him.

Animal caught a flicker of motion from the corner of his eye and looked up. There was a small black camera mounted in the ceiling that no one seemed to notice but him. "Hold up," he called out, but they had already crossed the threshold.

Jibs' eyes grew as wide as saucers when he saw all the money spread throughout the room. He had never seen that much money outside of television or movies.

"We done hit the motherload!" he said to Tech, but Tech didn't respond.

Jibs turned around and froze. Tech was standing behind him, but so were three other men holding guns. Two of the guns were trained on Jibs, and the third was pointed at Tech's head.

The men had been watching them on the camera and were waiting for them to make their move.

When Tech saw Jibs' grip on the shotgun tighten, he knew what the man meant to do. He shook his head, signaling for Jibs to be easy and not throw their lives away, but Jibs was determined to make a movie with Tech as the unwilling co-star.

"Die, niggas!" Jibs hoisted the shotgun.

Animal didn't see the gun go off, but he heard the shot and saw the blood splatter on the partially opened door to the count room. What was supposed to be an easy job had just become complicated.

For a long while, he just stood there in shock, looking at the strange patterns the blood splatter had made on the door. Inside the count room, he could hear screams and the sounds of combat. Though he would never admit it to another, he was terrified. Animal looked back and forth between the exit and the door Tech and Jibs had stepped through. He could go the other way and make it to freedom before anyone ever realized he was there. He had no love for Jibs, but he couldn't leave Tech. Leaving him wouldn't be honorable. Even if he died in the process, he had to at least try to repay Tech for his kindness.

As Animal stood near the doorway, preparing to do what he knew was necessary, the prayer Gladiator had taught him came to mind. *We are the damned and the damned are we. This is the role you've given us to play in life, and we accept it as the way of things. If we are to die here tonight, then let it be a soldier's death, so that we may look into the eyes of our killers in the final moments.* Taking a deep breath, he readied his gun and slipped inside the count room.

There was blood everywhere, even on the money that was sprawled out on the wooden tables. Jibs' lifeless body lay next to one of the tables, riddled with bullets. In his hand, he still clutched the smoldering shotgun. Near the door was a man who was missing half his torso. At least Jibs had taken one of theirs with him before he met his end.

Across the room, he saw Tech wedged behind a file cabinet, while two men advanced on him. They were focused on Tech, so they didn't even hear Animal come in the room. From the trail of blood, he knew that Tech had been wounded in the shootout. If Animal didn't do something, his comrade was dead.

"Hey, fellas." Animal announced himself. When the two men turned around, he opened fire. The recoil of the gun kicked so hard up his arms that he almost dropped it, but for the sake of all their lives, he held fast.

The man who had been standing closest to Animal got it the worst. A bullet tore through his throat, dropping him to his knees while he clutched at the wound, trying to stop the flow of blood. Animal walked up on him and shot him twice more in the back of his head, putting him down. The second man, who had been about to descend on Tech, spun and clapped two shots at Animal, which he avoided by leaping to the ground. With his adrenaline pumping, Animal scampered across the room on his hands and knees and hid under a desk.

From where Animal was hiding, he could see the legs of the second man coming toward him. As he rounded one side of the desk, Animal crawled out from the other side.

"You looking for me, homie?" Animal blasted him in the chest.

Animal was no longer nervous. He saw himself as a game hunter, and the men he was cutting down were his prey. Seeing the corpses spread on the floor and knowing he'd killed them made Animal giddy. It wasn't quite a happy feeling; it was more like a feeling of accomplishment. It was the same rush he'd gotten when he'd killed

Hammer and the same rush he'd gotten when Tech had blown Bump's head off. The more blood he spilled, the more comfortable he became with it. Since he'd lost his mother, this was the first time he'd ever felt like there wasn't a gaping hole in his soul. Looking over the blood and carnage, Animal realized that he had finally found something in life that he was not only good at but also made him happy—murder.

"You good?" Tech asked, noticing the peculiar grin on Animal's face.

"Never been better," Animal told him. "I should be asking you that, since you're the one bleeding all over the place."

Tech examined the wound on his arm. "This ain't 'bout shit. They just scratched me. I'm bulletproof, my nigga," he joked, but Animal could tell that he was in pain. Tech's eyes went to Jibs' corpse. "Damn, homie."

Animal came to stand next to Tech and looked down at Jibs. "It ain't on you that this happened. Jibs should've known to look before he leaped."

Tech didn't miss the coldness to Animal's voice. Between the time they entered the count room to then, something had changed in him that Tech couldn't quite put his finger on. "You're right, but that was still a homie. We'll make sure his family gets his cut from the robbery. Now help me gather up this money so we can bounce." He began collecting the scattered money and stuffing it into one of the plastic bags he'd had in his pocket.

"Man, that shit is all covered with blood, and you still wanna take it?" Animal frowned.

Tech looked over his shoulder at him. "Homie, you better act like you know what time it is. This money could be dipped in horse shit, but it'll still spend somewhere. The way you were letting that hammer bark, I didn't think you'd be squeamish about blood," he teased him. "Fuck it! If you don't wanna touch the money, make yourself useful and find those surveillance tapes. They're probably in the back office."

Animal went off to do as he was told. When he came back, he was carrying three small black tapes. Tech had managed to collect three nice-sized bags of money and had dragged them to the front door. When he saw Animal carrying the tapes, he gave him an approving smile.

"Looks like you may turn out to be a good soldier one of these days. Now help me get this shit outta here before somebody figures out it was us who ripped off this spot and we both find ourselves floating in the Hudson River. Mobsters don't take kindly to getting robbed."

Chapter 25

The heist had succeeded in doing two things: putting some real money in Animal's pockets for the first time and bringing him out of his shell. Even after Tech took the largest sum and broke Jibs' family off, Animal still made ten grand. He would have had to sell crack for Tango for months to make what he'd made in less than a half hour of work. He was officially turned out and eager to put in more work.

Over the next few months, Tech and Animal became the Batman and Robin of the underworld, leaving a trail of blood and empty pockets in their wake. They made good money doing freelance work for the Clarks and their associates, and when things got slow with the big-timers, Tech had a network of chicks in different cities that always had the 411 on whatever dudes were getting money. For a few dollars, they were more than willing to set cats up for Tech and Animal to knock down. Most of the time, the licks went smoothly, but when they met with opposition,

Tech let Animal off the leash. Animal was barely one hundred and fifty pounds soaking wet, but he had an appetite for blood that would make a vampire jealous. Life had been cruel to him, and in return, he was cruel to his enemies, turning even the simplest jobs into blood baths. The young boy had developed a knack for violence that sometimes made Tech uneasy.

It didn't take long for all the gunplay to bring the heat down on them. The two outlaws had managed to piss off quite a few people, including the police. Word had been sent to Tech that the excessive violence was starting to ruffle feathers, and it was "suggested" that they slow down for a while. Animal didn't like it. He felt like, as long as they had guns, no one should be able to tell them when or how to make money. Tech admired his zeal, but he was no fool. He understood hood politics and recognized a threat when he heard one, no matter how pretty the words were dressed. Part of Tech felt the same way Animal did, but he knew there was more at stake than pride. Tech was hardly a coward, but he needed to keep his relationships good with the heavyweights. Those relationships were how he ate, and to not at least show a measure of respect to their wishes would threaten those relationships. Wisely, he took a hiatus.

During their short break, Animal had time to sit back and enjoy some of the spoils of the personal war he had been waging on the streets. He invested in a new wardrobe, tricked off a few dollars on books and electronics, and bought himself some jewelry. The first thing he did was upgrade his gold teeth. He kept the original gold bridge Tango had gifted him and just had the jeweler add diamond cuts to it. When he was fitted with his grills, Animal smiled into the mirror, nodding in approval. Before Animal left the jewelry spot, he came across a chain and pendant that spoke to his soul. It was a small gold figurine of Animal, the insane, drum-playing Muppet he shared a name with. Small red stones ran over the figurine's head, while white ones made up his torso, filling out the tattered T-shirt and flowing into the tiny drumsticks in his outstretched hands. The stones were cheap, and the gold couldn't have been more than fourteen karats, but Animal didn't care. All he knew was that he wanted that piece, so he bought it. The moment he slipped it over his neck, it felt right. He didn't know it at the time, but it would go on to be one of his calling cards.

By the fall, the heat had started to die down, and Animal and Tech were back to work. It couldn't have happened at a more opportune time. The landlord of the building Tech's apartment was in had been indicted on a charge of fraud, so everyone who had rented under the table apartments from him was under a microscope. Tech probably could've gone through the motions with management and stayed, but he decided it'd be easier to just let it go and move to another spot.

Tech found another apartment and offered to let Animal continue to stay with him, but Animal declined. It wasn't that he wasn't grateful for the invitation or didn't enjoy having Tech as a roommate, but he was coming more into his own and needed more personal space. It was as if the older he got and the deeper into the game he sank, the more withdrawn he became. Animal was discovering that he preferred his own company to the gaggle of misfits that Tech kept in and out of his apartment. His new friends were cool, but Animal was different from the rest of them, and it was becoming more and more apparent by the day.

Animal wasn't old enough to sign off on his own apartment, and, since he was still a minor, the state had been looking for him since the death of his mother to put him in foster care, so Animal had to play this angle smart. Reluctantly, he reached out to his Aunt Rosa. She had washed her hands of her nephew after his stunt at the hospital and the fact that he'd skipped his mother's funeral, but Animal came speaking the universal language of cash, and he had a solution that would help both of them. Animal was willing to pay Rosa to agree to be his legal guardian, which would get social services off his back and provide her with a monthly foster care check. In addition to that, he agreed to pay her two thousand dollars per month to use the empty back bedroom as a mini-apartment, allowing him to come and go as he pleased. It was a lot to pay for just a room, but it would allow Animal the privacy he needed. For all the "family first" bullshit Rosa kicked, she happily took Animal's deal and his money.

Chapter 26

Animal's birthday started out just as any other day. He awoke, worked out, ate a light breakfast, and then hit the streets. Tech had hit him up that morning so they could start celebrating early. Animal jumped in a cab and headed to Tech's. He'd expected just Tech and him to sit around, sip a little bit and smoke some weed, but when he pulled up in front of Tech's building, he found it crowded with friends and associates. They had even set up a small grill in front of the building, and a white girl that Animal had never seen before was flipping burgers. The minute Animal stepped out of the taxi, he was greeted with hugs, pats on the back, and birthday well wishes from those assembled. Some of them Animal knew and some he didn't, but he just smiled and said, "Thanks."

"Happy B-day, Blood." Tech embraced Animal. "How does it feel to be another year older?"

Animal shrugged. "Good, I guess. I'm just happy to have lived to see it, because God knows there were times I didn't feel like I was going to make it another year."

"Well, you've made it through another year, and you're going to see many more for as long as I'm watching your back," Tech told him. "But dig, I want to introduce you to some people." He motioned to someone in the crowd.

Two females stepped forward, a black girl with dreads, dressed in baggy jeans and an oversized hoodie. In the right light, she could've passed for a young man. The other was the white girl who had been on the grill. Animal had to admit that, for a white girl, she was thick as hell. As their eyes locked, they both felt a small spark pass between them. Animal wasn't sure who the white girl was, but he was curious to find out.

"Animal," Tech continued, "this is Silk and China White." He pointed to the black girl and the white one, respectively. "They're going to be working with us," he informed Animal.

Animal didn't know how he felt about that. Since Jibs' death, it had just been him and Tech doing the big jobs. He didn't know Silk and China White and was distrustful of new people, but Tech was the leader of their gang, and what he said was law. Animal kept his opinions to himself and just nodded in greeting.

After the introductions, Tech sent two of the young runners to the liquor store and the weed spot. When they returned, they got the party started, right there on the stoop of Tech's building. About an hour into their celebration, a kid who ran errands for Tech came walking down the block. They called him Stump because he was born missing a hand. He was a cool dude who was always smiling, but that day, he had a worried expression on his face.

"What up, my nigga?" Tech asked Stump, noticing that something was wrong.

"Blood, I hate to interrupt the homie's celebration, but I gotta tell you something that you ain't gonna like," Stump said hesitantly.

"Don't be all mysterious about it. Spit it out!" Tech ordered.

"I was coming from the store, and I saw some li'l dude making a sale to a fiend," Stump told him.

Tech's face immediately darkened. Tech was a criminal, but one thing he didn't do was shit where he lived, and he didn't allow anyone else to do it either. This was part of the reason why the older people in the neighborhoods he lived in always overlooked his criminal behavior. They knew that as long as Tech lived in the area, they didn't have too much to worry about in the way of crime.

"Who is he?" Tech asked through gritted teeth.

"I ain't never seen him before, but from that blue rag hanging out of his pocket, I know he ain't from our side of the fence," Stump told him.

That was all Tech needed to hear.

"Say no more."

He retrieved his gun from the trash can near the building where he'd stashed it. Without saying a word, he started in the direction that Stump had told him he'd seen the kid. Animal and Stump fell in step behind him, with China and Silk bringing up the rear.

Animal spotted him first. He was wearing an oversized hoodie that concealed his face, but from the size of him, he couldn't have been any more than a kid. That didn't matter to Tech though. Young or old, if you violated his rules, Tech was going to get at you. Animal could tell from the evil expression on Tech's face that the situation was about to get ugly.

When the kid spotted the posse heading in his direction, he took off running. He had about a half block head start and was fast as hell, but China White was faster. The white girl shot off like a bullet, chasing the boy down and even-

tually overtaking him. Had China not chosen
the streets, she could've easily qualified for the
Olympic sprint team.

By the time they caught up with them, the boy
and China were struggling. China was bigger
than him, but the boy was putting up one hell of
a fight. The boy's hand dipped into his pocket,
and when it came back up, there was the familiar
flash of steel. He would've surely poked China
full of holes had Silk not stepped in and knocked
the knife out of his hand. She grabbed him by the
front of his shirt and gave him a good pop to
the mouth to calm him down. She was about
to sock him again when Tech stopped her.

"I got it from here, ma," Tech told her, taking
two fistfuls of the boy's shirt and slamming
him against the wall. "Little crab nigga, you
must've lost your fucking mind selling drugs in
my hood."

"Get your fucking hands off me before I kill
you." The little boy struggled from within the
folds of his oversized hoodie.

Something about the little boy's voice rang
familiar in Animal's head, but he was too focused
on the comedic spectacle to catch on. The boy
kicked Tech in the shins so hard that his grip
loosened, and the boy slipped completely out
of his hoodie. Now naked from the waist up, he

tried fleeing again, but Tech tripped him. Tech then straddled the boy and put his gun to his forehead.

"Kid, I should put a bullet in your fucking head for what you just did," Tech threatened.

"Do what the fuck you gotta do. I ain't scared to die," the boy spat. He was obviously outnumbered and outmuscled, but it didn't stop him from trying to fight until the inevitable end. If anything, he had heart.

Animal's curiosity got the best of him, and he moved forward to peek over Tech's shoulder and get a good look at the little hell-raiser. He had to do a double take when he saw who it was that Tech was about to pop.

"Ashanti?" He was shocked. The last he'd heard, Annie had sold him and his sister into bondage, and nobody knew where Ashanti had vanished to.

"You know this li'l nigga?" Tech asked Animal over his shoulder, still keeping his gun and eyes on the struggling Ashanti.

"Yeah, he from my hood. Let him up, Tech," Animal said.

Reluctantly, Tech got off of Ashanti, but he still kept his gun at the ready, in case he got any big ideas.

Animal extended his hand to Ashanti to help him up. Ashanti just stared at his hand, afraid that it was some trick. "It's okay, Ashanti. I ain't gonna do nothing to you," Animal promised.

Ashanti studied Animal's face for signs of deception, and when he found none, he allowed Animal to help him up. He kept his tough-guy scowl on, but secretly he was happy to see Animal. Ashanti was young, but he was no fool, and he realized that the situation could've gotten very ugly for him had Animal not stepped in.

"Thanks," he mumbled.

"It's all good," Animal said, handing him back the hoodie he'd been wearing.

Ashanti quickly slipped the hoodie over his head. Ashanti looked a little older and a little more worn than the last time Animal had seen him, and his teeth had grown back, but he could recognize that scowl anywhere.

"Say, Blood, I hate to interrupt your little reunion, but this nigga is still in violation," Silk pointed out. "Tech, how you wanna handle this?"

"He gets a pass," Animal answered for Tech, which drew curious stares from everyone.

"I know you and shorty got history, but he ain't from what we from, and he's clearly in violation of Tech's number one rule. He gotta at least catch a beating," Silk said.

"I ain't scared to fight nobody, not even some manly-ass-looking bitch!" Ashanti capped.

"You better watch your fucking mouth." Silk took a step toward Ashanti, but Animal got between them.

"This kid is from my neighborhood. I'm speaking for him, and I say he gets a pass," Animal said, a bit more sternly.

Tension hung in the air between Silk and Animal. Silk knew of Animal's growing reputation as a killer, but she was no coward. Both of them eyeballed each other, each daring the other to strike first. It was Tech who eventually broke the tension when he stepped up.

"Silk has a point," Tech said to Animal. "We just can't have anybody who feels like it thinking they can piss on my doorstep and it's all good."

"Tech, I know he's wrong, but give him a pass. He comes from what I come from, so I feel his pain. You once gave me a shot, and I'm asking you to do the same for him," Animal said.

Tech weighed it. "If I give him a pass, whatever comes of it is on you," he told Animal seriously.

"I'll wear that," Animal agreed.

Tech nodded. "Then so be it."

"Wait a minute. This li'l dude came over here flying an enemy flag and slanging stones, and you gonna let him walk?" Silk asked in disbelief.

Tech turned cold eyes to her. "Silk, you're a loyal soldier, but Animal is my brother. If he wants dude to get a pass, then he's got a pass and ain't no more to be said about it. Now let's get back to this food and this party before one of them greedy-ass niggas eat all the burgers." He walked off.

Silk didn't like it, but she didn't argue either. She felt slighted that Tech had taken Animal's side over hers, but she understood that he had seniority in the crew. Still, feeling like he had gotten one up on her didn't sit well. That one incident would be the first of many during their time together, and it would also be the beginning of a very rocky relationship.

Chapter 27

Animal had invited Ashanti to join him at his birthday celebration. Of course, there were some unhappy grumblings about it, but Animal didn't care. He and Ashanti had history that went further back than his ties with Tech's gang. Besides, they had a lot to catch up on.

Ashanti was leaning against the wall, scowling as usual, when Animal approached, carrying two burgers, offering one to Ashanti.

"Nah, I'm good," Ashanti lied.

"Bullshit. I saw the way you were staring at the grill. Don't let your pride make you starve." Animal held the burger out. Ashanti eventually took it and devoured it in three bites. "Damn! When is the last time you ate?"

"A day or so ago, I guess," Ashanti said, licking his fingers. Seeing how hungry he was, Animal gave Ashanti his burger too. This one he ate slower, savoring the flavor. "So, I hear you're a big man on the streets these days," he said between bites.

"Nah, I'm just out here trying to live. I been getting money with Tech and his crew since my mother died."

"Yeah, I heard about Marie. I'm sorry for your loss," Ashanti said sincerely.

Animal nodded in thanks. "It was rough for me for a time, but I'm coping with it now. How are you doing though? I heard about that cruddy shit your mom did. I'm sorry it happened to you."

"It was bad, man," Ashanti began. "Moms owed these dudes money, so she gave me and my sister to them until the debt was paid. They promised to keep us together, but they changed the plans and split us up. What Mama didn't know was that the dudes she gave us to as collateral were flesh peddlers. In addition to me and my sister, they had taken other kids too. They separated us by boys and girls and showcased us like slaves to people with money who were looking to buy kids on the black market. Thankfully social services and the police stepped in when they did, or ain't no telling where I'd be. I ain't never been so happy to see a cop in my life.

"Being that my mom was locked up, they put me in a home, but that joint was more like a prison for kids. I stayed there for a while before

I managed to escape. They eventually caught me, but I just ran again. I ain't never gonna stop running."

"And what happened to your sister?" Animal asked.

Ashanti's face saddened. "They never found her."

After hearing Ashanti's story, it gave Animal some insight into what kind of kid he was. Ashanti was a survivor, just like Animal.

"And what's up with that?" Animal motioned toward the blue bandana hanging out of Ashanti's pocket.

"This?" Ashanti took the bandana out and held it up. "These Crip dudes hustling the neighborhood recruited me to sell drugs for them."

"So you banging that?"

Ashanti shrugged. "I dunno. I was never officially down with them, but I fly their colors out of respect because they were feeding me."

"Well, I'm gonna feed you now. You're from the same dirt I was born from, and I'm gonna look out for you," Animal told him.

"Yo! I appreciate the burgers and stuff, but I'm not looking for a handout."

"And I don't plan on giving you any handouts. You'll earn every meal and every dollar you get under me, but we got rules over here. The first rule being: you bang that five or you bang *nothing*," Animal told him, sounding like a seasoned gang member, instead of the relative newborn that he was. Truth be told, his initiation had never really been made official, but Animal had put in so much work in the name of the Bloods that no one ever questioned his credibility. Animal saw Ashanti's hesitance.

"Look, I ain't trying to make you do nothing that you don't wanna do. I'm just telling you how it is with me and the dudes I roll with. The choice is yours at the end of the day."

Ashanti looked down at the bandana in his hand. He had only been hustling with the Crips for a few days and had no real ties to them, but Animal was from his hood. He knew where he came from and what he was about.

"Fuck it. I'm with you," Ashanti said, dropping the bandana to the ground.

"That's what I'm talking about." Animal proudly embraced him. "I'm about to show you a whole different side of the coin, my nigga."

Before they could get deeper into their conversation, a late model Honda with tinted windows pulled up to the curb. It was an unfamiliar car, so everyone was instantly on point, ready to pop off at a moment's notice. Surprisingly, a cute dark-skinned girl got out on the passenger's side and stepped onto the curb. She was carrying a large gift bag in her hand. "Anybody know where I can find Animal?"

Silk stepped up. "Nah, but I'm Silk if you're looking for a good time."

The girl rolled her eyes at Silk. "Sweetie, I'm strictly dickly, and I have a man. I just came to drop something off to Animal from a friend, so either you know where he is or you don't."

"I'm Animal." He stepped forward. As he got closer to the girl, he realized he had seen her before. She was the girl outside Hell who had told them about Tango getting killed.

The girl smiled and held out the bag. "This is from Kastro. She says to tell you happy birthday."

At the mention of Kastro's name, Animal's face lit up.

"How's she doing?" he asked as he accepted the bag.

"She's doing good, but she's been better. She's still locked up, fighting the case from the raid, but things are looking good for her," the girl informed him.

"I'm glad to hear it. I was worried about her," Animal said.

"No need to be. You know Kastro is a survivor," the girl replied.

"So what is it?" Animal hoisted the bag.

"I have no idea. She just said to make sure that I gave it to you and to tell you to open the gift when you're somewhere private. I've done my part, so I'm gone." The girl started back to the car, but Animal called after her.

"Thank you, and tell Kastro that I love her," Animal said.

The girl smiled. "I will. Happy birthday, Animal," she told him before getting back into her car and pulling off.

Animal stood there, peeking at the neatly wrapped box in the bag. "I wonder what it is," he thought out loud.

"Let's go upstairs and find out," Tech suggested.

Animal, Tech, and Ashanti went upstairs to Tech's apartment to open the gift. Animal's hands trembled nervously as he tore off the wrapping paper. It was a wooden box with a gold clasp and the words "for my favorite misfit" engraved into the top. When Animal opened the box and saw what was inside, his heart was aflutter. There were two Glocks, with rose-tinted barrels and rubber grips.

Ashanti whistled. "Now that's what I call a fucking birthday gift."

"Those have got to be the prettiest guns I've ever seen," Tech said, admiring the craftsmanship.

"They are, and that's what I'm going to call them—my Pretty Bitches." Animal took the guns from the box and held one in each hand.

"Pretty Bitches," Tech repeated. "I like that name for them. Man, you're gonna do some serious damage in the streets with those shits."

"Nah, these ain't for that. I've got special plans for these guns," Animal said.

"What are you going to do with them?" Ashanti asked.

Animal looked at his reflection in the rose chrome of the barrels. "One, I'm going to use on my biological father for abandoning us, and the other, I'm going to use on Eddie, the man who gave my mother the virus that killed her." It was the first time Animal had ever spoken publicly about how his mother had died.

Tech put his arm around Animal, comforting him. "We'll kill them together," he offered.

"Thanks, big homie, but this is something I have to do alone," Animal said. "I've been trying to get the rundown on Eddie for months. I haven't been able to find him, but I'll never stop looking."

"You mean crackhead Eddie that used to date your mother?" Ashanti asked.

Animal turned to him. "Yeah. Why?"

Ashanti smiled devilishly. "I know where he's been staying."

Chapter 28

Animal had spent many sleepless nights thinking about that moment, the time when would run up on Eddie and end his miserable existence. Now that it was upon him, he found his mouth watering, anticipating the kill.

According to Ashanti, Eddie had been holed up with some crack whore in a house in Stamford, Connecticut. He'd encountered him by chance during his stay there with his captors.

Tech got a friend of his to rent him a car, and they hit the I-95. It was Tech, Animal, and Ashanti who went along for the mission. Animal had wanted to go by himself, but Tech wouldn't hear of it. He knew how difficult the task ahead would be, and he wouldn't abandon his comrade. Besides, neither Animal nor Ashanti could drive, and it would've been too risky to take the train or bus while carrying guns.

For the whole ride, all Animal could do was stare at his Pretty Bitches. It was like they were singing a sweet serenade of murder that only he could hear.

They found the house, right where Ashanti said it would be, but there was no sign of Eddie. They spent all day watching the house, but he never showed. They'd assumed that Ashanti's information was wrong and were about to head back to New York when they spotted a blue minivan pull up to the house. A woman carrying grocery bags got out from behind the wheel. She was slender and brown-skinned with black hair. It looked like at one point she might've actually been pretty, but the drugs had taken hold of her, and she now looked worn out. Two men got out of the van next. One was fat and looked like he needed to get acquainted with a shower, and the other was the man of the hour, Eddie.

When Animal saw Eddie exit the van, his heart leaped into his chest. Had it not been for Tech holding him back, Animal would've jumped out and gunned Eddie down in front of the neighbors. Tech had laid out the perfect plan and didn't need Animal's temper ruining it. They would swoop in under the cover of darkness and do what they had to do. Animal didn't want to wait, but he understood what Tech was saying. None of them wanted to go to jail.

It seemed like it took forever for the sun to go down, but the moment had finally arrived.

"Animal, I know you're feeling in a way right now, but don't do anything stupid. We get in, kill Eddie, and get gone, understand?" Tech asked.

"Yeah, I got it," Animal said, sounding less than convincing. "You just remember that Eddie belongs to me." He got out of the car.

The plan was a simple one. Ashanti would knock on the door, carrying a box of chocolates, pretending to be a kid selling candy from school. Once he got them to open the door, Tech and Animal would rush the spot. They would subdue Eddie and take him somewhere remote to murder him.

With his box of candy tucked under his arm and his sweetest smile on, Ashanti knocked on the door and waited. They'd hoped that it would've been Eddie to answer the door, so they could snatch him without having to go into the house, but they would have no such luck. The fat dude who they had seen getting out of the van was the one who answered.

"Fuck you want?" the fat man snapped at Ashanti. He was wearing a white T-shirt that was past the point of being washed and should've just been burned.

"How are you, sir? My name is Paul, and I'm with a group of kids in the neighborhood who are selling candy today to raise money for basketball uniforms," Ashanti lied.

The fat man looked at him suspiciously. "What kind of damn school sends kids to this side of town at night, selling candy?"

"A desperate one," Ashanti told him.

"A'ight, what you got?" the fat man asked.

"A little bit of everything," Ashanti said, opening the box of candy so the fat man could see what he was selling. "Each candy bar is a dollar, but I'm willing to give you six for five dollars."

"Ain't you the little hustler?" The fat man rummaged through the box, taking out two hands full of candy. "How about I take these and instead of paying for them, I won't kick your little ass for being on the wrong side of town at the wrong time."

"C'mon, mister! Don't do me like that. If I come back short, my mom has to pay the difference." Ashanti was laying it on thick.

"They should've thought about that before they sent you down to this muthafucka. Now get the fuck off my porch before I kick a bone out your ass." He laughed, but it was cut short when Tech and Animal jumped from the bushes, guns drawn.

"Man, you gotta be a low-ass nigga if you're willing to steal candy from a baby." Animal pointed one of the Pretty Bitches at the fat man's face. The fat man opened his mouth to speak, but Animal raised his finger for him to remain silent. "Where's Eddie?"

The fat man nodded over his shoulder, indicating that Eddie was inside.

"Take me to him," Animal ordered.

With the Glock placed firmly against the back of his head, the fat man led Animal inside the house, with Tech and Ashanti following.

The inside of the house was a mess. The once green carpet was now leaning toward brown and worn nearly to the floor beneath in certain spots. In the center of the living room sat a coffee table littered with overflowing ashtrays, abandoned cups, and toys.

Behind the table sat the woman who had been driving the van. She was so busy loading her crack pipe that she didn't even notice she had company. Animal watched in disgust as she fired up her pipe and took a deep hit. Her eyes rolled in ecstasy as the blast took effect. Watching her getting high reminded Animal of his mother, sitting in their living room, smoking crack, while he sat on the floor a few feet away playing with his toys. She was about to take a second hit when Animal slapped the crack pipe out of her hand, breaking it.

"What the—"

Her eyes snapped up, mouth twisted, ready to curse whoever had ruined her high, but whatever sharp words she had died in her throat when she saw the murderous young men with their guns, standing in her living room.

"Where is he? Where is Eddie?" Animal pressed her.

"Who the hell is Eddie? Don't no Eddie live here," the woman said, a bit too loud for Animal's liking.

Animal grabbed her by the throat, pinning her to the couch. He pressed his gun to her eye so hard that she thought he was trying to squash it into the socket. "Lady, don't play with me. I only came for Eddie, but as God is my witness, I'll splatter you and anybody else I find in here to get to him. Now stop fucking around and tell me where he is!"

Just then, Eddie came out of the kitchen, holding a forty ounce and three cups.

"What the hell is all that noise out here? I hope y'all ain't smoked all my shit, because if you did, I'm gonna . . ."

Eddie's words trailed off. When he saw Tech and Ashanti standing near the door, he thought they were getting robbed, but when his eyes landed on Animal, he knew it was no robbery.

"Speak the devil's name, and he shall appear." Animal smiled like a proud son, before turning his gun from the woman on the couch to Eddie. "My mother sends her regards." He opened fire.

Eddie hit the floor just before the bullets struck the wall above him. He scrambled on all fours to the bedroom.

Seeing Animal was unexpected. When he found out that he had infected Marie with the HIV virus, he knew there would be repercussions, but he had always thought it would be Justice who would come looking to avenge his mother's death. Never in a million years would he have thought he would be running for his life from a boy whom he had terrorized for over a decade.

Animal rounded the corner just before Eddie made it to the bedroom door. He took aim and fired, striking Eddie in the shoulder and sending him spilling into the darkened bedroom. Animal moved cautiously toward the bedroom door and pushed it open. He could hear Eddie's breathing, but it was too dark to see exactly where he was. Keeping his gun raised and ready, he felt along the wall with his free hand until he found the light switch.

When he flicked it, the room was illuminated. It was a child's room. He could tell from the toys scattered on the floor and the cartoon decals on the walls. On one side of the room, there was an unmade pink princess bed. On the other side, Eddie cowered near the window. In his arms, he held a little girl. He held a knife to her neck.

"You take one more step and I'll cut her," Eddie threatened. The little girl looked terrified, and tears ran from her sleep-heavy eyes.

"You're a killer and a coward, Eddie," Animal spat.

"Yeah, and I'm also a survivor," Eddie said. "Now back the fuck up or I'm gonna split this little bitch open."

"This is between me and you, Eddie. Let that child go and take your medicine like a man," Animal challenged. He wanted to tear Eddie up bad as hell, but he didn't want to risk hitting the little girl.

Eddie laughed. "Nigga, you done seen one movie too many. Ain't no happy endings in the ghetto, and ain't no honor among thieves. What's gonna happen next is you're gonna put that gun down, and me and this kid are gonna walk out of here unharmed."

"And what makes you think I won't just smoke you and her?" Animal asked.

"Because I know you," Eddie said matter-of-factly. "I hear you're making a name for yourself in the streets, but that heart of yours is still tender. For as bad as you wanna kill me, you're more worried about hitting this kid by accident. Now drop that burner so I can be on my way, and if I have to ask you again, I might slip and cut her throat by accident."

Animal hesitated for a moment before finally dropping his gun. He was furious not only because he would miss his chance to kill Eddie, but because this many years later, Eddie was still able to play on his insecurities and come out on top.

"You know I'm going to hunt you to the ends of the earth, right? Even if I don't get you tonight, I'll get you eventually," he promised.

"I believe you'll give it your best shot, but as you can see, ol' Eddie ain't so easy to kill. Now if you'll excuse me—"

Eddie's body went stiff. He released the little girl and began clawing at his back. When he turned, Animal saw two things: a pair of scissors sticking out of Eddie's back, and Ashanti. During the standoff, he'd snuck around to the side of the house and climbed in through the first floor window of the child's room and got the drop on Eddie. He was the only one of the three who entered the house that didn't have a gun, but he'd snatched a pair of scissors from the living room, thinking they might come in handy, and they did.

Seizing the moment, Animal scooped the Pretty Bitch off the ground and let it rock. The first bullet hit Eddie high in the chest and bounced him off the wall. Animal hit him again and again, causing Eddie's body to do a little dance before falling to the ground.

Eddie was down but still breathing. Animal walked over to Eddie and stood over him. His eyes were rolling around in his head, trying to find something to focus on.

"Look at me," Animal ordered. Eddie's eyes instinctively went to the voice. "On behalf of my mother and every other person whose life you've ever ruined, I cast you back to the pit of hell that you crawled out of." He fired two shots into Eddie's face, ending his existence. "May God show no mercy on your soul." Animal shot him once more for good measure.

When Tech saw Animal come into the living room, cradling a little girl with blood-splattered pajamas, he knew things had gone from bad to worse. He looked to Ashanti for an explanation, but the youngster couldn't meet his gaze. He was clearly shaken up. For as much time as Ashanti had spent in the streets, this was the first time he had ever seen someone murdered, and it had rattled him to the core.

When the woman saw Animal carrying her child, she became frantic. "Please, don't hurt my baby."

Animal's dark eyes turned to the woman. "I'm not the monster. I'm the monster killer," he told her as he set the child down gently on the couch next to her.

"You handle your business, Blood?" Tech asked Animal.

Animal nodded. "It's done."

"Cool. Let's clean up the rest of this mess and get out of here." Tech raised his gun and shot the fat man in the head, knocking him into the wall, before his body fell in front of the terrified mother and child. The woman clutched the child to her chest and pleaded for hers and the life of her child, but mercy was a foreign concept to Tech. Before he could pull the trigger, Animal placed a calming hand on his arm.

"There is no honor in killing women and children," Animal told him.

"Fuck honor! They saw us. We could all get the needle for this," Tech reasoned.

"I said no women and children!" Animal's voice boomed.

The look in his eyes said that he was willing to go the extra mile to defend what he believed, so Tech left it alone. Animal walked over to the couch and knelt before the woman and the little girl. Gently, he turned the little girl's face so that she was looking him in the eyes.

"Who am I?"

The little girl wiped the tears from her eyes, trying to not be afraid and sobbed. "The monster killer."

"Right." Animal nodded. "And the monster killer keeps little girls safe from bad men, just like I did today. Do you understand?"

The little girl nodded.

Animal picked up a loose piece of mail and turned to the woman, holding it up so that she could see that he now had her full name and address. "I don't know what you're going to tell the police when they come, but if I were you, I'd make it a good story. If I even think you tried to roll over on us, I'll be back to collect the life of another monster."

"As God is my witness, I won't say a word," the woman cried.

"Little girls need their mothers, and I'd hate to see yours grow up without hers. Take this second chance at life and get your shit together." Animal stood to leave, but he had some parting words for the woman. "If you were fucking Eddie without a condom, you might want to go and get tested. Don't wait until it's too late to find out your status."

Epilogue

They didn't talk much on the ride back. Everyone was pretty much in their own thoughts. Every so often, Tech would glance over at Animal, who had just been staring out the window aimlessly. His body was in the car with them, but his mind was somewhere else. Until then, Tech had thought that he'd known Animal better than anybody else, but that night, he'd found out different. Inside the sweet kid who had slept on his living room floor lurked a demon, and for the first time, Tech had gotten a glimpse of his face.

When they pulled up in front of Tech's building, everybody was outside. Tech, Ashanti, and Animal had disappeared early that morning without telling a soul where they were going, so people had begun to worry.

Animal picked his way through the crowd toward Tech's building in a zone, as if he didn't even notice them. When he got to the entrance, China White was leaning against the doorframe.

Animal looked up at her, and his tired eyes told the story of his life within a few seconds. The pain in them hit China like a punch to the chest. Surprising Animal and herself, she leaned forward and hugged him. She wasn't sure why she did it, other than the fact that he looked like he needed it.

Tech had managed to get rid of everyone, and now it was just him, Animal, and Ashanti in his apartment. Ashanti sat on the couch with a half-eaten sandwich on his lap. After what he'd seen at the house, he didn't have much of an appetite. Watching Animal commit cold-blooded murder had both frightened and fascinated him.

Animal was sitting on the floor in the corner with the wooden box he'd gotten from Kastro between his legs. He gently placed the gun he'd shot Eddie with back inside the box, running his finger over it tenderly.

Leaving the box lid open, Animal got up and went into the bathroom. A few seconds later, Tech heard the shower water turn on. Just beneath the loud spray of water, he could hear his friend sobbing. Years of pent-up anger and hurt were finally let go in a river of tears.

"That was some cold shit, wasn't it?" Ashanti asked Tech after Animal was out of earshot.

"Cold indeed, but I'm glad he got it out of his system," Tech said.

Ashanti looked from the bathroom door back to Tech. "So now that Eddie is gone, I guess it's over, right?"

Tech's eyes drifted to the second gun in the wooden box and thought of the vow Animal made when he'd received the gifts. There would definitely be more bloodshed before it was said and done. "Nah, man. I think this is only the beginning."

THE BEGINNING...

ORDER FORM
URBAN BOOKS, LLC
97 N. 18th Street
Wyandanch, NY 11798

Name (please print):_____

Address:_____

City/State:_____

Zip:_____

QTY	TITLES	PRICE

Shipping and handling-add $3.50 for 1st book, then $1.75 for each additional book.

Please send a check payable to:

Urban Books, LLC

Please allow 4-6 weeks for delivery